"FASTEN YOUR SEAT BELT! CA... A STIMULATING, FAST-
PACED NOVEL BRIMMING WI...
—Joe Weber, bestsellin...

CARRIER

HELLFIRE

Book Twenty in the Acclaimed Naval Aviation Series

KEITH DOUGLASS

Author of the Seal Team Seven series

JOVE

$5.99 U.S.
$8.99 CAN

ISBN 0-515-13348-5

9 780515 133486

5 0 5 9 9 >

S EAN

CARRIER

These are the stories of the Carrier Battle Group Fourteen—a force including a supercarrier, amphibious unit, guided missile cruiser, and destroyer. And these are the novels that capture the blistering reality of international combat. Exciting. Authentic. Explosive.

CARRIER . . . The smash debut thriller about the ultimate military nightmare: the takeover of a U.S. Intelligence ship.

VIPER STRIKE . . . A renegade Chinese fighter group penetrates Thai airspace—and launches a full-scale invasion.

ARMAGEDDON MODE . . . With India and Pakistan on the verge of nuclear destruction, the Carrier Battle Group Fourteen must prevent a final showdown.

FLAME-OUT . . . The Soviet Union is reborn in a military takeover—and their strike force shows no mercy.

MAELSTROM . . . The Soviet occupation of Scandinavia leads the Carrier Battle Group Fourteen into conventional weapons combat—and possible all-out war.

COUNTDOWN . . . Carrier Battle Group Fourteen must prevent the deployment of Russian submarines. The problem is: They have nukes.

AFTERBURN . . . Carrier Battle Group Fourteen receives orders to enter the Black Sea—in the middle of a Russian civil war.

ALPHA STRIKE . . . When American and Chinese interests collide in the South China Sea, the superpowers risk waging a third world war.

ARCTIC FIRE . . . A Russian splinter group has occupied the Aleutian Islands off the coast of Alaska—in the ultimate invasion of U.S. soil.

continued on next page . . .

ARSENAL . . . Magruder and his crew are trapped between Cuban revolutionaries . . . and a U.S. power play that's spun wildly out of control.

NUKE ZONE . . . When a nuclear missile is launched against the U.S. Sixth Fleet, Magruder must face a frightening question: In an age of computer warfare, how do you tell friends from enemies?

CHAIN OF COMMAND . . . Magruder enters the jungles of Vietnam, looking for answers about his missing father. Little does he know that another bloody war is about to be unleashed . . .

BRINK OF WAR . . . Friendly war games with the Russians take a deadly turn, and Carrier Battle Group Fourteen must prevent war from erupting in the skies.

TYPHOON . . . An American yacht is attacked by a Chinese helicopter in international waters, and the Carrier Team is called to the front lines of what may be the start of a war between the superpowers . . .

ENEMY OF MY ENEMY . . . A Greek pilot unwittingly downs a news chopper, and Magruder must keep the peace between Greece and the breakaway republic of Macedonia. But what no one knows is that it wasn't an accident at all . . .

JOINT OPERATIONS . . . China launches a surprise attack on Hawaii—and the Carrier Team can't handle it alone. As Tombstone and his fleet take charge of the air, Lieutenant Murdock and his SEALs are called in to work ashore . . .

THE ART OF WAR . . . When Iranian militants take the first bloody step toward toppling the decadent West, the Carrier group are the only ones who can stop the madmen . . .

ISLAND WARRIORS . . . China launches a full-scale invasion on its tiny capitalist island neighbor—and Carrier Battle Group Fourteen is the only hope to stop them . . .

FIRST STRIKE . . . A group of radical Russian military officers are planning a nuclear attack on the United States, but Carrier Battle Group has been called in to make sure the Cold War ends without a bang . . .

book twenty

CARRIER

Hellfire

KEITH DOUGLASS

JOVE BOOKS, NEW YORK

This is a work of fiction. Names, characters, places, and incidents either are the product of the author's imagination or are used fictitiously, and any resemblance to actual persons, living or dead, business establishments, events, or locales is entirely coincidental.

CARRIER: HELLFIRE

A Jove Book / published by arrangement with
the author

PRINTING HISTORY
Jove edition / August 2002

Visit our website at
www.penguinputnam.com

ISBN: 0-515-13348-5

A JOVE BOOK®
Jove Books are published by The Berkley Publishing Group,
a division of Penguin Putnam Inc.,
375 Hudson Street, New York, New York 10014.
JOVE and the "J" design
are trademarks belonging to Penguin Putnam Inc.

PRINTED IN THE UNITED STATES OF AMERICA

10 9 8 7 6 5 4 3 2 1

ONE

Russian General Vasily Groshenko dreamed. He was in the hills, bivouacked with his men. He was a junior officer, one only recently trusted off on his own, and this was his first mission in command of his company. He had been careful, so careful, in his planning—every detail examined, every potential problem anticipated. Or, at least he'd thought so.

It wasn't like he was entirely on his own, not like he would be on a real mission. Certainly, he had radio contact with higher authority, and could call for a helicopter should a medical emergency arise, or some other unforeseen incident. Unlike the earlier days of the Soviet Union, today's Russia had the luxury of training time. In fact, it was almost all they had. Less money, less fuel—the only thing they had was time and terrain.

Overhead, the stars were blinding. He had never seen them so close or so bright, large pinwheels of light against the blackness. There was no moon, no light from a nearby city. Just complete, utter blackness and the stars reaching down at him.

The camp was practicing covert operations and all lights were extinguished. Even the sentries depended on their night-adapted eyes to find their way around, the flashlights hanging unused at their sides. The training was a valid tactical objective, but its secondary purpose was conserving the few batteries they had.

Although the general could not see them, he could hear his men around him. Hear their breathing, the occasional muttered expletive of a sleeper disturbed by dreams, a mournful groan as another tried to find a comfortable spot on the ground. The sleeping bags were Arctic issue, shaped like a shroud, with attached hoods to go over the occupants' heads. They were too hot for the season, although the general had not noticed it earlier. It was only recently that he became aware of the sweat running down his sides and dampening the liner of the sleeping bag. He knew a trickle of frustration, that he could plan everything else so carefully and still have the men bring the wrong equipment for the climate.

But now it wasn't the sleeping bags. It was the stars. They were moving closer, almost so close he could touch them now, their hard fiery heat beating down on him. The light was blinding, so blinding. It illuminated every crack of the landscape, drawing harsh shadows in seemingly random directions, making a mockery of his carefully practiced darkened camp procedures.

A cluster of stars from one constellation moved together, merging into a single blinding mass. It hovered directly above him, the heat almost unbearable now. His eyebrows were singed and his skin bubbled as the fire penetrated through fragile flesh to sear his bones. He tried not to scream, tried not to give away their position to the enemy who was surely watching nearby. With all his will, he bit down on his lower lip, screaming inside as his flesh charred away from his bones. Finally, unable to bear it any longer, he let a scream rip out from the corner of his mouth, a sick keening sound that no human should ever make. In that one note, he knew that all was lost. The guns were centering on him now, bearing down just behind the light of the stars. He had betrayed them all.

With a start, the general awoke. His sheets were clammy

with sweat, twisted into strange forms around him. He took a few moments to remember where he was, disoriented at the abrupt transition from dreams to wakefulness. In the first second that his eyes were open, he thought he was in a coffin. It was dark, so dark, an enclosed space. He started to scream again, not sure he was even awake, and then reality crashed in on him.

Not a coffin. A ship. Perhaps the equivalent for an army officer, if truth be known.

Now fully oriented and awake, he slid back down on the bed, peeling back the top sheet to allow the sweat to dry. He was clad in an undershirt and boxer shorts, the former being a new habit ever since the nightmares—night terrors—had started.

He held still for moment, waiting for his heart to slow down. Finally, when it was beating at a normal pace and his breathing had slowed, he swung his feet over onto the cold linoleum.

The prospect of another two months on board the ship, and continuing nightmares, was almost more than he could bear. Yes, he had wanted this. Yes, it was necessary that he supervise all phases of the operation. The nightmares, the cramped quarters—all necessary evils, as was the gear located in two special trailers located on the aft deck.

Special equipment—such an innocuous name. Intellectually, he knew that it was the source of his nightmares. Somehow his subconscious mind was convinced that the anti-satellite targeting laser contained in one of the trailers were targeted at him.

How had it come to this? It was not Russia's fault, not this time. No, the Americans were responsible for this. Their determination to build a missile defense shield, beginning with one deployed at sea, had destabilized the entire balance of power so carefully worked out during the decades of relative peace. Why had they done it? Hadn't they realized what would happen?

No matter. That was for the politicians to decide. His mission was simply to demonstrate to the Americans, in no uncertain terms, just how dangerous their actions were. If they deployed the system, made it operational, then Russia had to be prepared to retaliate. From what he understood, the diplomats had made that point eminently clear in the carefully worded statements that were the diplomatic equivalent of hardware. It had had no effect. A more explicit demonstration was necessary.

Tomorrow night. It will all be over tomorrow night. And then, perhaps, the nightmares will stop.

Did Captain First Rank Pietro Bolshovich have nightmares? It was possible, he supposed, although he doubted it. The officer commanding the amphibious transport seemed to be a stolid, rather dull man. Or perhaps that was just his way of expressing his displeasure at having an army officer on board and in tactical command. For whatever reason, he had struck Vasily as somewhat dense. Not the sort of man given to fanciful imaginings about stars and lasers.

Tomorrow, the demonstration. A short one, just to show the Americans that no matter how well their system worked, Russia was ahead of them. Again. Like Soyuz and the first man in space. Like the development of tactical nuclear weapons. Russia's planning process linked civilian and military assets and resources into a potent developmental force. The nation had one focus, one priority, unlike the United States, splintered by profit motives and self-interest.

The American forces at sea would see the Russian laser spiking the heavens, although Vasily doubted that they'd be told what it was. They hadn't a need to know—Russia intended the message for those higher up the chain of command.

The demonstration, then a few weeks of monitoring the American tests, watching for weaknesses and vulnerabilities. Those would be long hours, not only for the scientists on board but for the more mundane sailors as well. Keeping within range to monitor the Americans while maintaining a safe distance and observing international safety-at-sea conventions would take some precision navigation. Then a few more weeks at sea to return to their home port. When he thought about the weeks ahead of him, marooned on this ship with only naval officers such as Bolshovich for company, the general's spirits sank.

While Groshenko had overall responsibility and authority

for the testing program, Bolshovich was responsible for the safety of his ship and crew. The Russian naval officer had ordered the ship to an increased state of readiness, and planned to be prepared for immediate retaliation by American forces. The general thought that unnecessary, but he demurred. It was, after all, the captain's ship.

Could Bolshovich really be as dull as he seemed? Was it possible to be stupid and rise to command of a ship of this size, much less be entrusted with the testing of Russia's missile defense system? Perhaps, but traditional Russian paranoia demanded that the general consider the possibility that he might have underestimated the captain.

The general paced the small compartment for a bit, letting the heat leach out of his body through his feet on the cold linoleum, then he washed his face and tried to clear his mind. He changed his T-shirt and was comforted by the clean, crisp feel of fresh cotton against his skin. Finally, he lay down on top of his blanket and pulled it around him, avoiding the clammy sheets. Like all good ground troops, he was capable of making use of almost any opportunity to sleep. Old habits kicked in, his mind stilled, and he drifted back off to sleep. His final thought before he fell asleep was to wonder if Bolshovich was sleeping, too.

TWO

Pamela Drake's first thought upon meeting Cary Winston was that her boobs couldn't possibly be real. Nature simply didn't make them that rounded and jutting. Nor did nature, in Drake's experience, ever couple that attribute with exceptionally translucent skin, sky blue eyes, and gold hair. Nature wouldn't: it simply wouldn't be fair.

"Hi." Cary's voice was low and warm. "What an honor to meet you, Miss Drake. I've been a fan of yours since grade school. And now to have a chance to work with you—well, it's more than I could have ever dreamed." Winston fluttered her improbably long lashes at Drake, her expression one of complete awe.

"Thank you, I'm sure," Drake murmured, seething. *Since grade school. And that would imply precisely what?* That Drake herself had been knocking around different parts of the world since before Winston was potty trained?

"I hope you don't mind if I've got a lot of questions," Winston continued, apparently oblivious to the effect she was having on Drake. "Gosh, I don't even know where to start." Her blue eyes looked up with hero worship shining.

But it was true, wasn't it? Winston had been drafted deep from the ranks of regional news programs in the Southwest, after only two years' experience on network. Two years, plus four for college, plus four for high school—yes, ten years. She could easily have been in grade school, or at least middle school, when Drake had started at ACN.

"Of course," Drake said, not allowing her emotions to show in her voice. She was acutely aware of the rest of the newsroom crew watching, and could almost feel the effort it was taking for them to choke back snorts of laughter. Winston may not have known what impact her remarks had, but none of it was lost on the rest of the cynical, world-weary reporters there.

Or maybe, Drake thought, scrutinizing Winston more closely, the young woman *did* know exactly what she was doing. She couldn't be a completely brainless idiot, could she? Not and have risen that quickly through the ranks of regional news organizations. No, she had to have more on the ball than Drake was seeing right now.

Give her some time and see what develops. Maybe it's just nerves.

Then again, if the bitch was going to declare war on anyone, she'd better watch out. Drake had not survived in this bastion of male superiority without developing a few guerrilla combat techniques of her own. And foremost among them was niceness.

"Anything I can do to help," Drake said, her voice suddenly sweet. She put one arm around the younger woman's shoulders and gave her a warm hug, only accidentally throwing her off balance in her high heel shoes. "Of course, it was such a long time ago that I was as—well—new as you are, wasn't it?" Her green eyes ringed with gold bore in on Winston's blue ones, and just for a moment, the new reporter looked shaken. "And there is so much to learn, isn't there? The technical information, how to get around in the world—not to mention contacts. Even learning to get along with the rest of the staff can be a challenge, don't you think?" Drake stepped up the intensity of her stare that was quickly turning into a glare. "After all, it's all a matter of teamwork, isn't it?"

Winston smiled uncertainly. "Of course. And with all your experience—" she started, evidently setting up for another jab, but Pamela leaned forward and accidentally stepped on her toe. Winston yelped and drew back. Pamela reached across her to pick up a catalog. She handed it to Winston and smiled. "Oh, I'm sorry. I do hope I didn't hurt you."

"Not at all." Winston drew herself up to her full height, her face hard. The steel beneath the attractive exterior was now showing.

"Because the smallest injury can really set you back," Pamela said, her gaze locked on the other woman's eyes. "I mean, a broken toe or something—well, it's not like you can do much traveling if you can't run, is it? The sort of places we go, you never know when you'll need to get out of the way."

"I wouldn't let a broken toe slow me down."

Drake shook her head, amused. "Ah, no. *You* wouldn't. But first off, Hank would never allow you out of the country until you had medical clearance. And second, even if he did, it would be very dangerous. You never know when the shit is going to hit the fan and you have to be able to run for your life. If it comes down to it. And it sometimes does." She turned back to survey the other reporters, now watching them enjoy the interaction. "Isn't that right, guys?" A chorus of nods and agreement answered her. Sure, they were enjoying the tiff, but they knew which side their bread was buttered on. Drake was a powerhouse and Winston was just the new kid on the block.

Besides, Drake was right. The cameramen would have enough to do with getting their own gear clear of trouble without worrying about a reporter with a bum leg.

"So, for starters," Drake said briskly, her point made, "you need more comfortable shoes for around here." She tapped the catalog she'd given Winston. "I ordered from these guys. Spring for the steel-toed field shoes—they come in handy, particularly if you're on a ship."

"Thank you, I will," Winston said. For a moment, all the fight seemed to have gone out of her. Then her temper flared again. "So tell me, Miss Drake—Pamela—is there any truth to the rumor that you've picked up where you left off with

Admiral Magruder? After all, I understand he's available now."

There was a moment of shocked, appalled silence, and Winston immediately saw that she'd overstepped her bounds. But there was no way to recover, not with the entire newsroom staring at her. Drake herself was a model of icy composure.

"First off, as you should know, he's no longer an admiral. He's just a civilian now. And no, I am not quite ill-bred enough to, quote, pick up, unquote, as you put it with a man whose wife is missing in action."

"It's been a year," Winston said. "Surely he's preparing to go on with his life and accept the inevitable. After all, she hasn't been heard from at all since she was shot down."

Pamela did not move. "A parachute was sighted when she ejected. While the conclusion that she was killed in action may seem the only correct one to you, I can assure you that all of us—and I mean *all* of us—are hoping and praying that she is eventually found. To do less would be rather despicable, don't you think?" Behind her, the rest of the newsroom murmured its agreement.

Winston considered that for moment, then a flush crept up her cheeks. "You know," she said, a new note in her voice, "I wonder if I could ask you an enormous favor. Just this once."

Drake shrugged, her anger boiling white hot inside her. "Besides advice on your footwear?"

Winston nodded slowly. "Yes." She was still speaking loudly enough for everyone in the newsroom to hear. "I seem to have this really awful tendency to make a complete and utter ass out of myself when I first meet people." Her blue-eyed gaze locked on Pamela's, the eyes calm but with a hint of defiance. "I think that's something I need to get over. Perhaps you could give me some pointers."

Drake regarded her for a moment, her expression softening only slightly in the face of the other woman's apparently sincere embarrassment. She could sense the mood of the newsroom swinging behind Winston now, and to hammer Winston again in the face of an attempted apology, however oblique, would be to concede the round to her.

"I think I just did," Drake said calmly. She stuck out her

hand, taking the sting out of her words with a genuine smile. "Welcome aboard, Cary." This time, her words were warm. "What are you doing for lunch today?"

USS **Jefferson**
0300 local (GMT-9)
Mid-Pacific Ocean

Airman Lance Irving enjoyed midwatches. It was the only time he was certain he would be left alone.

The USS *Jefferson* was steaming through the warm night air. Irving knew they were somewhere between Hawaii and San Diego, but he wasn't sure exactly where. The other Navy ships and commercial vessels were mere specks of light on the horizon, the Navy ships in the battle groups spaced out around the carrier at twenty-mile intervals, the civilian ships wandering in and out between them, oblivious to the formation. In a few hours, the opening evolutions of an exercise known as Kernel Blitz would begin.

Irving saw the lights of the USS *Lake Champlain* shift slightly. The cruiser was the closest Navy ship to the carrier. From what Irving could see, it was changing course slightly to move away from a cruise ship blazing with lights, lit up like a carnival. Smart move. If the cruise ship was dumb enough to be in the vicinity of a naval exercise, then it was probably dumb enough to collide with the minimally lit *Lake Champlain*.

Irving was reasonably certain that the operations specialist in CDC would have already noticed the change in the cruiser's course, but standing orders called for him to report his observations. With all the electronics and link systems in use, the Navy still relied on the old Mark One Mod Zero eyeball for a sanity check on radars and computers. Irving keyed his sound-powered phone. "Surface Plot, Port. Aspect change on the cruise ship."

A laconic "Roger, got it" came back immediately. "That cruise ship is the *Montego Bay*—bet they've got better food than we do, you think?"

"Yeah, I bet." *Got it. These guys don't sweat the load, not the way the airdales do. I could get used to being a surface sailor real easy.* Irving's division officer, division chief, and a leading petty officer all seemed to have it in for him. Day in and day out, they were on his back, and all because he hadn't yet finished his basic qualifications as plane captain.

Oh, sure, he was trying. He spent numerous hours on the flight deck, trying to pick up what was going on. But everyone was moving so fast in so many directions at once! And the aircraft—in his most private moments, he would admit that being around them on the flight deck terrified him. The stories of sailors who got caught up in the jet blast and went overboard, or, even worse, were sucked into the jet engines and ground up like chopped liver, kept him awake at night. The nightmares were becoming increasingly terrifying. As much as he wanted to be part of the gang, he found himself more and more often thinking longingly about the quiet office jobs on the ship—a disbursing clerk, a yeoman, perhaps an aviation supply rating—something civilized, a job that dealt with people instead of tons and tons of hot, screaming metal.

Irving scanned his sector of the ocean, his binoculars focused and attentive. Although he might not have been suited to be a plane captain, that didn't mean he was a slacker. No, someday soon he would screw up his courage and tell the chief just how he felt about being on the flight deck. And, from the expression he'd seen on the chief's face today, his confession might not be that much of a surprise.

Admiral Kurashov
0202 local (GMT-9)

Groshenko stood in the center of the ship's command center, one deck below the flight deck. Much of the tactical chatter around him made little sense, but the calm professional tones were evidence of a highly trained and competent crew. Unprepared crews, like soldiers, either panicked or got belligerent. There was a peculiarly distinctive tone of voice that walked the line between tension and confidence that was the hallmark of anything done well.

Despite his personal dislike of the ship's commander, Captain First Rank Bolshovich, Groshenko had to admit that the man appeared to be competent. A command was always a reflection of its commander, an infallible window into the inner workings of its most senior officer. Perhaps they would never be friends, but they would be comrades in arms.

Finally, the last checklist was completed, the last pre-operational test performed. The circuits fell silent. The tactical officer turned to look at Bolshovich. "All systems ready, sir. Request weapons free."

The silence was palpable. Every warrant officer at a radar screen seemed to be holding his breath. Bolshovich let the tension build for a few moments, and Groshenko felt a familiar flash of irritation. It was one thing to take time to consider one's decision, another entirely to grandstand.

"Weapons free." Groshenko's voice was pure confidence, and the bracing effect on the crew was immediately evident, the surge of adrenaline palpable.

"Weapons free, aye-aye." The tactical officer turned back to his console and clicked his communications circuit. "Special units, you are weapons free. Execute operational test two three."

Groshenko thought he could hear a hum build within the hull of the ship, but it was so faint as to be virtually undetectable to his untrained senses. He glanced at Bolshovich and saw him nod.

Two indicators on a small makeshift panel flashed yellow, then green. The monitor mounted high in one corner of the compartment flashed a line of light so brief in duration that at first Groshenko thought it was his imagination.

"Again," Boshovich ordered. The panel lights flashed again, and this time Groshenko was certain he saw the spear of light on the monitor.

The hum stopped. The compartment was silent.

Low Earth Orbit
Track 2459
0203 local (GMT-9)

To the men and women who monitored her, the satellite was known as Betty Lou. She was located at an altitude of five thousand miles and maintained a geosynchronous position just north of Hawaii. She was an older satellite, one not equipped with some of the newer downloading capabilities of later ones, but she had been in place for fifteen years and had proved to be exceptionally reliable.

Just before dawn, Betty Lou's sensors picked up a flash of light lancing upward from the middle of the Pacific Ocean. It was a blue-green spear, its beam tight, focused, and unusually stable. It pulsed just once, the duration measured in milliseconds.

Betty Lou recorded the event, buffered it, and squirt it out to a monitoring station located at Naval Station Pearl Harbor. There, the satellite data was digitally transformed into a picture, given a quick look by both the duty officer and a photo-intelligence specialist, then sent out to the numerous civilian and military units that relied on the data daily.

Four microseconds after Betty had downloaded the data, the laser pulsed again, this time sweeping a tight beam across her outer shell. The effect was instantaneous and disastrous. The beam of light smashed into Betty Lou's solar panels, instantly disrupting the delicate crystalline layers. It heated up the metal casing of the satellite, destroying control circuits designed to work in the subzero temperatures of outer space, then proceeded to fuse the delicate, if antique, circuitry inside her. Within the first few moments of the light striking the pitted and dull hull of the satellite, Betty Lou was reduced to a chunk of space debris.

USS Jefferson
0204 local (GMT-9)

Just as Irving was starting to sweep the forward segment of his area, the sky cracked in half. An arrow of blue light shot up from the horizon and divided the sky into two equal parts. It seemed to go on and on forever, as high as the eye could see. The light stunned his dark-adapted eyes. Then, just as suddenly as it had appeared, it was gone.

He grabbed the sound-powered phone hanging around his neck and depressed the transmit button. "Deck, port lookout, reporting a blue light in the sky," he said, his words tumbling over one another. Just what the hell had it been? There had been nothing like that in his lookout indoctrination training.

"Port, we saw it!" a voice said sharply. "Keep your eyes peeled, okay?"

It had looked like one of the lasers he'd seen at a concert recently, except that the ones at the concert had been red and yellow. Had there been blue or green lights? He wasn't sure. But it had been the same sharply defined beam, the same blinding brilliance. He keyed his mike again. "Deck, port. It looked like a laser."

"That's what we think it was," the voice said. "And for future reference, the—"

The man's voice cut off abruptly. There was a chorus of clicks on the line, as others listening waited for the rest of the explanation. Finally, the voice said, "Wait. Out"

Yeah. Like I've got anything else to do.

Admiral Kurashov
0205 local (GMT-9)

Groshenko waited, again irritated at Bolshovich's predilection for the dramatic. If the navy captain had been working for him, this nonsense would have been put to a stop immediately. But he wasn't, was he? At least not completely.

Finally, Bolshovich broke the silence with "Well done!" He turned to his executive officer, grinning broadly. "Exceptionally well done."

The executive officer visibly relaxed, tendering his own small, tight smile. "It seemed to go well," he said self-consciously.

Gorshenko kept his face carefully impassive. How could

they tell it went well? There had been little to see on the screen, and not much more from outside on the weather-decks. One brief flash of blinding light, gone before you could be entirely certain it was there. That was all. Had he blinked at the wrong moment, he would have missed it entirely.

"We will, of course, have to wait for final confirmation of the success of a shot." The captain glanced at the general, checking to see if he understood the difficulty. "We have no capability for evaluating whether or not there was a hard or even soft kill on the satellite. She is old, of course. Our intelligence people who monitor such things may be able to tell when she does not transmit her downlink at the usual time. Then again, the opportunities for detecting her down-link are relatively narrow." The captain shrugged, dismissing the matter. "I suspect we will know more quickly from the American reaction and the press."

"Unless they decide not to say anything," Gorshenko said.

"Always the possibility. But even if they do, their defense establishment is full of leaks. Sooner or later, we will know." Bolshovich was ebullient now, triumphant, and the crew was picking up his mood.

"We will know even more quickly if the American carrier opens fire on us," Gorshenko observed.

"Exactly. That is the reason we're still on alert, General." Bolshovich managed to be simultaneously condescending and nominally respectful. "I imagine they will have seen the flash of the laser, even if they're not exactly certain what it is. They will report it, of course. How much they are told by their superiors in response is anyone's guess."

Just as how much you'll be told is my *decision. And under the circumstances, I don't think it will be much.* Gorshenko allowed his face to relax into a congratulatory smile, knowing that the navy captain would never know exactly what was behind the test.

USS **Jefferson**
TFCC
0206 local (GMT-9)

Coyote had just dozed off when he heard a gentle tap on his door. He blinked hard twice, sat up in bed, and switched on the light. The admiral's cabin was a large one and was between TFCC and the flag mess. His duty officers had had instructions to wake him under certain specified conditions or if anything unusual happened, and he had always emphasized that he would rather be woken up in error than surprised later. Thus, though he silently swore as he heard the door open, he kept his thoughts to himself.

Commander Brian Hanson stood there, a worried look on his face. Hanson was an experienced officer, and one whose judgment Coyote trusted. If he thought it was worth waking the admiral up, it probably was.

Coyote swung his feet to the deck and reached for the shirt hung neatly over the back of a chair. "Talk to me."

"The lookout and officer at the deck reported seeing a blue laser over the horizon," Hanson said. "All reports are consistent with a laser. I sent the messenger to wake up Commander Busby."

"Good move." Coyote started to button the shirt as he slipped on his shoes. He stopped, kicked the shoes back off, and pulled on his pants. "And?"

"And the position is consistent with the position of the Russian carrier," Hanson finished.

"And why am I not surprised?" Coyote muttered. "Some sort of show of force, it has to be. It's not like they'd sit quietly while we test ours. They just had to show us, didn't they?" He shot Hanson a sharp look. "The Russian carrier, though . . ." He let Hanson finish the sentence.

"The Russian amphibious transport," Hanson said, correcting his earlier terminology.

In terms of warfare capabilities, it was largely a distinction without a difference. The *Admiral Kurashov* amphibious transport was the Russian equivalent of an aircraft carrier, although carrying only vertical launch fighter/attack aircraft and helicopters, and fewer of those than her American counterpart. Still, it was important for international political repercussions to characterize the ship correctly—amphibious transport, not an aircraft carrier. God knows why it made a difference, but it did, and Coyote and his staff tried to remember to use the politically correct terminology.

"Okay, get Lab Rat on it. You already got the message drafted?"

Hanson nodded. "The watch officer has started on it. We made an initial voice report to Third Fleet and CINCPAC before I came to wake you up."

And that's what I like to see. Hanson is aggressive, professional—he already knows what I'm going to ask them to do and he's got his watch officer completing the action checklists while he briefs me. Good man. Aloud, he said, "Any information back from either of them?"

"No, Admiral. Then again, I suspect if they have anything, it needs to be on the intelligence circuits."

"You're right about that." Now completely dressed, Coyote headed for the door. Hanson held it open and stepped back to let the admiral precede him.

A funny thing, that there's information you can't even say over a top secret encrypted circuit. But that's the way the world is these days. More and more stuff is secret, and more highly classified. Hell, I bet next our toilet paper usage report is moved up to secret. As it is, it's confidential, since it's logistic data. They're worried that the Russians can figure out how many people are on board from how much toilet paper we use. Like they couldn't find out by looking at Jefferson's web page.

Inside TFCC, there was no panic. The watch officer, Lieutenant Bailey Kates, appeared calm and in control. He maintained control of the flow of information, juggling ten or fifteen actions at once, all the while keeping his gaze glued to the tactical screen. He said, "Good evening, Admiral," almost without taking a breath as he monitored the lookout reports and checked the message that awaited the admiral's signature.

Not bad. Not bad at all. Coyote made a mental note to keep track of the lieutenant and make sure he got the mentoring he needed to move up quickly. Hanson was a good man to start Kates under.

Lab Rat burst into TFCC, still buttoning his shirt. "Evening, Admiral. Anything else?" he asked, already edging back for the hatch, heading for the compartment next to TFCC. The SCIF, or specially compartmented information, was staffed by sailors with stratospheric security clearances. It was the equivalent of TFCC in the top secret intelligence world.

"Nothing new, sir," Kates said. There was a lull in the action, and he swung his chair around to face Hanson. He handed him a clipboard. "Rough on the message, sir."

Coyote resisted the impulse to read over Hanson's shoulder, and instead followed Lab Rat to SCIF. Any explanation might never make it out of that black hole. Frustrating sometimes, but officers were used to not always getting the full story.

Inside SCIF, the air of frustration was immediately evident. Sailors spoke softly over four radio circuits, murmuring into their headsets. Another two ran queries through databases, searching for anything similar. In a few words, the watch officer briefed Lab Rat. "Nothing yet, sir, Admiral. CINCPAC is looking into it as is Seventh Fleet. It's already gone up to JCS—the JCS watch officer just notified the JCS TAO."

"Wonderful," Coyote muttered yet again. There was nothing like having DC and JCS maintain an electronic presence on board the ship. They'd been pinging on *Jeff* and Coyote particularly hard as the date for the laser test approached.

Trust the Russians to want to beat us to it. It's Soyuz all over again.

Well, no matter. Even if the Russian system worked, Coyote had no doubt that the American system would be far more accurate and deadly. And on balance, it wasn't a bad idea if the Russians had one as well, was it? Wasn't that the whole point of missile defense systems, that they would eliminate the insane race for offense arms in the world?

One of the sailors turned to Lab Rat and peeled off his headset. "Sir? They'd like to speak to you."

"Who is it?"

"JCS."

Lab Rat slipped the headset on. He identified himself, and fell silent as he listened. He motioned to the sailor, who passed him a clipboard and pencil. Lab Rat began taking notes. Finally, after about sixty seconds, he said, "Aye-aye, Admiral. I will pass it on to Admiral Gránt."

There was another silence, then Lab Rat said, "Yes, Admiral. I understand."

With a sigh, Lab Rat pulled off his headset and handed it back to the sailor. "They want to finish up the coordination issues with you." He turned to Coyote and continued with "JCS says they have no information on this. However, they want complete silence maintained. Not a word anywhere. I'm to personally debrief each lookout and have him sign a non-disclosure agreement."

"Wow. And they're not saying anything about it?" Coyote asked.

"Zero, Admiral. That was Rear Admiral Larson I was speaking to. He's the duty officer."

"Better you than me," Coyote answered. Larson was a surface sailor and had a reputation for being exceptionally acerbic with battle group commanders.

"This doesn't change anything, does it, Admiral?" Lab Rat asked. "We still solid on our test schedule?"

"Yeah, as far as I know. They want it all kept secret, though." Coyote sighed, contemplating the improbability and sheer lunacy of trying to keep the Russian laser test a secret. That would be only slightly more improbable than keeping their own tests secret. "Okay, make it happen. Everybody signs the damned paper, but make sure the lookouts know what they're looking for, okay?"

USS **Jefferson**
Port Lookout Station
0217 local (GMT-9)

Fifteen minutes after Irving had first reported the laser, a new voice spoke up on his sound-powered phone headset. The voice was older, more authoritarian than the officer of the deck, and for a few moments Irving couldn't exactly place it. "All stations, listen up. Some of you reported seeing a blue flash in the sky. It was simply a helicopter searchlight at an odd angle to the ship. Nothing unusual. Forget you even saw it. And all lookouts and bridge watchstanders are to report to Commander Busby in CVIC immediately after being relieved."

A helicopter searchlight? Irving shook his head. Not likely. Besides, they had secured from flight quarters several hours ago, and there were no helicopters airborne. Perhaps off the cruiser or something—no, they would've known that, too, as one of the lookouts would have seen it launch and reported it.

What, did they think he was stupid? A searchlight—yeah, right. What a bunch of horseshit. Some of the officers couldn't even use a computer, and had never been to a laser light show, and they expected him to believe that story? Well, he wasn't blind. He knew what he had seen, and it wasn't a searchlight.

The remaining hours of his watch passed quickly as he kept alert for anything else in the sky. He fully expected to see the laser again. Any second now, and he would miss it if he blinked at the wrong time. He kept up an excellent watch, but no matter how hard he stared, the light did not reappear.

THREE

The cruise ship *Montego Bay* had seen better days. Once the flagship of her fleet, she was now starting to show her age. On more modern ships, gas turbines replaced the steam boilers *Montego Bay* used for power. Her wooden decking had been stripped, sanded, and refinished so many times that it was now perceptibly lower than the interior of the ship. The cabins were smaller than those found on modern ships, and contained fewer amenities. While the cruise ship company had done what it could to keep her updated and attractive, the *Montego Bay* was trapped somewhere between a claim to old world charm and sleek modern convenience.

Despite her deficiencies, *Montego Bay*'s revenues were always positive. She was the favorite of a large class of passengers who enjoyed cruises but found the prices of the newer liners simply beyond their means. *Montego Bay* provided an acceptable compromise.

Montego Bay was currently working the pineapple run, the voyage between San Pedro Island in Southern California and the Hawaiian island chain. She'd made the trip many times, always uneventfully. This time, through no fault of her own, that would not be the case.

Her captain, Eric Gaspert, had been her master for the last ten years. He knew every sound she made, had walked her through her most recent renovations, and enjoyed being her master. The passengers were far more reasonable to deal with than the very rich. Gaspert liked his job and looked forward to several more years of it.

Gaspert was also a diligent captain, entirely professional and conscientious. This morning, he was on the bridge, reviewing the weather forecasts, notices to mariners, and other operational reports. The notices to mariners, or NOTAMS, particularly caught his attention. These were promulgated by the United States Coast Guard and contained warnings about military operations or other hazards at sea.

"If we stay on our present course, we'll be right along the edge of this warning area," his navigator said, tapping the chart in the center of an area outlined in red pencil. "And I think we'd like to stay well clear. Last night they were doing those random zigzags they like to practice—no talking to us, even though they saw us on the radar, no warning. We were never too close, but it'd be nice to know when they're going to do something like that. Then all at once—*wham*. One of them, the Russians or the Americans, starts shooting lasers up in the air."

Gaspert chuckled. "Bet that scared the crap out of the night crew."

"I was down in the engine room and I heard the deck officer yell. Wonder what it was."

"The NOTAM says they're doing some Kernel Blitz missile testing exercises today," Gaspert said. "It's probably related to that, and if it's missile testing, we won't have to worry about staying clear. They'll be all over us to clear the area before they take a shot."

"Yes, of course," the navigator said. "But this time, it may be a bit more complicated. The Russians are keeping a close eye on them. And they've been keeping station just to the east of the operating area."

"They know something we don't?" Gaspert asked.

The navigator nodded. "Probably. No less than we do, anyway."

Wonder why the Russians are so interested in this exercise? Sure, they conduct surveillance on most military operations, but normally with one of their spy trawlers masquerading as a fishing boat. Hardly ever with a complete battle group including one of their own operational carriers. "They must be making the Navy nervous," he said out loud. Gaspert had started his own career at sea in the United States Navy, and had a good idea of what was probably going on within the American battle group with the Russians so close. "INCOS is getting a workout."

INCOS, or the International Concord to Avoid Incidents at Sea, was an agreement signed by both Russia and the United States. It covered conduct between the navies when meeting in open ocean and was designed to prevent misunderstandings that could escalate into conflicts. Prior to IN-COS, there had been many instances where posturing and seemingly innocent but fairly hostile acts had almost led to tragedy. Recognizing the need for stricter rules between enemies during the Cold War, the Concord had been developed with the help of military and civilian law-of-the-sea experts. Since nobody wanted a war, particularly not now, both sides respected its provisions.

"Well, they're big enough that we'll see them on radar," Gaspert said, checking the formations one last time. "But put a note in the night orders to notify me if we come within twenty miles of either group." INCOS might cover Russian and U.S. military forces, but it said nothing about conduct toward cruise ships.

"Aye-aye, sir." The navigator proceeded to brief the weather, which looked exceptionally pleasant. No hurricanes, not even a low-pressure system between the ship and her final destination, nor was one expected to move in. This was good news. The *Montego Bay* lacked the advanced stabilizers of more modern hulls, and although she rode the seas well, she could not provide the rock-steady deck that many passengers seemed to expect under all conditions. "We'd hate to interfere with shuffleboard, wouldn't we?"

There was nothing more of particular interest in Gaspert's

morning brief. A few emergencies involving the passengers.
One now in sick bay for a possible heart attack. A twisted
ankle, a few cases of seasickness—and how was that possible, in this most gentle of seas? One case of what looked
like the flu. The ordinary run of accidents and illnesses expected on any trip.

Captain Gaspert followed his usual sequence of dealing
with paperwork, approving engineering and maintenance requests, making his rounds among the passengers, seeing and
being seen and providing a sense of presence that reassured
the most nervous of them. By the time he went below to tour
the ship's engineering plant, he had every reason to feel confident that the voyage would proceed uneventfully.

USS **Jefferson**
0800 local (GMT-9)

The morning brief on board the carrier was proceeding according to plan. Each department head ran through the status
report of the areas under his or her responsibility, the remarks
backed up by slides projected from a computer onto a large
screen. Engineering, operations, intelligence, and so forth,
each one bringing Coyote current on what had transpired
since the previous evening brief.

The very last department to report was always the ocean-
ographer, who also served as the meteorologist. Coyote had
decreed the order of the briefers, saying the weather and the
ocean environment were of critical importance to every department on the ship. Privately, Lab Rat suspected that the
admiral had scheduled it as a show closer because the presentation was always boring enough to convince even the
most gung-ho brown-noser present that it was time for the
brief to wrap up.

"Another four days of this weather," Lieutenant Commander Mason Wyatt said, entirely too chattily for Lab Rat's
taste. Whenever Wyatt briefed, Lab Rat got the distinct impression that he was auditioning for a spot on the Weather
Channel. "Looks like terrific weather for the steel beach
planned for the Fourth of July." Wyatt beamed as though

personally guaranteeing good weather for the gigantic cook-out and celebration planned on the flight deck, the steel beach.

He proceeded to run through a number of graphs depicting the sound velocity profile of the ocean, the major weather fronts and high- and low-pressure areas across the Pacific, maintaining the same informal, breezy tone so at odds with the no-nonsense seriousness of every other department. Still, Lab Rat reflected, Mason was a hell of a meteorologist. If he said they were in for good weather, there would be good weather. Personally, Lab Rat thought that the *Jefferson* was due for some decent weather just to make up for the rest of the cruise.

Jefferson, along with her escorts, had departed San Diego six weeks ago. They were supposedly deployed to participate in a major war game staged for the Pacific theater, known as Kernel Blitz. At least, that was the story put out to all but a few with the need to know.

Lab Rat was one of those with a need to know.

It wasn't as if it were a complete cover-up. There *was* an exercise named Kernel Blitz under way, and *Jefferson was* in the data link with units around the world, as was the Naval War College. Most of the ship's crew was frantically planning and executing theoretical strikes and amphibious landings as well as other evolutions designed to ensure that every part of the battle group had a chance to practice the skills they'd need in actual war.

But a small group located in the bowels of Lab Rat's department was engaged in something far more critical to the nation's defense: the operational test of a new theater ballistic missile defense system.

Lab Rat had been chosen to head up the operation on board *Jefferson,* partly because he possessed the necessary clearances and it fell within his areas of responsibility as intelligence officer for the ship. Additionally, he was all too familiar with lasers and ballistic missile defense. During the last cruise, Senior Chief Armstrong, Lab Rat's right-hand man, had showed him just how potent a land-based defense system could be. Only three weeks before, the senior chief had retired from the Navy and left *Jefferson* to begin his new civilian career with Omicron, the defense contractor with the primary contract for the TBMD laser.

To complicate matters, a Russian battle group centered around the *Admiral Kurashov,* what the Russians called an amphibious transport but what was really an aircraft carrier, was located thirty miles to the east. The laser blast arrowing up into the sky last night had caught them all off guard. The low-level intelligence reports said that they were there to monitor Kernel Blitz. But Lab Rat suspected that somewhere in the bowels of the organization would be a group similar to his, watching the TBMD tests and evaluating the impact of a success on the balance of power. Because, when you got right down to it, nothing was ever as secret as you thought it was.

There was, however, one primary problem with any land-based system: no matter how secret, no matter how covert, its location eventually became known. And once known, it was immediately targeted by America's enemies.

The same reasoning that had led the United States to base a third of its nuclear triad on silent nuclear submarines had also spurred the development of sea-based ballistic missile defense systems. Omicron was again the lead contractor, as they had been for the land-based system, although this time through one of its wholly owned subsidiaries. Judging from the message traffic Lab Rat had seen that morning, Senior Chief Armstrong would soon be back aboard *Jefferson,* but this time as a very senior project manager whose equivalent military grade was several grades higher than Lab Rat's rank.

"Finally," Mason said, still holding his genial smile and staring at his audience while tapping the chart with his pointer—and just how did he do that, Lab Rat wondered, manage to nail exactly the correct spot without looking at it—"meteorologists all over the world are saying a fond fare-well to a satellite known as Betty Lou. Last night, at approximately 0230, one final transmission was received from Betty Lou. After that, she no longer responded to control commands."

"Okay, anything else?" Coyote asked briskly, tapping his number two pencil on the legal pad in front of him. Everyone on his staff knew that this was a sign that the admiral's attention span had just been exceeded. Mason was the only one who never seemed to understand that, and to Coyote's dismay, Mason continued.

"Odd circumstances, too," he went on blithely. "In fact, Commander Busby, some of your folks are looking into it now. Just before Betty Lou passed away, she detected a— well, we don't know exactly what it is. It's being correlated with other intelligence sources now, I suppose. But it looked like a bolt of lightning."

Shit. We're supposed to be keeping a lid on this. Maybe he'll take the hint if I blow it off. Coyote had talked to the midwatch TFCC crew and made sure that they all knew the laser incident was strictly hush-hush. If the lookouts kept their mouths shut, they might just pull off the secrecy bit for a while longer.

"Lightning?" Coyote queried. "In space? Right."

"A sharp, short blast of light. Probably an internal short circuit of some sort that created an artifact, Admiral." Mason was positively gloating over the fact that Coyote had shown enough interest to comment. Most of the time, his questions came from the destroyer squadron, or DESRON, who maintained an intense and somewhat anal interest in the intricate temperature profiles within the ocean.

"Well," Coyote said, clearly a dismissal. "Unless there are any questions." His tone of voice made it clear that none were expected. "Commander Busby, I'll see you in CDC in ten minutes."

"Yes, Admiral," Lab Rat replied.

They're testing their systems.

Of course, it could be one of those odd coincidences that keeps popping up around the world, and making a hash of the best intelligence estimates that money could buy. Lady Luck always had her hand in the works. But losing a satellite to something that looked like lightning just when *Jefferson* was testing out her systems and Russians were watching— or maybe even testing their own—well, that was just a little bit too much, wasn't it?

Well, significant or not, it would have to wait. Lab Rat had eight minutes before he was supposed to meet the admiral in CDC to go over the final details for the test of their own system tonight. Sure, it was bad news that the Russians were testing their own version, not only from a correlation-of-forces point of view but simply as a matter of muddying up the playing field.

"Sir?" a voice just behind him asked. "Is there anything I can do?" Lab Rat turned to shake his head at Lieutenant Bill Strain, the new assistant intelligence officer who had checked in just before they'd deployed. Strain was a tall, lanky fellow, built like the college basketball player he was. Word had it that Strain had had a full scholarship at Notre Dame, a fact that was readily confirmed by the alumni on board. A few squadrons had already made a bid for him to join their in-tramural teams, but so far Strain had been pleading the need to concentrate on his duties in CVIC. Maybe later, after the deployment. Lab Rat suspected that his new lieutenant pre-ferred more intellectual leisure activities and would probably continue to find excuses not to join until the interest died down. Nothing wrong with that, although Lab Rat found himself faintly envious of Strain for having a choice. At five-feet, six-inches tall, Lab Rat had long since resigned himself to signing up for bantam-weight sports.

"Not yet," Lab Rat answered. "Not unless you know some way we can reach out and touch that system of theirs from here. And without getting caught."

"Nothing comes to mind, but I'll give it some thought." Strain passed him a few sheets out of an intelligence update, information on the probable status of Russian laser defense systems. Lab Rat hadn't known he wanted them until Strain handed them to him.

Sharp, real sharp. New, just like Bailey Kates, but already a front runner. We're growing the next generation right here, our own replacements. And the Navy's giving us some damned fine material to work with.

"Thanks." Lab Rat glanced through them, refreshing his memory. It'd been a while since he'd looked at Russian ca-pabilities, and it wouldn't hurt to sound smart if Coyote had any technical questions. The admiral had a knack for sur-prising his officers with the depth of his knowledge on arcane subjects.

Maybe they're done with their test. Maybe taking out the satellite was enough for them. Not that there won't be hell to pay for that—in fact, I'm surprised we're not already seeing warning orders on it. In some contexts, that would be a clear enough act of war to start a nasty little exchange of weapons.

But it was an older satellite, wasn't it? One that wasn't all that useful anyway. And maybe, with the U.S. concentrating their resources and efforts on fighting worldwide terrorism, the Russians' cooperation was worth more than a little outdated chunk of metal in the sky.

And we're just going to let them get away with it? Lab Rat shook his head in disgust. Not so long ago, destroying an American satellite would have been grounds for a declaration of war.

"I wonder what made them pick out Betty Lou," Strain mused. "Old satellite, of course—were they walking some sort of line between pissing us off and proving that they could do it? A few years ago, they never would have dared. Seems like nothing's sacred anymore."

The changes that had been wrought in American society by the hideous events of September 11, 2001, were deep and profound. The legal system was already infringing on constitutional rights that just a few months before the attack were virtually untouchable. With U.S. military forces treading heavily around the restrictions on *posse comitatus,* the restriction on using the military inside the U.S. for law enforcement, a lot of things were giving way to the need to hunt down terrorists. Maybe that included not being quite so worried about one satellite and not being willing to risk war over it.

If the tests tonight proved out, the U.S. would be a long way toward perfecting the continental missile defense system. And if it worked, it would free up assets normally occupied with mutual assured destruction, or MAD, to concentrate on the war on terrorism.

Coyote entered the compartment, and Strain moved quietly to a corner. That was another thing about the newly promoted lieutenant that Lab Rat liked, his ability to fade into the background until he was needed. Hard to do when you were Strain's size, too.

"Your people ready?" Coyote asked. "I got to tell you, there's a lot more riding on this test now than there was a few hours ago."

Lab Rat ran his hand over his scalp, feeling the small bristles poking into his palm. "It'll work. It's got to."

"You sound sure about that."

"I am, Admiral."

"Well." Coyote stared at the computer screen showing the relative positions of all the ships in this part of the ocean. The symbols formed a neat geometric pattern on the screen, courses and speed represented by speed leaders. Too bad reality wasn't as orderly. "The sooner we get it over with, the better I'll feel. Especially when we COD the civilians off the ship." He glanced over at Lab Rat. "They're a pain in the ass."

"Yes, Admiral. But they own the gear until we sign off on the formal acceptance of it."

Coyote waved him off irritably. "I know, I know. As much as we've paid them for developing the damn thing, you think they'd be easier to get along with." The defense contractors had been cluttering up the flag mess for weeks.

"We'll know tonight, Admiral. As soon as it tests sat, I'll have them secure all the gear and pack up their stuff. We'll have them out on the next COD."

Coyote stared moodily at the screen. "Yeah, I know." He stood and stretched, feeling the long hours seeping into his bones. "The sooner the better. DESRON wants the ASW module back, and the techs are bitching about the power distribution panels and the new wiring harnesses, and the chief engineer is going hermitile over the voltage drop in there. That shit draws a hell of a lot of power."

"First COD," Lab Rat promised.

"Let's hope that's soon enough. Call me if there are any changes." Coyote took one last look at the tactical plot before leaving.

Strain moved quietly to Lab Rat's side. "I'll go through the pre-op checklist again, sir."

Lab Rat shook his head. "No. We're ready. If you really
want to do something useful—"

"Yes, sir."

"—then go check on the COD availability. I have a feeling
the admiral's going to be more interested in that than another
checklist."

Washington, DC
The Beltway
0900 local (GMT-5)

Tombstone pulled his cherry red muscle car into the parking
lot. The office building was typical of the structures that were
home to a multitude of small defense contractors known as
the Beltway Bandits. The design had been modern fifteen
years ago, when defense industry money seemed to be an
endless stream of cash and new defense contractors and con-
sultants would pop up overnight. It featured an impressive
foyer replete with a waterfall and large plants, marbled floors
and express elevators. The entire impression of the lobby was
one of luxury.

Not so for the floors farther up the sixteen-story building.
At least half had absolutely no windows. The target occupants required areas that could satisfy the Department of Defense regulations for security, and the building specifications
required to house top secret material. Each floor was separated from the others by a layer of steel, and the concrete
brick of the structure was designed to prevent eavesdropping
and electronic surveillance.

The sixteenth floor was particularly secure. The rents
charged were commensurate with the degree of security the
floor afforded its occupants, and ranged from merely high to
absolutely outrageous. Nevertheless, the building never had
a shortage of potential renters for the sixteenth-floor facilities.

That Advanced Analysis had been able to obtain a small
suite of rooms was something of a curiosity to the other
occupants. Normally, one spent months, perhaps years on the
waiting list. How it was that Advanced Analysis had man-

aged to move in immediately just eight months ago was a
mystery. No one had ever heard of them and no one had ever
worked with them before their appearance on the scene.

A few of the more knowledgeable defense contractors quietly took note of that, along with the priority given to their
tenancy, glanced at the sign-in log in the lobby, and noted
that few visitors ever came to Advanced Analysis. And finally, they took in the occasional appearance of two very
familiar faces in the passageway and elevators: retired Admiral Thomas Magruder and his nephew, retired Vice Admiral Matthew Magruder.

While other defense contractors speculated on Advanced
Analysis's projects and complained about their intrusion into
the sixteenth floor—one small computer company had
wanted the spaces to expand their own operations—the wiser
among them kept their collective mouths shut. They had seen
this before and knew what it meant, more often in the bad
old days of the Cold War than now, but the pattern was all
too familiar. In all probability, Advanced Analysis was not
a normal aspiring defense contractor. Not with those two men
involved. Advanced Analysis was most probably a front for
the CIA or perhaps another agency with an interest in certain
special operations. There were always things that needed doing that no one in the established military structure wanted
to be responsible for. Sure, they recognized the necessity,
even suggested particular operations, but when it came down
to committing forces to the operations, the enthusiasm evap-
orated.

The outer office and lobby of Advanced Analysis was
done in traditional colors and style. Mauve and sky blue pre-
dominated, with modern pictures composed of interesting
fabrics and textures gracing the walls. The waiting room had
several comfortable chairs, a plastic and slightly dusty small
tree in one corner, and a few outdated magazines carefully
arranged on the side tables. It gave little evidence of ever
being used.

To date, Advanced Analysis had only four employees: the
two Magruders, another Tomcat pilot named Jeremy Greene,
and a receptionist, Janice Hall. Greene was technically a ci-

vilian, and had accepted a discharge from the Navy with the understanding that if he left Advanced Analysis he would be immediately recalled to active duty. Hall was a quiet, sharp woman, adept at maintaining the outer facade of the company. She fielded incoming calls, collected the resumes dropped off by job hunters and kept the small refrigerator stocked. Of the four, only Hall had regular hours. The other three worked insane hours when a mission was prepping and stood down between missions.

Tombstone had just returned from two weeks in Africa. There had been some indications that his wife, the former Tomboy Flynn, had been taken there as a prisoner following her ejection at sea. Tomboy, as the commanding officer of VF 95, had punched out when her aircraft was fatally damaged.

A month before, a Navy captain had risked her career to provide him with photo-intelligence shots of a rebel camp. In one of them, Tombstone could clearly make out Tomboy's face, lifted up toward the sky. It was a procedure that all aviators were taught, to expose their faces to the sky in hopes that a satellite or reconnaissance aircraft would be able to identify them. Analysis indicated that she was probably at a rebel camp in Africa. Tombstone had few contacts in the area, but that did not prevent him from going there personally and imposing on every possible government official to gain access to the interior.

"Good morning, sir," Hall said as Tombstone strode into the waiting room. "Your uncle is already here."

"And Jeremy?" Tombstone asked.

Hall shook her head. "Traffic, probably."

"Probably. Again," Tombstone said. None of them punched a clock at Advanced Analysis, but certain standards of behavior were expected when an operation was in the offing. Even during downtimes, they were expected to stay in contact with the office, ready for immediate recall. Since the last mission, Greene had been increasingly restless and sometimes difficult to locate when needed.

Tombstone knew what was at the heart of the younger aviator's attitude. Jeremy was a pilot and he wanted to fly.

When he accepted the offer to join Advanced Analysis, he had been assured that he would be flying, and in more dangerous situations than he would in the fleet. It hadn't worked out that way, and too much of it had been Tombstone's fault.

I should have taken a RIO, not another pilot. And I should get him more stick time.

Damn it all, it was so hard to turn over the controls. But how was Jeremy going to get the experience that Tombstone had without—well, experience?

I'll talk to Uncle about it. Get a couple of RIOs and start planning on two aircraft missions. Otherwise, we're going to lose him. I can feel it.

The security door opened as Hall let him in. Tombstone strode down the short passageway to his office, checked for messages, and then headed for the conference room. A few hours catching up on paperwork, and he would be done.

His uncle was already there, perusing a thin brown folder. "Morning," Tombstone said. "Anything up?"

"Maybe." His uncle sighed heavily, shut the folder, and shoved it across the table to Tombstone. "Although I'm not sure what we can do about it. We might not even be involved."

Before he took the folder, Tombstone paused to study his uncle. In the last three months, his uncle's boundless enthusiasm for Advanced Analysis and its mission seemed to have waned. Instead of presenting the ruddy, cheerful face he normally did to the world, his uncle had lost a good deal of color. His face tended to look gray and drawn now, and he appeared older than he had in years.

"Is anything wrong?" Tombstone asked, his hand still on the closed folder. "You don't look so hot."

"I'm fine," his uncle said.

"You sure?"

His uncle glared at him, his eyes piercing under his heavy eyebrows. There was a grim set to his face, a determination that Tombstone knew very well. It was an expression he'd seen often during his uncle's days as chief of naval operations, but less often since he had retired from active duty. Now, seeing the same expression again, Tombstone felt uneasy. "What is it?"

"Nothing."

Tombstone recognized that tone in his uncle's voice. Questioning him further would just result in an argument. Whatever was going on—and Tombstone was convinced something was—he would have to wait for his uncle to reveal it in his own time.

Tombstone opened the folder. A satellite photo was on top, and Tombstone spent a few minutes trying to puzzle it out before referring to the attached analysis sheet. Photo-intelligence interpretation was a highly specialized skill, more art than science, and it took trained eyes to extract the most information from a picture.

He glanced at the technical data before getting to the analyst's comments. The picture was taken at nighttime by an older geosynchronous satellite and showed a large portion of the Atlantic Ocean. There was a sharp line running across the center on it, linking the top right and bottom left corners. Tombstone had assumed it was a scratch of some sort, or a processing anomaly or gap in the data.

After reading the analyst's comments, he flipped back to the photo with renewed interest. "A laser shot," he said, impressed. "And from a Russian ship. Just why did they let us see this? They know when the satellites are going to be overhead, and what areas are covered by geosynchronous assets. Why test it on a clear day when you know a satellite is watching?"

"Exactly. But keep reading—there's more."

Tombstone skipped the rest of the report and leafed through the later materials. Just after the analyst's report was a top secret message from the National Atmospheric and Oceanographic Observatory. It announced the termination of the satellite that had taken the first photo. The cause was listed as unknown, possibly a mechanical failure. The message was classified top secret.

The message after it went one step further, both in classification and in explanation. It was specially compartmented information, eyes only. Readers had to have a cosmic purple clearance even to know that those messages existed.

And the contents were stunning. Tombstone whistled softly as he read. "Laser . . . intentional termination . . . possible experiment and response to theater ballistic missile testing . . ." When he finished reading, Tombstone looked up with concern in his eyes. "They think the Russians nailed the satellite? But why? How does that tie in with the theater ballistic missile defense system?"

"Pretty tightly, if you ask me. You saw the storm of worldwide protest when President Bush first announced that the United States would be pursuing an anti-missile defense system. Well, the rest of the world has had a few years to think about that while we worked on developing an operationally reliable system. It relies on early detection of launches and laser targeting and weaponry for soft kill operations. It makes perfect sense as a tactical system. The first thing anyone would want to do would be eliminate the detection and targeting systems, and that means taking out the space-based lasers. What better weapon to use against a laser than another laser?"

"Fight fire with fire?" Tombstone mused.

His uncle nodded. "Exactly. It's very much like the development of the mutually assured destruction, or MAD, program. If you recall, the think tanks were tasked with coming up with a solution to the possibility of nuclear attack from Russia. They spent years considering defense systems just like this, but the technology didn't exist then. Finally, some smart kid ran the numbers and came up with the answer— within the budget restraints, the only way to fight the Russian ballistic missiles system was to develop our own. Fire with fire, as you say. That resulted in the insanity of the Cold War. We made it so costly for the Russians to attack that they never did—although they did test our resolve on numerous occasions, not believing that an American would have the guts to push the button.

"But while the system worked, the downside was that it insured there would be an arms race. And that, as you know, eventually led to nuclear weapons in the hands of rogue states." His uncle shook his head sadly. "Sometimes I think it would have been better if we'd never uncorked that particular genie."

"Maybe if we hadn't relied on MAD, more research would have been poured into defense systems like the laser," Tombstone added. "So why are the Russians so dead set against a missile defense system?"

"Because, to their mind, it means we can attack and not suffer the consequences of MAD. There's a huge cultural gap between Russia and the United States, don't ever forget that."

"Right. So we're testing a missile laser system at sea—"

His uncle interrupted him. "They're shadowing *Jefferson,* which is testing our own sea-based ballistic missile defense system. That's the official story. In response to every query, Russia says it is simply in the same area testing its own systems."

"So they planned to use the battle group for surveillance anyway?" Tombstone asked.

"The thinking is that the Russians are worried enough about the test to stage a little demonstration of their own power. They picked an older satellite, one that wouldn't have remained in service much longer, and took her out. Maybe they thought they would destroy it before it detected the laser, or that it wouldn't be able to transmit after being targeted. But fortunately, although her optical capabilities were burned out immediately, she did manage one last data downlink. That picture."

"So where do we come in?" Tombstone asked.

"I don't know yet. For now, this is all background briefing." His uncle looked even more troubled and seemed about to continue, then just shook his head. "It's a complicated situation, Tombstone. More so than I can tell you right now."

"I see."

"Yeah. I know you don't like it, but for now you'll have to let it ride. I'll fill you in when I can."

"No problem." Tombstone turned his attention back to the message traffic, but had a hard time staying focused. The discomfort on his uncle's face hinted that there was much more to this than he was letting on. And given the discomfort it was causing the elder Magruder, Tombstone wasn't so sure he really wanted to know what it was about.

I really don't want to know. Tombstone stared at the message in front of him, not seeing it, as he realized how much he meant it. *Maybe I'm finally realizing I'm retired. Or*

*maybe it's just all too much. I've spent so much time trying
to track down Tomboy, following every lead, worrying about
her—maybe there's just no room left for anything else. There
was a time when I had to know every detail, had to. Maybe
I can finally put the load down.*

He glanced across at his uncle, who appeared lost in his
own thoughts, and felt a flash of guilt. Tombstone might be
able to avoid whatever it was, but his uncle couldn't.

USS Jefferson
CDC
2208 local (GMT-9)

Blair Edwards was one of the men that Coyote thought of
first when the admiral contemplated the indignities of having
civilian defense contractors on board his ship. Edwards was
a large man, one built on the scale everyone would expect
from a Texan. He was almost six and a half feet tall, with
broad shoulders narrowing to a solidly muscled waist and
legs. As a quarterback at Texas A&M, he had accumulated
an impressive record, and had followed it up with a string
of business successes as well. Armed with an electrical engineering degree, Edwards had struck out on his own during
the height of the Cold War, building from the ground up an
electronics and weapons design firm that was second to none.
He kept it small so he could control every aspect of the
company. While it might not be a household name, everyone
in the defense industry knew Edwards Electronics.

Edwards had been a golden boy during the Reagan era. In
a series of top secret contracts, his company had been funded
to conduct the initial research and testing on Reagan's dream
of a missile defense system. But the technology had not been
there, not then. Reagan had had the dream, but others would
have to build the computers to make it possible. When the
Star Wars projects had been abandoned, many had thought
that Edwards would be crushed.

Those who knew him well knew better. His closest com-
petitors in France watched him sit back, take stock, and qui-

etly continue his own research. He kept track of all the new technology that might support a missile defense system, updating his designs, keeping a marketing plan so current that some said it was reviewed daily. When the time finally came and technology and leadership collided to produce a favorable environment, Edwards was ready.

Edwards had long since lost touch with the details of the tactical side of things. As much as he enjoyed them, newer and brighter minds now dealt with the details. Edwards was at his most effective as a front man for the company, the CEO out there shaking hands and kissing babies, wining and dining senators and congresspeople in order to keep his name in front of them.

It wasn't that Edwards minded that part of his job, not at all. By nature he was gregarious and found he had a lot in common with the politicians he befriended. Occasionally he missed the early days when he had been intimately involved in every technical decision, but he was mature enough to know that he was more valuable where he was.

One prerogative that he insisted on was his right to be present at every operational test. Edwards was one of those men who always seem like they've been in the military, but have never actually served. He affected a military style of speech and had a flight jacket. When he was on board ship or traveling with the ground unit, he took some pains to ensure he never appeared ignorant or inexperienced. This often required hours of staff briefing. But as a result, when he wandered into *Jefferson*'s CDC, Edwards looked at home.

"You boys ready to do this?" he asked, his voice carrying to every corner of Combat. " 'Cause I'm telling you, *we're* ready." He slapped his hand on the arm of one of the elevated chairs as though he'd made a joke. Several sailors smiled. Edwards's enthusiasm was contagious. "I'm telling you, we're going to smash that—"

"Sir!" A voice at his side, an elbow in his ribs.

"What the hell?"

"Sir, over here." Lab Rat touched Edwards gently on the elbow to get his attention. "This console."

Edwards looked slightly abashed. He had been briefed on

security measures, but had forgotten that not everyone on the ship, not even all the Combat watchstanders, knew what was going on. "Whenever you say, son." He followed Lab Rat into a compartment located just off Combat. Lab Rat stood aside to allow Edwards to go in first. Once they were both in, Lab Rat swung the heavy hatch shut and slid the dogging bar home.

Two technicians were sitting at consoles monitoring self-tests in the laser gear. Speakers set high in the corner hissed static broken only occasionally by a cryptic report from an aircraft or shore station.

"Sorry about that out there," Edwards said, gesturing vaguely toward the main compartment. "Don't think anybody noticed anyhow."

Edwards was aware of Lab Rat's cool, light blue eyes studying him carefully. It was an uncomfortable feeling. Edwards was the one that stared people down and made them uneasy. It wasn't done to him. He was just about to protest, figuring out what to say—after all, it didn't make much sense to say, "Quit looking at me like that"—when Lab Rat broke the silence.

"You're right. I don't think anyone noticed. If they did, I'll deal with it." Lab Rat turned back to the two technicians. "Anything happening?"

One shook his head. "Not a thing, sir. No indication that anything is out of the ordinary. We're running system checks every twenty minutes and so far everything is clean."

"Good, good. No surprises, okay?" Lab Rat said, a faint note of relief in his voice. He turned back to Edwards. "Come sit over here." He pointed at a chair mounted in front of a large console in the center of the room. "This is where I will be when we run the actual test."

Edwards slid his bulk into the chair, feeling slightly confined. He noticed the seat belt dangling from the seat. What kind of seas could make a ship this big so unsteady that you'd need a belt? He shuddered at the thought.

Lab Rat stood behind him. "Standard data link input," he said. "Here we are, and here are the Russians." He pointed at a set of contacts on the screen. "They've been keeping their distance. During the actual test, we're not going to be

able to hide the laser light. But by then, it shouldn't make
any difference."

"How close are they?" Edwards asked.

"About ten miles right now," Lab Rat said. "Closer than
we'd like. The captain was just going to ask them to stand
off a bit. Ten miles may sound like a lot of distance, but it's
not. Especially not when you're conducting flight operations
and have to run into the wind."

"So what will the fellows sitting here do?" Edwards asked.
He touched the trackball embedded in the keyboard and
moved the cursor around on the screen. "I'm not going to
start World War III, am I?"

Lab Rat grinned. "No. The console is signed off right now.
Your input isn't going into the link. So feel free to fool
around with it. If you've got any questions, speak up."

Lab Rat moved back over to the technicians and began
discussing some small detail of the upcoming exercise. They
quickly progressed beyond terminology that Edwards recognized, and he began to get bored.

That was the thing about the ship, the close quarters. Except for the flight deck, there was nowhere you could really
sort of spread out, Texas style. And as for the decks below
the water line, well—it just wasn't natural. The only way he
could feel safe down there was to consciously try to forget
just how far below the surface of the water he was.

Curious by nature, Edwards let his fingers roam over the
keys, pulling up menus and submenus, examining the options
for each. They'd tinkered with his system some, but for the
better. Sure, it still had a few rough spots—this organization
of options didn't make sense, for instance. Why not move
them over here with the targeting functions?

He pulled up the display of the sensors and checked the
status of each. By now, his boredom was becoming serious.
This was a completed system, one that no longer needed
working on—nothing more boring than a system that worked
as advertised.

He flipped through the radar options, marveling at just how
many sensors were on board the carrier. That one there he
recognized as a fire control radar. He scrolled down to it and
called up details. There were a number of different modes

for both search and targeting functions. He toggled through them, his fingers dancing lightly on the keys. He experimented with selecting different options, and noted that a few places required two mouse clicks and others required one to change the default settings. Sloppy programming—why hadn't he caught that? No matter, it would be an easy fix when his folks dove back into the guts of the program.

Off to Edwards's left, an inadequately shielded high-voltage line arced across a sixteenth of an inch of dead space to energize another circuit. Eight hundred feet overhead, the massive SPS-49 radar shivered slightly. If it had been a sailor, it might have objected to the changes being cycled through its programming. It might have wondered what sort of operational sequence could possibly require search, track, and targeting modes so quickly, particularly when the data wasn't being relayed to another unit. It probably would have objected to the orders it was receiving, or at least asked for verification.

But radar so finely tuned to capture every bit of metal in the air was not a sailor. Its electronics had no problem keeping pace with the changes that were ordered. As Edwards crawled through each option below, simply highlighting a mode for the radar, a bug in the program automatically switched the radar to that mode. The console wasn't transmitting data, not into the link anyway. But its link to the radars was still enabled and simply looking at an option on the screen was sufficient to activate it.

"Okay, I think we're done," Lab Rat said, turning back to Edwards. "Any questions about the changes we've made?"

Edward shook his head. "Couple of places I'd change a single click to a double, but nothing real important." Edwards then launched into a series of questions about the configuration of the load out and targeting menus, eventually appearing satisfied by Lab Rat's explanations.

"Well, then." Lab Rat unlocked a heavy door. "Intelligence brief in fifteen minutes, Mr. Edwards. I do hope you'll excuse me so I can prepare. If you'd like to join us, we'll be in CVIC."

Edwards stretched and yawned. "Might see if I can get outside for bit," he said. "Get some air."

Lab Rat nodded. "You should have time. We don't start flight operations for another two hours. Plenty of time to get in a run, if that's what you're thinking. Just watch out for the pad eyes on the deck—nasty road rash if you fall on non-skid."

Edwards chuckled. "Don't I know it."

Lab Rat swung the door shut behind them. "I'll probably see you after your run, then," he said.

Eight hundred feet overhead, the SPS-49 radar pulsed once then fell silent.

Admiral Kurashov
2209 local (GMT-9)

Lieutenant Ilya Rotenyo was standing his watch in his normal fashion. Rotenyo was an experienced officer, one respected by both his subordinates and seniors. Promotions came more slowly in the Russian Navy than in her American counterpart, and paychecks even more so. For some time, he had been debating whether or not to leave the navy and try to find a civilian job. Perhaps in the shipyard or in one of the defense industries. He would probably make more money, at least after the first training.

Still, did he really want to leave this? His gaze swept over the crowded electronics compartment, assessing each individual's readiness and recalling the status of all equipment. He knew what he was doing in here, knew it so well that most decisions were made by reflex rather than requiring much thought. Did he really want to trade going to sea for landlocked life?

Not really. But then again, he did have responsibilities, didn't he? And officers in the Russian Navy had not been paid for two months now. Without socialism, his family would be starving.

He mulled over the options for perhaps the millionth time in his mind, trying to decide what he should do. The more he thought about it, the more tiresome it became. But his wife Irini was pushing for decisions, and he said that when he got back from this cruise he needed to make the change.

Suddenly, a buzzer snapped to life, followed immediately by the intercom system. He snatched at the handset. "What was that?" he demanded.

"Sir, fire control radar—yes, we verified it. It's coming from the aircraft carrier."

"Are you sure?" he asked incredulously. A fire control radar—they knew better than that. Targeting another vessel with fire control radar was an act of war and strictly forbidden. "Could it have been anything else?"

"No, sir," the voice said, offended.

"Very well." Rotenyo put down the handset and surveyed the shocked faces staring at him around Combat. "Set general quarters. We've been targeted." He turned to his weapons officer. "Prepare for snapshot return of fire."

All around him, the men sprang into action. They had done this drill so many times that there was no confusion, no hesitation. An edge of adrenaline made them move a bit faster, knowing that this time it wasn't the drill.

Or was it? The captain could have arranged the buzzer. And the telephone call—perhaps the electronics warfare people were in on it, too. Perhaps it was just a drill, another exercise of their capabilities. Rotenyo tried to believe that, tried to ignore the fact that no one in his right mind would set general quarters this close to the American battle group, and that the weapons officer looked just as worried as he did.

USS **Jefferson**
2210 local (GMT-9)

Petty Officer Joe Warner had just popped open his first candy bar of the watch when the ESM data console in front of him beeped a warning. The electronics warfare technician swore quietly and punched the mouse for the details of the offending signal, while peeling back the candy bar wrapper with his teeth.

Just as he'd thought. No different from the hundreds of other warnings it had insisted were threats in the last hour.

The last software upgrade had turned his normally reliable console into a sensitive bitch, and the number of false alarms had quadrupled.

He scanned the details again. The specs were consistent with a Russian fire control radar and there was nothing else in the area that the gear could have confused it with.

Better safe than sorry. He toggled on his comm circuit. "TAO, EW—got a brief shot of a fire control radar off them. It's out now."

"Roger, I see it," the TAO acknowledged. "Any other indications of launch?" There was worry in the TAO's voice. This could be a spurious detection, a mistake on the part of some poorly trained Russian sailor—or the beginning of a world of shit.

"Nothing further, sir," the EW replied. Warner sighed. New officers were always too paranoid. Until they got the hang of it, they freaked out over every false alarm. It made for a tense and uncomfortable watch. Warner took one last look at his scope. Nothing else.

Warner glanced over and saw the TAO staring at his screen, his finger poised over a fire control switch. Like that would do any good, even if it were the real thing. An attack at this close range would leave virtually no time for reaction. It would be up to CIWS, with its independent radar and fire control system, to detect any incoming missile and react. Even if CIWS did kill the main body of it, the shrapnel would do serious damage.

Neither man considered the possibility that it had been a radar signal from their own ship that had provoked the warning signal. The EW's console was programmed to ignore his own ship radiations.

USS **Jefferson**
CVIC
2211 local (GMT-9)

Forty frames astern of CDC, the carrier intelligence center, or CVIC, kept watch on all signals, including those emitted by the carrier herself. Under normal conditions, every console was manned and a watch supervisor roamed the SIGINT, or signals intelligence, processing center. But tonight one of the intelligence specialists had tuned one monitor to a replay of a Cubs game—one that the Cubs *won*—and most of the watch section was popping over there at least intermittently to check out the action.

Most of the watch section, but not all of it. Bill Johnson was tired of being on watch. In fact, he was pretty much tired of the Navy altogether. While everyone else was watching the Cubs, Johnson was responsible for keeping an eye on the consoles and logging the alerts generated. Help was just a few steps away if he needed it.

So when the electronics warfare console warning went off, it was more of an irritation. The EW gear was so sensitive that if you left the audible alert turned on, the warning buzzer sounded at least once a minute. More often, usually. And it seemed to have worse judgment than a sailor on liberty, often alerting on commercial radar and tentatively classifying them as threats, sounding the buzzer, and then immediately downgrading the contact to a friendly or neutral. As a result, except for drills and special exercises, the buzzer was turned off and the techs relied on the flashing red light that replaced it.

Johnson stole a wistful look at the almost-empty plate of doughnuts on the table five feet away. There had been at least two dozen of them when the baker dropped them off, and they'd quickly disappeared. Only two were left, one glazed and one sprinkled with cinnamon sugar. The latter was a particular favorite of his. But here he was, anchored to a console, and there it was, out of reach and everyone else gone, already stuffed with *their* own favorites.

But no one was watching right now, were they? He stole another look at the doughnuts, and seemed to hear them calling to him. The red light flashed again. He checked the console, quickly locating the false signal, and then hit the reset button. Every twenty seconds now. And for this he'd gone to a year of school?

From the outer room, he heard a ripple of laughter, and his feeling of being left out deepened. Why did he always get left behind? If there was only one person at the console, shouldn't it be somebody more senior?

He reached a decision. He slipped his headphones off quickly, shoved his chair back, and in one quick motion snagged the cinnamon doughnut. He started to settle back into his chair, and then reached and grabbed the other one as well. Let *them* be the ones to come back into the compartment to an empty tray for a change.

He had taken his eyes off his console for no more than eight seconds or so. He slid back into the chair, the doughnuts warm and greasy in his fingers. He could almost feel the warmth seeping into his skin.

He slipped the headphones back on and saw that the red light was on once again. Right on time. He mashed the reset button with his right hand, getting a little smear of sugar on it. He quickly polished that off with his sleeve, then wiped his fingers on his pants.

The warning symbol and threat parameters that flashed on-screen when the red light flashed also disappeared. He had a vague impression that he should have looked at them, and then decided it was simply his guilty conscience. The others got away with a lot more than he did, didn't they? It wasn't like they were at war or something, was it?

He broke the glazed doughnut in half and took a bite. It was just as light and warm as he'd expected, and he groaned with pleasure as it slid down his throat. He finished off the rest of it, savoring every bite, and then turned his attention to the cinnamon and sugar one. He licked the edge of it first, tasting the pungent combination, letting the anticipation build. Then, one tiny nibble after another. He closed his eyes to concentrate, and saw the red light strobe at him behind his eyelids. He opened them, checked the screen again, and mashed reset.

Five minutes later, the rest of the watch section returned. By then, the only trace of the doughnuts was two greasy streaks on his pants and a sprinkling of sugar and cinnamon on the deck. And a very short but valid detection of a fire control radar radiating, and not from the Russians but from the USS *Jefferson*. Ignored, negligently relegated to the massive history data banks, the signal was digitally recorded on the CD when the watch section backed up the database prior to watch relief. No one else even noticed it.

SS Montego Bay
2215 local (GMT-9)

Captain Gaspert stared at the ships in the distance. The Russians were just dark blots on the horizon. The American ships were farther away and he could just make out a few running lights. Still, the computer gave a clear record of their track. They were heading away, and *Montego Bay* would be well clear of them even if they reversed course right now.

But there was something about the geometry that made him uneasy. He couldn't pinpoint it exactly, hard as he tried. Perhaps it was the instinctive reaction to being the burdened vessel in any encounter with ships in military operations. Normally, the *Montego Bay* would be the privileged vehicle, the ship entitled to right-of-way should there be any conflict between her course and that of another vessel.

But the Russians were conducting flight operations and had to maintain a particular angle into the wind in order to launch and recover safely. That made the *Admiral Kurashov* the privileged vehicle, and *Montego Bay* the burdened vehicle ship.

Why am I even thinking there's a situation? We're opening, not closing. There is no reason to be concerned.

Still, he stayed on the bridge, watching the Russian ship as daylight faded. An hour after dark, he instructed the officer of the day to change course by fifteen degrees, increasing the distance between the Russian ship and *Montego Bay*. Again, he had no real reason to do this, but somehow the added margin of safety made him feel slightly better.

Gaspert watched the screen as the distance between his ship and the Russians increased. He should be feeling much better, but he wasn't.

Admiral Kurashov
2216 local (GMT-9)

General Gorshenko reached Combat just a few steps behind
Captain Bolshovick. Any question the general had about
whether or not the general alarm was a drill was answered
the moment he looked at the captain's face. The navy captain's normal expression of supreme confidence was gone.

*Mistake, that. They should never see you show concern or
alarm.*

"Captain!" The young lieutenant's voice was sharp. "A fire
control radar has been detected. We are being targeted, sir!"

"What radar? From which platform?" the captain asked.

"The SPS-48 from the carrier, sir. In targeting mode for
only a brief moment, but definitely a fire control radar locked
on."

"And now?"

"Normal search mode, sir."

"That is exactly how they would fire a Harpoon," the captain snapped. "A brief flash for targeting data, then launch
the weapon. The missile has its own seeker head, complete
with re-attack circuitry, and would need no further guidance." Bolshovick paused for a moment as though considering his options.

Gorshenko swore quietly. "And nothing further? Just one
radar sweep, no more? No additional aircraft in the air, no
signs of targeting or manuevering?"

"None of that, General," the lieutenant answered, steady-
ing visibly in response to the general's calm, no-nonsense
tone.

"Irrelevant," the navy captain said, clearly annoyed at the
general's interference. "Weapons officer, weapons release
authority. One round, targeting the carrier."

Before Bolshovick could foul things up further with his
infernal grandstanding, Gorshenko reached his decision.
"No." His voice carried the unconscious assumption that he
would be obeyed. The lieutenant froze. "There is no evidence
they are attacking."

"Captain?" the lieutenant asked. Gorshenko could hear the
uncertainty in his voice, and it was reflected in the faces of

the rest of the men in Combat. The warrant officers and petty officers stared at the captain, aghast.

"If I wait until the missile is visible to our radar, it will be too late," the captain said.

"They are not attacking," the general said. "You, weapons person—do not fire."

"We destroyed their satellite! Of course they are attacking!"

The lieutenant held his finger still poised over the button. He kept his gaze locked on his captain, ignoring the general except for the fact he had not yet fired. It was clear that if the captain so much as nodded, he would depress the button.

The damned fool. The Americans are not attacking, not unless something has gone terribly wrong. If Bolshovich only knew—no, I cannot tell him. He would not believe me now.

"There is much you do not know," Gorshenko said, crossing the compartment in a few steps to stand beside the lieutenant's console. "Captain, you must not shoot. I forbid it."

"I am in command here," the captain snapped, moving to Rotenyo's other side. "Lieutenant, you will obey my orders."

Gorshenko saw in the lieutenant's face that the young officer had reached a decision. Before Rotenyo's finger could twitch, the general slammed into him, smashing him out of the chair. By reflex, Rotenyo's finger jabbed down at the fire control button, even as the general's palm slapped down on the console keyboard in an effort to abort the attack.

When the laser had fired, there had been no indication inside the ship of its operation—no warning buzzer, no vibration, no sound, nothing. With the anti-ship missile, however, it was different. All personnel had been recalled inside the skin of the ship for the laser exercise and for general quarters. The entire forward part of the ship rumbled, and exhaust from the rocket billowed from the launch canister, sweeping across the deck. The rumble built for two seconds, then white fire ignited inside the cloud. The missile emerged from the fire, a thin, white pole, and seemed to hang in the air for a few moments, before it shot off toward the horizon.

USS **Lake Champlain**
2216 local (GMT-9)

On board the cruiser, Lieutenant Commander Alan Simms, the tactical action officer, or TAO, was double-checking a closest-point-of-approach solution showing his ship would pass well aft of the *Montego Bay*. He'd had the operations specialists work out the solution manually as well, figuring any opportunity for real live training shouldn't be missed. All in all, it was a quiet night watch, and Simms figured they'd have plenty of time to work out the final preparations for the Kernel Blitz evolutions scheduled for the next day.

All that changed in an instant. As TAO, Simms had weapons release authority and full responsibility for protecting the ship when the captain was not in Combat. With the ships so close together there was no time to think, no time to call the captain or ask for a second opinion. The reflexes implanted by hours of training and countless drills kicked in.

At the very moment that Gorshenko was first realizing what Bolshovich had done, Simms flipped his fire control key to the launch position and sounded general quarters. As Gorshenko attempted to abort the launch, Simms ordered weapons free, and the chief manning the weapons console manually designated the launch cell from the vertical launch system. By the time the Russian general knocked the sailor out of his chair, the *Lake Champlain* had fired two anti-air missiles at the Russian missile already in the air. Once clear of the ship, the *Champlain*'s missiles locked on to the Russian missile and began boring in on it.

Admiral Kurashov
2217 local (GMT-9)

"You fool," Gorshenko raged. "I did not authorize you to fire. Abort the missile—do it now!"

"*You* are the fool," the captain responded. "I'm authorized to take such action to preserve the safety of the ship, even if you are in tactical command."

"Captain!" Rotenyo stared at the screen in horror. "Sir, the missile is off course!"

Both the captain and the general spun around to check the large screen in the front of the compartment. The symbol for the missile, which had been inching toward the carrier, had changed direction. As they watched, the symbol for a hostile missile launch appeared next to the American cruiser, the arrowhead of the speed leader aimed directly for the *Kurashov*.

"You're responsible for that," the captain said, his voice soft and menacing. "When you hit the keyboard, you disrupted the programmed launch order. God knows where it's going—and what it will hit."

On the screen, the Russian missile changed course again. The American missile changed course also, tracking it. As they both veered north, Gorshenko saw that their trajectories put them directly overhead the SS *Montego Bay*.

Gorshenko stared at the screen in horror, his mind in turmoil. What had he done? *What had he done?*

FOUR

SS Montego Bay
2215 local (GMT-9)

Most of the passengers were on the main deck or weather-decks. A good portion had exercised their option of eating at the casual grill on the fantail, and even more lounged around the small jewel of a pool with hamburgers, club sandwiches, and a large selection of alcoholic beverages. Many of the passengers had been drinking steadily all day. On each cruise there were a couple of people who could not decide when it was time to quit.

John and Erica Cabot were on their second honeymoon, hoping desperately to patch up their differences. Erica, whose tolerance for alcohol was significantly lower than John's, was not in a mood to try particularly hard.

"We should have gone to the dining room," she said for the seventh time. "I like the people at our table. That's why you don't want to go, isn't it? I was having too much fun."

"That's not it at all, as I told you. I just thought that since it's such a nice night, we might—"

"Sit by the pool and watch half-naked women?" Erica sneered. "Well, two can play that game." She bounced away to the other side of the pool, sat down on an empty deck seat in the middle of three men, and started talking to them.

John started after her, and stopped. What was the use? She was right. What would it have hurt for him to go along with the dining room routine? Just because he didn't like dressing up didn't mean he shouldn't compromise from time to time.

Emboldened by the alcohol, he rounded the pool and sat down on Erica's chair. The three men who had been chatting with her immediately backed off. Erica shot him a scornful look.

"You're right," he said rapidly, trying to get it all out before he changed his mind. "It was selfish of me to insist on coming to the pool. Come on, if we hurry, we can get dressed and still make it for dessert."

Amazement followed by love dashed across her face. "Thank you," she said. "Oh, John, thank you."

She left her hamburger sitting on the table as she rose to join him. Hand in hand, hips and elbows touching, they walked back into the interior ship and headed forward toward their cabin.

SS **Montego Bay**
Bridge
2216 local (GMT-9)

Suddenly, off to the right of the screen, a new contact popped up. Ten miles away, but it had come up so suddenly that it had to be an extremely tiny contact. Perhaps a cabin cruiser, or one of the foolish small boats that regularly made the trip between California and Hawaii. On more than one occasion, Gaspert had had to slow to provide assistance to them in the form of fresh water, fuel, or simply sailing directions to Hawaii.

"What is—" Gaspert started to ask, intending to have the officer of the deck raise the new contact on the radio. But before he could finish the sentence, the contact jumped across the screen, closing the distance from *Montego Bay* to half of what it had been a second earlier.

"*Montego Bay,* this is *Jefferson!*" The voice from the carrier cut through the static on the ship-to-ship radar.

"Roger, *Jefferson,* what the—*shit!*" The truth took a few seconds to sink in. His first thought was that there had been a radar malfunction, and a picture had simply corrected itself. If that was the case, the contact was within five miles of the cruise ship and it was even more critical that they keep a close eye on her.

Then the forward lookout began howling. "Contact, bearing zero four five relative, position angle three—Captain, it's a missile!"

"General alarm," Gaspert snapped, ordering the civilian equivalent of general quarters. A gong began sounding immediately, and a recorded voice directed all passengers to return to their staterooms. Gaspert ran to the bridge wing, as though there were some way he could ward it off by his mere presence there. He could see it now, too, without the binoculars. It looked like a white sliver against the field of stars now emerging in the sky. But it was a deadly splinter, a contrail marking its course through the air. It was homing in on *Montego Bay,* closing the distance every microsecond.

This can't be happening. Not with four hundred and twenty-seven passengers on board.

Unlike her military counterparts, the *Montego Bay* was not built with watertight integrity throughout the ship. Certainly, her hull kept the ocean at bay, and there were a few watertight doors between decks. But she was riddled with elevator shafts, passageways, and large areas of space divided by only the flimsiest bulkheads. She was not designed to take much damage and keep floating.

"*Montego Bay*, this is *Jefferson!*"

Gaspert keyed the mike as he shouted out damage control and maneuvering commands.

USS **Jefferson**
2216 local (GMT-9)

Coyote slouched in the elevated chair in the center of the compartment. His truncated sleeping hours were starting to catch up with him. "Any coffee left, Chief?" he asked the senior mess management specialist, who had come into TFCC to see when the admiral wanted to eat.

"Yes, sir. And what will you . . . ?" A startled yelp from Commander Hanson, the flag TAO, stopped him.

"Vampires inbound!" The TAO's voice cut through the activity immediately.

"What the bloody hell?" Coyote said. The hard gong of general quarters began sounding throughout the ship.

"Missile launch, from the Russian ship," Hanson said. "It's headed our way, Admiral." Without pausing, he began conferring with the officer of the deck, ordering last-minute maneuvers that would probably be futile.

"Set EMCON Echo! Nothing radiating, nothing. *Now!*" Coyote could already hear the odd patches of silence as sensor operators began shutting down their gear. The constant background noise was noticeable only in its absence.

If the missile was targeting one of the rich sources of electromagnetic energy radiating from the carrier, shutting down all the radars and sensors could make it go stupid. There was nothing more really to do at this point, but Coyote could not bring himself to sit in his chair and simply watch. He paced behind Hanson and the watch officer, itching to give an order, any order. But it wasn't necessary.

As he watched, the speed leader pointed directly at the carrier. It inched forward steadily. The computer evaluated the continuous radar hits, and then corrected the display. The speed leader was now pointed away from the carrier at a sixty-degree angle, and at a new target.

"*Jefferson, Lake Champlain* TAO. Snapshot procedure— two birds launched. Be advised we are standing by to launch additional rounds." The TAO's voice shivered slightly, as though the speaker had just realized what he'd done.

"Dear Lord," Hanson breathed. He grabbed the marine radio mike and said, "*Montego Bay,* this is *Jefferson.* Do you copy?"

The ship-to-ship circuit was a babble of shouted commands and answers from the cruise liner. The mike was keyed, but no one answered the carrier's call-up.

Just then, the speed leaders from the American missile intercepted the speed leaders from the Russian missile, directly over the symbol marking *Montego Bay*'s location. The circuit went dead.

FIVE

SS Montego Bay
2219 local (GMT-9)

On the fantail, one of the men Erica had been flirting with muttered, "Bitch." He turned to stare out at the sea. A flash of light caught his attention. He perked up immediately. "Hey, fireworks!" He had just tapped his buddy on the shoulder to get him to turn around when the first missile struck.

After flashing through the air at almost impossible speeds, it penetrated the skin of the ship just above the waterline. From there, it continued through the ship for twenty feet before the delayed fuse detonated the warhead. This particular fuse was guaranteed to ensure the missile exploded deep inside a ship where it could create the most damage rather than simply piercing the outer compartments.

The compartment it finally entered was the main engineering space. This compartment housed the four boilers that were connected to steam turbines, as well as the reduction gear and the beginning of the propeller shaft.

Three engineers were in the compartment, although the normal watch required only one. One was working on a bilge pump, garnering some overtime. The man on watch was monitoring the gauges and dials that spelled out every detail of the ship's engineering plant. A third was studying his emergency procedures book in preparation for the next Coast Guard classification exam.

They had just a split second to hear the soul-shattering noise of metal crumpling and twisting before the warhead detonated. The engineer on watch stood, and had taken one step toward his console when the warheads detonated.

Four point five kilograms of heavy explosive converted the metal immediately around it into molten fluid and shrapnel, and catapulted those droplets in all directions at once. They ripped through everything in their path, piercing more metal, until one shard punctured a fuel line.

The body of the missile continued on through the compartment, shoving the rest of the flaming debris in front of it. The remaining propulsion fuel in the weapon's main body was ignited by a fireball, and contributed to the devastation.

The men in the compartment were flashed into charred corpses. They never knew that something had gone very, very wrong.

Although the engine compartment itself was surrounded by watertight compartments, it was not designed to withstand this assault. Additionally, none of the damage control hatches had been secured. The expanding ball of fire and hot gasses blew them off their hinges, and superheated steam, burning fuel, and fire poured to the upper decks, consuming everything in their path.

The explosion rocked the ship, not hard enough to throw people off their feet but enough to alert them that something was seriously wrong. Immediately, alarms began screaming at every console. The propeller shaft, no longer attached to the rest to the ship, with both of its shock-mounted seals breached, careened through the aft section of the ship. The drag of the water on the propeller began pulling it out of the ship, and it broke the watertight seals, allowing seawater to pour into the ship.

The fire was already burning through the decks and into the upper compartments, and smoke was billowing out of the stacks. On the fantail, a first few seconds of stunned silence gave way to immediate panic. As the sea poured into the hull and the ship took on a list, men and women clad in swimsuits crawled over each other in a mad stampede to move forward.

Jack and Erica, who were inside the ship at the time of the impact, were thrown against a bulkhead. The stampede of people now coming down their passageway was an angry, panicked mob.

Gaspert was operating on reflex, as any sailor must do in the first few critical seconds in order to prevent complete disaster. He shouted orders to damage control teams and ordered the rest of the crew into their preplanned roles in controlling the passengers and preparing for abandon ship. But it was difficult to round them all up and get them to their assigned lifeboat stations, much less ensure that they all had their safety gear on. Ninety percent of the passengers were in one of the three dining areas, and some were five decks away from their life preservers—even if they had remembered how to use them after the quick five-minute brief by their assigned abandon ship crew member.

Gaspert got on the ship's intercom and tried to head off the hysteria. "Ladies and gentlemen, we have a serious problem on the ship. No one is injured, but you must remain calm and follow the orders of my crew exactly as they are given in order to ensure your own safety. Please stay where you are. Senior crew members, take charge and execute general plan number two." Plan two was the contingency developed to cover just this situation. It involved an immediate flood of crew members to break up groups of passengers into smaller, more controllable elements. Regardless of their assigned damage control station, the passengers would be dispatched to one of several areas.

Montego Bay was listing hard to port now, and the officer of the day was rapping out an oral message over the distress channel, informing all vessels in the area as well as Coast Guard stations in California and Hawaii of their exact situation. They were closer to Hawaii than California, but not by much. In fact, their nearest source of assistance was the Russian battle group, followed closely by the American one.

As the ship lurched hard to port, Gaspert finally accepted the inevitable. They were going to be abandoning ship. The operations officer on the USS *Jefferson* came on the distress channel and they began coordinating rescue operations.

Admiral **Kurashov**
2220 local (GMT-9)

The general stared aghast at the screen. The disaster was all too evident, especially given the call over the marine circuit from *Jefferson* to *Montego Bay*.

"What have you done?" he shouted at the captain. "A civilian ship!"

"You interfered with our operations," the captain responded. "This is your fault, General. Do not expect me to take the blame for this."

Gorshenko stared at the screen, his gut churning. Finally, he said, "I think there will be enough blame to go around, Captain. Now contact the Americans and offer your assistance."

SS **Montego Bay**
Lifeboat Number 10
2225 local (GMT-9)

Gaspert ran aft down the starboard weatherdeck, pausing briefly at each lifeboat station to make sure that his crew had the situation in hand. There was surprisingly little panic. His crew had been firm, confident, and forceful. The passengers were assembled, in most cases already loaded into the boats, and a few were already in the process of being lowered to the sea.

The damage to the stern was too severe to permit him to cross to the other side of the ship, so he returned forward, and cut through the main stairwell to the other side. There, the situation was a bit more difficult, since that side of the ship was high. The angle made it difficult to lower the lifeboats without banging into the side of the ship, but again, the crew was managing astoundingly well.

Finally, convinced that he could do no more, Gaspert returned to his own lifeboat. All the passengers and crew were loaded, and they were waiting for him. He took his place, then activated the winch that would lower them to the sea.

Once that was done, he turned to the next senior man present. "Report."

"Twenty on board, three slightly injured, two seriously. One unconscious, having difficulty breathing. I think it may be a heart attack. The other serious is a broken leg."

Gaspert surveyed the passengers and saw pale, frightened faces staring back him. One man was stretched out flat on his back, eyes closed. A few of the passengers who knew first aid were hovering over him, apparently ready to start CPR.

The boat hit the water, coming down harder than it should have. Gaspert and another crewman cast off the lines and shoved the boat away from the dying ship while the engineer started the engines. Within moments, the engine sputtered and caught and they were under way. All along the starboard side and, Gaspert hoped, on the port as well, the other boats were doing the same thing.

A series of explosions rocked *Montego Bay* and rained debris on them. Gaspert shouted, but the noise was deafening. Between the fire and the explosions, no one could hear him.

That was when the real value of the training became apparent. No orders were necessary—the helmsman simply jammed the throttles forward and turned them at right angles to the ship, putting as much distance between them as possible. The other boats followed his lead, and soon they were far enough away that they could resume trying to navigate.

A hundred yards from the cruise ship, the noise was significantly reduced. Gaspert shouted, "Astern!" and pointed toward the aft end of the ship. That would be the mustering point. His boat led the way, and the others followed, moving slowly and keeping a safe distance between them. There was no point in surviving abandon ship only to collide with each other.

As they reassembled astern, the radio reports started coming in. One by one, each boat reported a full and complete muster. As he listened to the numbers rolling in, Gaspert felt sick. Not a single boat had everyone on it that it was supposed to.

Overhead, helicopters were on the horizon, a string of

them making a beeline for them. Gaspert breathed a prayer of thanksgiving then turned to the navigator. "Assign each boat a sector. I want every square inch of this water searched, consistent with safety. And get me *Jefferson* on the radio."

USS Jefferson
2226 local (GMT-9)

From the moment the decision was made to go to EMCON condition Echo, an odd silence settled over in TFCC. The religious were praying, and everyone else focused his or her thoughts on just one objective, offering it up to whoever might be in charge of things, if indeed there was anybody. Both the religious and nonreligious pleas and prayers were remarkably similar.

Please, please, don't let it hit the cruise ship. Let it be a dud, a typical example of Russian engineering. Let there be a fishing boat, anything, but please, please not the cruise ship.

The prayers went unanswered, as did the pleas and threats. Deprived of its rich, tempting target radiating energy on so many bands, the seeker had cast about until it found another source. Not nearly as enticing, certainly. A meager meal compared to the aircraft carrier and her escorts. But, approaching the missile equivalent of starvation, the secondary target would have to do.

It did not require much of a change of course for the missile to intercept *Montego Bay*. It twitched slightly in that air, tipped over, descended to barely above the waves and bore in.

"Flight deck, TAO! Set flight quarters for rescue-at-sea operations!" Hanson rapped out a series of orders to the other ships, turning them toward the cruise liner and ordering them to flight quarters.

"*Jefferson,* this is the captain of *Montego Bay,*" a tightly controlled voice said. "I am preparing to abandon ship. We've taken two hits in our stern. We have a main space fire out of control. I estimate I have approximately ten minutes to get everyone off the ship and into the water, one way or another."

The admiral picked up the handset. "Roger, *Montego Bay,* copy all. I have all units en route to your position to render assistance. Just get them in the water, sir—we'll take care of you."

Just then, a rough foreign voice broke in. "We, also, can help." Hearing the Russian accent froze everyone's blood.

"That will not be necessary," the admiral replied, ice in his voice. "If you attempt to interfere with rescue operations under my command, we will open fire. And if we do, it will be far less despicable than attacking an unarmed cruise ship. Now clear this circuit before you get more people killed.

"Montego Bay, Jefferson. We're deploying rescue helicopters with SAR swimmers, as well as small boats, in your direction. Estimate the helicopters overhead in approximately five mikes. The small boats are proceeding at flank speed and estimate fifteen mikes. What other assistance can we render at this time, sir?"

There was no immediate answer, although a cacophony of commands, screams, and shouts came over the circuit. Evidently the captain had keyed the mike but could not yet take the time to speak to them.

Finally, Gaspert said, "We shall expect you shortly, then. Request you search the area for individuals in the water while I organize the lifeboats into some form of convoy. Suggest one of your small ships stay upwind to create a lee for lifeboat launches. When we've got them all in the water, we'll proceed in your direction at best speed."

"How long to get the platform deployed?" the admiral asked Hanson.

"Twenty minutes, maybe less."

"Make it ten." The admiral turned his attention back to Gaspert. "We will be prepared to receive your boats when you get here."

"Medical teams, casualty teams," Gaspert continued. There was more background chatter over the circuit, and from what the admiral could gather, the damage control efforts were being abandoned completely. "We are leaving the circuit, will contact you from the radio in the lifeboat as soon as possible. *Montego Bay,* out."

The Russian returned to the circuit. "We did not intend to fire on the cruise ship."

"Nor on us," the admiral said acidly. "Funny, that doesn't make it any better. Now clear the circuit, sir, or I will open fire."

SIX

For once, the president heard about a military disaster from his joint chiefs of staff rather than CNN. It was an unusual situation, one that allowed him several moments to gather his thoughts and formulate a response without a camera staring him in the face. His first reaction was to use the secure hotline to grant the president of Russia the same breathing space before CNN picked up the story. Surely there was some explanation other than a Russian fighter firing on a defenseless American cruise ship. But as he reached for the hotline, a pointed little cough from the chairman, JCS, brought him up short.

"What?" the president demanded.

"Mr. President, that would be premature." The chairman, a man noted for his bluntness, had nevertheless proved to be an excellent chairman. No, he was not a political creature, just an old artillery man who had come up through the ranks the hard way.

"And you believe this because . . . ?" the president said, leaving the sentence unfinished.

"Because I believe we'll find those bastards are at fault."

The president took his hand off the hotline and leaned back in his chair. Reflexively, he started to interlace his hands behind his head, but he immediately felt a surge of inchoate discomfort at having his midsection unprotected while the chairman was in the room. He dropped his arms back down and rested his hands on the desk, annoyed at his own reaction.

Just why the hell did the chairman make him so nervous? Yes, he had picked the man, and had kept him in the position after his last term. And he'd come to rely even more on the general's advice during the last two years. And yes, if he was reelected—not that that seemed improbable, but one never knew—he would ask this man to continue on, or at least to give him some advice on a successor.

Despite all that, there was something in the chairman's bearing and the way he spoke and the way he carried himself that made any other man just a bit uneasy about exposing his midsection too much. Because no matter how civilized he was, how immaculate his uniform or courteous his bearing, you never, ever had any doubt that the chairman could kill you in a New York minute. Not that he would, of course. And still, as uneasy as the general's deadly air made the president, it was the one thing that he really liked about the general as well. You always knew where you stood with him.

"Regardless of whether they are or not," the president said carefully, "we will have to talk to them sooner or later. Taking the offensive"—the chairman was always big on taking the offensive—"means we get to select the terrain. Right?" There was a shade more of an actual question in the president's voice than he would have liked, but the chairman ignored it. When it came to matters of military tactics, the chairman had few compunctions about treating the president as though he were the junior captain he had been when he left the Army.

"Too soon, sir," the general said shortly. "We're still at the deception stage. Sure, shots have been fired, but the fog of war is too pervasive right now. We know what's happened, but they don't know we know. Sir, lay low for now. See if they make the first move. After all, it looks like they're the ones who attacked. They ought to be the ones calling us.

We stay in our fortress, don't come outside. Not yet."

"I see," the president said. "Very well, then—what do I tell the media when they start calling? And call they will, you can be sure of that."

"Nothing. You tell them nothing." The general was very firm on the point.

The president sighed and shook his head. "That won't work long. It just won't."

"It doesn't have to work for long, Mr. President. Not long at all. Buy yourself some time to get that gal up in New York to find out what's going on from her perspective. Never ask the Russians a question you don't know the answer to."

Gal. I wonder if I will tell Sarah Wexler that the chairman of the joint chiefs of staff calls her a "gal." If I do, I think I'll make sure I'm out of arm's reach. Then again, I get the feeling that may be about the highest compliment he ever pays a woman.

"What you need, Mr. President, is time."

"Time to find out what happened, I suppose."

To his surprise, the general shook his head. "No, sir. Enough time to get reelected."

Now, that was a puzzler! Who would've ever thought the general gave a damn about the election? I don't even know what party he is. Or how he votes.

But it's not like I really care.

"Thank you, sir," the president said slowly, in the unusual position of being enormously flattered by the compliment he'd been paid. Heady stuff for the young Army captain who was now president of the most powerful nation on the earth.

"I want what is best for this country," the general said bluntly. "Right now, that means you sitting in that chair."

"This has the potential to cut both ways, though," the president said, his mind racing. His national security council— he had to have them in on this. "We run the risk of looking soft on this. And that's the one thing I can't have happen."

"I realize that, sir. And you'll have people who can better advise you on that point. But I consider it critical that you be reelected next month, and I don't want this incident to keep that from happening." The general stood abruptly. "If I

hear anything else, Mr. President, I'll let you know immediately."

"Thank you." The president stood and walked the general
to the door. "And I will take your take on this to the security
council. I appreciate your candor."

After the general had gone, the president turned to his
chief of staff and said, "Mike, get Sarah Wexler on the secure
line. No, better yet—get her down here. Within the next couple of hours if possible."

ACN Headquarters
1400 local (GMT-5)

When Hank Carter stormed into the ACN newsroom, he
made his presence felt immediately. Carter was one of the
two old-style journalists who'd successfully made the transition to the twin paradigms of computers and international
coverage. At heart, he was the stereotype of a hard-drinking,
cigar-smoking, out-of-shape, cynical reporter turning out
tight, elegant prose on a manual typewriter. But Carter had
decided that was not who he wanted to be, and thus he
wasn't. In his early fifties, he was trim, muscular, and in
excellent shape. There was not an ounce of fat on his lean
body.

Carter was slightly taller than average, but his build made
him look well over six feet tall. His hair was steel gray and
close-cut, and tended to spike even without gel or mousse.
His face with smooth, deeply tanned, with only a few lines
around his eyes. He glowed with good health. His eyebrows
were heavy and deep, hanging over a set of piercing gray
eyes. The rest of his features were strong, jutting planes and
acute angles, with an unexpectedly full and generous mouth.

Carter was originally from Alabama, and he retained the
smooth vowels and consonants of his youth. Whether or not
it was an act Drake had never been able to figure out, but
she'd seen more than one person underestimate him based
solely on his accent. She had never made that mistake herself, and she considered warning Winston against it, but then

thought better. Carter had been a prime force in Winston's hiring, and not just for her looks.

When Drake had been informed of his decision, she had immediately assumed that he had hired her for appearance only.

Now Carter's Southern accent dropped away as he responded: "I'm going to forget you said that, Drake." His eyes were cold, a Northern Sea during winter. She could almost see the ice creep over the rest of his face, and could hear it in his voice. "Of all people to assume that—what, are you having flashbacks to your own first days here?"

"That's not why I was hired," Drake said, her voice level.

Carter drove his point home. "No, it wasn't. You were hired because my bosses could see the way things were headed. We had no women on the staff, not in the on-air department. In order to make sure we stayed in step with the times, we had to have a female presence on the front lines. And we picked you to be that person." His gaze never waivered as he delivered this brutal assessment.

"So you say." Drake was just as implacable.

Carter conceded gracefully, his point made. "But whatever the original reasons, they hardly matter now, do they? When it comes to delivering a headline story, you beat the pants off of everyone—male, female, everyone. You're a pro, Drake. One of the best, as you well know. If you weren't, you'd never get away with half the shit you pull in the field."

"I deliver the story. That's what matters, right?"

Carter sighed. "At least half the time, you're *part of the story*. Cuba, Greece, Turkey," he ticked off the different conflicts on his fingers. In Cuba, she'd been held hostage as a human shield by renegade militia forces. In Greece, she'd been personally involved with the leader of the rebel forces. And in Turkey, she'd forced the United States Navy to conduct an at-sea rescue in order to get on board the carrier to get the story. That little incident had almost resulted in charges being filed against her, but ACN's massive legal team, coupled with a not insignificant legal budget, had finally bailed her out.

"I don't start these wars."

"And it doesn't matter," Carter said, ignoring her protest.

"Because our audience bit, and they bit big. They love you. All they see is this stunning woman caught up in the middle of things. They don't think about whether or not you violate any sort of journalistic ethics by getting involved with these people. All they do is identify with you. The men in our audience see somebody they need to go rescue, and they're cheering on the rest of the world as they do that. The women identify with you even more, like your life is some sort of action-adventure romance story." He held up one hand to forestall protest. "I'm not blaming you. The people love that—they love you. And that means an increased market share."

"So why did you hire her?" Drake asked. There was too much truth in what he said.

"Because she's good," Carter said, gazing at her steadily. "If you want, take a look at her tapes." He fished around the bookcase behind him and produced two videocassettes. "One hard news, one human interest. She did the research, put the whole thing together. You look at them and then come back and bitch about my decision."

"She was regional. This is the big league."

"And I think she's ready for it." Carter's gaze softened slightly. "You've done enough for female reporters, Drake. However you got your start, you've carved out a broad path for the women coming up behind you—no pun intended. You've made it so that a kid like Cary has a shot based on her ability. Now, the outside package does matter, but it's the same for men as well. It's part of on-camera presence. The important thing is that she didn't have to screw anybody to get this job, and that's in part thanks to you."

"Great."

"So," Carter continued, ignoring the mutinous expression on his star reporter's face, "I expect you to show her the ropes. Sure, you may have to step on her a couple of times. I heard what happened out there. There's no way she's got the people skills yet to get in some of the places that you can. I don't expect you to share your entire contact book with her, either. She'll have to develop her own. But at least give her a shot, Drake. You know that if she ever pushed it to the breaking point, we'd take you over her without a second thought. She's not a threat to you."

"I'm not afraid of her," Drake said. She picked up the two videocassettes. "I'll take a look. See what's she's got. Then I'll decide."

Just then, Winston knocked once, then stepped into the room. She strolled over to Carter's desk and handed him a computer printout. Then turning to include Pamela, she said, "It's your ship. The *Jefferson*. The Russians just shot up a cruise liner right next to her."

"Let's roll," Carter snapped, still staring at the printout as he spoke. "Drake, you're on it. Take your own camera people and whoever else you want. Marcia, arranged transportation. Jim, get on the phone and get the usual clearances. I want a presence on that ship within the next twelve hours, people. So move!"

Around him, people sprang into action, following a well-practiced drill. Marcia, Carter's personal assistant, picked up the telephone and speed dialed ACN's travel department. "Party of two?" she asked, looking at her boss.

Carter didn't answer immediately and Drake felt her heart sinking. *No, not right now. Not on this one.* "Carter, I can—" she started.

"No. Three. Drake, one camera, and Winston. Might as well hit the deck running, Cary."

Drake groaned silently, but turned to face Winston with a calm, professional expression. "Get moving. Pants, comfortable shoes, personal items for two weeks. Two bags, no more. On-camera outfits, a dress if you want—you won't need it, but take one anyway." She pointed at Winston's high-heeled shoes. "One pair, no more. Now move. I'll meet you at the airport in three hours," she continued, mentally running through the flight schedules in her mind. "Marcia will have us take a direct flight to San Diego, and from there we'll try to get Navy transport. We may have to continue on to Hawaii and fly out from there, but that'll get us out with the State Department and the military."

Winston's jaw was hanging open. She recovered and began scribbling notes on her notepad. "So we're going to—"

"Two hours," Drake said. "At the airport. That's all you need to know right now."

Carter regarded her with a slight smile. "If you ever call me high-handed again, I want you to think about this little incident."

"Who the hell do you think I learned it from?" Drake snapped.

SEVEN

Ambassador Wexler was having a hard time concentrating on the debate raging across the floor of the general assembly of the United Nations. The gist of it was a conflict that seemed to involve most of the eastern part of Africa. The differences that divided the factions went deeper than religion or race, although in public those were the most hotly contended issues. But the real problem lay far deeper.

For more centuries than most nations could count, the continent had been primarily tribal in nature. Ancient societies had grown and flourished around leaders who could unify factions, and a sense of identity that came with a strong tribal system provided a real source of stability. But the transition from a strongly decentralized government to the form of unified nation government that was necessary to conduct business in the modern age had proved troublesome for the continent. As a result, other nations had imposed their wills on her, along with their governments and their cultures, without looking beneath the surface of the "heathen" culture.

Other nations' answers were not the right answers for Africa, no more then America's answers were right for Russia. The peoples of each region had to find their own way, their own expression of community line that reflected the culture from which they had grown.

The ambassador had a sense, watching the debate raging around her, that points were being made by either side in ways that she only vaguely understood. Water rights, land, yes—those she understood. But she could tell from the reaction of other African nations that she was missing many of the subtleties.

Well, no doubt the State Department analysts would be over in the morning to fill her in on their interpretation. There were some good people there, people who had lived and worked in the countries they studied, and she valued them for their ability to provide some context to the arguments, insight into what was really going on.

But the problem with State was that sometimes they identified a little too strongly with their areas of expertise. They were ready to send in the troops—American troops—as a universal solution. And military force wasn't, not really. Peace came from within, not imposed from outside.

If there ever really were such a thing as peace. There were days when she suspected that war was simply an innate part of human nature, one that could never be successfully repressed for long. She shook her head, marveling at the reasons people found to kill each other. But then again, an outsider looking into the United States would probably find some of her hot spots equally baffling.

There would be no votes called on the arguments presented today. She shifted in her chair, careful to keep her expression neutral. She had no clear sense of what the United States stand should be on any of the issues addressed, and she didn't want to inadvertently signal a position that didn't exist.

Her aide, Brad, appeared by her side. He crouched down next to her and passed her a hastily written note. "President wants you in DC ASAP," it said. She lifted one eyebrow while her mind ran across the various possibilities. Nothing immediately sprang to mind. The world seemed oddly quiet at the moment, at least as far as America's concerns went.

Brad shook his head. He was only the messenger boy on this one. "No details. He just wants you there."

ASAP. And just what does that mean? Leave the floor during the debate, giving the impression that America isn't concerned?

She glanced up at the clock, and saw that only five more minutes remained in this session. She flashed five fingers at Brad, who nodded. He would get back to the office and let the White House know, and five minutes seemed a small delay under the circumstances.

As the debate built to a climax, with all parties realizing that time was limited, and trying to get in the last word, she knew it had been the right decision.

The White House
1500 local (GMT-5)

The president was alone in the Oval Office. As alone as a president ever is, of course. Secret Service agents were stationed outside his door, not entirely comfortable with being excluded, but reassured because they were on home ground. The senior agent had worked for three presidents, and understood well that at times the constant surveillance and company, even though quiet and unobtrusive, could drive a man crazy. Every president that he had served with had moments when he simply insisted that he'd be alone, even if just for a few minutes. So the president was granted his privacy and, behind the closed doors, was luxuriating in it.

The White House was never entirely silent. The rumble of the air-conditioning, small noises from the kitchens below, the soft steps of Secret Service in the passageway—you could sense the movement all around. But just for these few moments, the president could at least pretend that he was alone.

And he was in more ways than one, wasn't he? The general's briefing and the general's concern over his reelection were clashing in his head. He was self-aware enough to realize it was the ultimate in egotism to believe that he was the only one who could run the country during these times. The United States had managed to survive under even the most incompetent presidents, and he had no doubt that even if the idiot who was running for the other party won, America would survive him, too.

Still, the presidency was a different order of magnitude in the nuclear age, wasn't it? The world was a much more dangerous place than any of his predecessors had ever dreamed. His detractors could call it egotism if they wanted, but he truly believed that at this moment in history he was the one best equipped to lead the country.

And that's the crux of the problem, isn't it? He had to deal with this crisis, and deal forcefully with it. That was what was best for the country. But it was also best for the country if he survived it, and possibilities for this going very wrong were too great.

So how to balance it? Wexler would have one answer, the general another. He reflected on the contradictory advice that would shortly be coming his way, staring out through the bulletproof glass at the night sky. An earlier summer thunderstorm had cleared, leaving clean, fresh air in its wake. The stars seem particularly bright tonight, although his view of them was somewhat obscured by the lights that were constantly on around the exterior of the White House. Another trade-off for security, like his privacy.

Was there a way around this? Maybe. His mind lined up the options, ranging from a full-out confrontation (quickly dismissed) to a more covert special operation intervention. That was a possibility, certainly.

But no. Although he had used special operations with great success on occasion, there was too much risk of the details leaking to the public. The last thing he needed right now was the congressional oversight committee questioning his motives. No, this had to be handled very quietly.

The answer came to him, stunning in its simplicity. Why hadn't he thought of it before? He picked up the telephone, and a familiar voice in the White House communications office answered immediately. "Yes, Mr. President?"

"Track down Admiral Magruder—the older one, the one that was chief of naval operations. Tell him I want to see him at his very earliest convenience—like tonight, if he's free."

"Yes, Mr. President."

The president hung up, chuckling slightly at the disingenuous request. *Tonight, if he's free. Right. As if a retired admiral—or, really, anybody for that matter—would ever tell the president of the United States that a meeting time was not convenient.*

Maybe someday somebody would. Sarah Wexler's face flashed through his mind. He grinned at the thought. Maybe Wexler would be the one to do it.

The United Nations
1600 local (GMT-9)

As Wexler stepped outside the assembly room, Brad appeared at her side carrying a briefcase and a small bag. "The car is waiting." Carrying her emergency traveling gear, Brad led her out and down to the waiting town car. She slipped into it and was whisked away to the airport, and twenty minutes later was boarding a waiting jet. When they touched down in DC, a helo waited to take her to the White House.

By the time she reached the Oval Office, she had heard the same news reports that the president had and had an idea why she'd been summoned. Things big enough to get her summoned to the White House just didn't stay quiet that long.

Just as the helo touched down, the details became available on the radio. "We have just learned from the Coast Guard station in San Diego, California, that there has been a major disaster at sea involving the SS *Montego Bay*. A luxury cruise liner, the *Montego Bay* was making her normal run between San Pedro and Hawaii. According to preliminary reports, the cruise liner has suffered some sort of casualty. The situation remains unclear, and there is no word on deaths or injuries."

A cruise liner. So what had happened—hostages? A collision? Please, not one involving our Navy.

Montego Bay—she hadn't been aboard her but had been on a sister ship years ago. How many years ago—twenty, perhaps? She remembered the ship had seemed so very glamorous at the time.

"Come right in, Madam Ambassador," the president's chief of staff said as he met her outside the Oval Office. "He's waiting for you."

He was behind his desk, scribbling through some papers, but looked up as she walked in. Relief flashed across his face and then the worried lines reappeared. "It's breaking now," he said, pointing at the TV in the corner. A newscaster was flashing up what appeared to be file photos of the SS *Montego Bay,* a chart with her current location on it, and then brief bios of the captain and crew. All this background information meant only one thing—they were stalling, killing time until they could figure out what the Coast Guard reports meant. Or, better yet, until they could get their people on scene. As a last resort, if any ship in the area were in cell phone range, they would settle for a very informative and highly unauthorized cell phone call from some sailor to the mainland.

"Three hours ago," the president began, "the Russian aircraft carrier opened fire on *Montego Bay.* Or, to be more precise, the *Admiral Kurashov* launched a surface attack missile at *Montego Bay.* It struck near the stern, causing massive damage. The captain wisely elected to execute an immediate abandon ship, and probably saved a lot of lives that way."

"The Russians fired on a cruise liner?" Wexler repeated, stunned. "That doesn't make sense. What possible reason could they have for doing that?"

The president shook his head. "I was hoping you could tell me."

"Not a clue, Mr. President. Not a clue. Casualties?" she asked.

"All the passengers have been taken aboard the USS *Jefferson.* A complete tally is still pending, but it looks like there are a number of people missing, presumed dead. Primarily crew members that were belowdecks, either off shift or working near the engineering spaces. There are probably more."

"How many passengers?"

"Four hundred and twenty seven. Two hundred crewmen.

As of the last report, five hundred and forty-three people are accounted for."

"Dear God." Wexler said a silent prayer, stunned. "And what do the Russians have to say about it?"

"I haven't talked to them yet." The president's voice was impassive.

"You haven't—why in the world not? You've got to, don't you? That's the whole point of the hotline and of all the arrangements made for immediate communication between the two of you."

"The Cold War is over, Sarah."

"But—Mr. President, surely you can see this makes no sense. You've got to talk to them. Something like this can get out of hand so fast that there's no controlling it."

Wexler stopped, aware that she was starting to babble. It wasn't that she wasn't making sense. She was, and she had worked with the president too long to believe he didn't understand her point. So why hadn't he called the Russians? What possible reason could he have?

As she studied him and saw him look away from her, saw a faint line of red creep across his jaw, she knew. With a heartsick lurch in her gut, she knew. He had proved himself beyond this before, but evidently he wasn't the man she thought he was.

"There's a problem," he said finally. "Evidently one of our cruisers fired anti-air missiles at the missile launched by the Russians, intending to intercept and destroy it before it could hit anything. It may—*may*—have intercepted the other missile in the vicinity of the *Montego Bay*."

So that's it. You are pretty sure the Russians are at fault, but you can't prove that our missile didn't hit the cruise liner. And right now, that's got you more worried than the people that died.

"What do you think the public perception of this is going to be?" she asked, careful to keep all traces of horror and disgust out of her voice. "How is the best way to approach this?"

"It's hard to say," he said neutrally, but it was too late. She had already seen a flicker of relief on his face as he decided she understood what his concern was. "On the face of it, it appears completely outrageous. But it's dangerous to work off first assumptions without a complete report. For now, see what you can find out from their side. I'll talk to their president soon, but I'd like to be a step ahead of him when I do."

"I understand, of course," she said. "I'll call you as soon as I know anything."

The president stood and the ambassador followed suit. He came around the desk and laid one hand on her shoulder as he escorted her to the door. "Thank you, Sarah. Let me know as soon as you can."

As she stood in the hallway outside the Oval Office, Wexler wondered just what was going on.

After she left, the president stared down at the papers in front of him, trying to concentrate. There would be nothing critically important in the pile—officer appointments, routine matters, a few personal letters his chief of staff had decided he should sign. Anything of substance, such as legislation, would have been hand-carried in to his office by the appropriate action officer, and he would have been rebriefed on the importance of it before he signed it.

Not that everything of importance got signed in front of his staff. Much as they might not like it, the president did have some matters pending that his staff knew nothing about. Oh, they'd caught hints that something was afoot, but he'd managed to deflect their suspicions, and for the most part, his staff believed that Betty Lou was entirely more human than she was.

"Mr. President?" his chief of staff asked. "Admiral Magruder is here."

"Send him in. And keep everyone else out," the president said, holding up his hand to forestall protest from his chief of staff and from the Secret Service. "Just do it."

"Admiral," the president said warmly as the senior Magruder entered the room. "Thank you for coming."

"I am always at your disposal. You know that."

"Sit." The president waited until Magruder was seated, then said with a sigh, "That satellite business. It's not going to stop there, is it? The Russians have really screwed the pooch on this one."

"It was a risk," Magruder conceded. "We knew that from the start."

"I know, I know. Still, now that things are hosed up, what do you recommend?"

"We do nothing," Magruder said promptly. "After all, we haven't yet evaluated the Russians' information, have we? And until we do, there's no point in second-guessing ourselves on allowing them to take out the satellite."

"That's true. So when will we know something about their quid pro quo?"

The senior Magruder smiled, a wintry expression settling in around his eyes. "In a few days Mr. President. In a few days. We'll also know more about what happened with our missiles and theirs and the *Montego Bay*. But even if we had final answers to those questions, I wouldn't want to move until we knew the rest of the answers."

The president sighed. "I know you're right. But I'm going to be getting a lot of pressure here real soon."

"I know. Let them think you're just worried about the election. Or that you're having some sort of illicit relationship with this Betty Lou." Magruder stopped, seeing the look of distaste on the president's face. "Just stall, Mr. President. Just for a few days."

"Okay. I can do that. But get back to me as soon as you can on the other stuff. If they're feeding us disinformation, I'm going to haul their asses into international court over that satellite."

After Magruder left, the president forced himself to concentrate on the innocuous papers still needing his signature. The important matters, like the decision to let the Russians test their laser system on an obsolete American satellite, were never committed to paper.

EIGHT

When all the commercial flights had proved full, Carter had sprung for using the network's corporate jet. The two women, plus their cameraman and baggage, flew in royal comfort from Denver to San Diego's Lindbergh Field. There, the local affiliate had had a rental car and driver waiting for them. They had been picked up and were now being transported to the North Island Naval Air Station operations center.

"There's a COD leaving today, but no one is exactly certain when," their escort said, briefing them on their latest travel arrangements as he drove. He passed a brown envelope to Drake. "Those are your orders, shot records, clearance information. The usual stuff."

"Like the clearance will make a difference," she said, as she passed out the papers to the appropriate people. "They never tell us anything classified. At least not intentionally."

"What's a COD?" Winston asked. The cameraman smirked, and Drake turned away, a smile of amusement on her face. "Carrier on-board delivery. We'll be CODing out to *Jefferson,* of course. It's a lot of fun."

"I see." Winston's voice belied her statement, but she asked no further questions. Pamela grinned.

Fun. Damn right. If you consider a controlled crash at one hundred and forty miles an hour onto a steel deck in the middle of nowhere fun, then I guess it qualifies. And do that facing backwards in what seems to be the flimsiest aircraft you have ever been in. But she'll have to get used to it, just like the rest of us did.

Now, sitting on the hard plastic chairs in the operation center, their stomachs full of hot dogs from the snack bar, they waited. And waited and waited. The cameraman and Pamela took some background shots, then so did Winston. That accomplished, Pamela settled down and opened a book to read.

Winston had not brought anything to read. She shifted uneasily in her chair, watching the sailors pass. Finally she asked, "What the crap are we waiting for?"

"Who, probably. Not what," Drake said, not looking up from her book. "Getting a seat on the COD right at the beginning of something is primarily a function of how much water you draw. Everybody wants to be on the scene right away, including a lot of people that are actually useful. Like them," she said, gesturing at the junior sailors and technicians that made up most of the passengers. "But sometimes they don't get out until the top brass and senior officer and reporters are on board the carrier."

"Who, then?" Winston said, clearly bored and trying to prolong the conversation.

"No telling."

"Don't you even have a theory?"

Drake sighed and closed her book, using her finger to mark the spot. "No, I don't. Lesson learned, Winston. A lot of waiting is part of it. Be prepared for it. Now, unless there was something else?" Drake waited politely for a moment before returning to her book. Winston sighed in frustration.

Suddenly, the noise level near the entrance picked up markedly. In one smooth motion, Drake snapped her book shut, jammed it in her bag, and darted off to shove her way through the crowd to the front door. Two Marine Corps sergeants entered, blazing a path through the waiting crowd for the man behind them.

"Who is it?" Winston asked, struggling to catch up with Drake and the cameraman, who had already positioned himself to get a shot of whoever was entering.

Tombstone Magruder stepped through the door. The tall, lean frame, those piercing dark gray eyes, the short clipped hair now going gray at the temples. She had every line of his face—indeed, of his body—memorized. Her fingers had touched every inch of his skin and she knew his body as well as she knew her own.

Even after all these years since she'd broken off their engagement, she still found herself short of breath when she saw him. No one had ever come close to him, in bed or out of it, and over the years she had become resigned to the fact that no one ever would.

One of the reasons she had been so angry at Winston's callous remarks about Tombstone's availability was that that thought had crossed her own mind more than once. She had been foolish, so foolish, not to marry him when she had the chance. Sure, it would have meant compromises in her career, but if she had known how much she would miss him, she would have been willing to make them.

But the compromises only went one way, didn't they? There was no way he was willing to settle down, no way he would've been happy without flying around the world every couple of weeks. Somehow Tomboy, with her own career in the Navy, had been able to stand it. Drake knew she couldn't have. There was never any hope of a future for them, not as long as Tombstone refused to compromise.

But there could have been, one part of her mind insisted. *He would have changed, I know he would. And he's not in the Navy anymore. He's retired now, a civilian, although it's hard to tell it by looking at him.*

Indeed, even in civilian clothes, Tombstone Magruder looked every inch the admiral. His erect posture, the ease with which he moved through the crowd of sailors, the lazy way his eyes were half closed as he surveyed the crowd— all said that this was an officer who was used to command and accustomed to being obeyed.

Pamela felt her breathing grow unsteady as he turned in her direction. His eyes passed over her lightly, and then came back to her. They widened slightly and he nodded in acknowledgment of her presence. There was no smile or any change in his expression.

What do you expect from a man nicknamed Tombstone? She shoved her way through the crowd, which didn't give way for her as it had for him. She stepped in front him, almost too close, and looked up at him. His familiar musk smell reached her.

"Good afternoon, Admiral. Are you headed out to *Jefferson*?" she asked, holding the mike unobtrusively at her side. It was sensitive enough to pick up any comments he might make.

Tombstone just looked at her for a long moment then said, "I assume you're waiting for the COD?"

"And I assume it's waiting for you, isn't it?"

He studied her for a moment, his gaze lingering over her features, and she knew he was remembering how well they knew each other. With a flash of insight, she realized how desperately lonely he must be these days. Tomboy had seemed to complete part of him, and although he carried on in her absence, there was always a sense that he was withdrawn.

There was a commotion at her side, and then Winston stepped up beside Drake, elbowing her slightly as she did so. She smiled brightly and held out her hand. "You must be Admiral Magruder," she said. "Cary Winston. I'm working with Pamela now."

"For. Not with." Pamela corrected the preposition immediately, and she saw a flash of amusement on Tombstone's face. As she had known he would, he picked up instantly on the tension between the two women. With just a hint of sardonic amusement in his eyes, he said, "How do you do, Ms. Winston. If you'll excuse me, I need to check in. I'm certain we'll have a chance to speak later." He turned away without saying any more to Drake, and she could have kicked him in the shins. It was evident what he was doing, at least to her and her cameraman. But not so to Winston.

Winston turned back to her, a bemused expression on her face. "Wow. He's really something." *Another one bites the dust. Just what is it about Tombstone?*

Ten minutes later, the check-in clerk was calling out names and leading passengers with their luggage out to the waiting COD. Tombstone was not in line. Then again, Drake did not expect he would have to go through the same procedures that they did. He was probably already on board, perhaps up front talking to the pilots.

But when they followed the clerk across the hot tarmac, piled their luggage as directed, and then proceeded to board through the tail ramp, she was surprised still not to see him. She grabbed a petty officer helping the passengers to their seats and asked, "Isn't Admiral Magruder on this flight?"

The sailor regarded her levelly. "I'm sorry, ma'am. The movements of senior officials are always classified."

"Yes, but I saw him in the terminal."

"If you'd proceed to board, ma'am."

Frustrated, she started toward the ramp and paused to let Cary Winston and the cameraman precede her. She trotted back to her luggage, as though she'd forgotten something, and took a quick look around the airfield. Sure enough, about four hundred feet away, she saw Tombstone climbing up the boarding ladder and into the cockpit of a Tomcat. She turned back to the crewman who had refused to answer her questions, a grin on her face. As he started for her, she waved to Tombstone, and then trotted back to the COD's ramp. "Sorry. I forgot my book."

So he's flying out in a Tomcat, is he? I wonder how he stays current. And I wonder why the Navy is letting a retired admiral get stick time anyway? Surely they have plenty of pilots who are dying for some stick time. What's going on here?

"Maybe he's taking the later flight," Winston said, disappointment in her voice.

"Maybe," Drake said. She fastened the restraining harness, tightened the straps, and opened her book. *And then again, I bet he beats us out there.*

Tomcat 201
2105 local (GMT-9)

"Who's that?" Jeremy Greene asked, pointing across the tarmac. Tombstone, halfway up the boarding ladder, twisted
around to see Drake's familiar figure standing near the COD.

*Pamela, dammit—why do you always have to be every-
where I am? And why are you here when Tomboy isn't?*

It made no sense at all, the intrusive train of thought that
started every time he saw her. Pamela was not responsible
for Tomboy being gone. He knew that, kept repeating it to
himself. Yet every time he saw his former fiancée, he felt a
completely irrational flash of rage that she was here, dogging
his footsteps, and Tomboy wasn't. Tombstone looked down
at Greene, who had already completed his preflight and was
strapped into his ejection seat. "Ignore her."

"Civilian, right? Maybe we'll see her on the boat."

"Maybe you ought to be a RIO instead of a pilot," Tombstone said. "You didn't recognize her?"

"I don't wear glasses," Greene said hotly. Then he remembered exactly who was in the front seat. Retired or not, you
had to be polite to an admiral.

"That, my friend, was the esteemed Pamela Drake. And
when we get on board, you'll say nothing to her. Not a word.
Zip. Nada." The plane captain who had followed Tombstone
up the boarding ladder double-checked Tombstone's straps
then pulled the safeties that kept the ejection seat from firing
on the ground and held them up for Tombstone's inspection.
Tombstone counted them out loud, as was his habit, and then
nodded.

"I'm not a RIO, I'm a pilot," Greene grumbled. "And
speaking of being a pilot—"

"You're not current, are you?" Tombstone said calmly. "If
you had been in shape to fly, you could have gotten your
quals out of the way yesterday. I told you I'd make sure
you'd get more stick time."

"A touch of the flu," Greene muttered. Not exactly true,
since the alcohol he'd consumed the night before had killed
off any germs.

"Right. Pre-start checklist," Tombstone said, and opened

his flight manual to begin to run through it. "Ready?"

With a sigh, Greene opened his own manual. He knew Tombstone did not believe him, and he couldn't blame him. Yes, he should have gotten his quals taken care of yesterday, but what the heck? After all, there would be time on the boat, wouldn't there?

But it's your own fault. You missed the chance to fly out there, one small part of his mind insisted. *Tombstone is never out of qual, is he? He makes time.*

Responding automatically to Tombstone's questions as he completed the backseat pre-flight actions, Jeremy mulled that thought over for a moment.

Technically, Jeremy Greene was not on active duty. When he agreed to become part of the small, highly specialized special operations group that Tombstone and his uncle headed up, he had been discharged from the Navy and offered a civilian contract with the company. True, should he leave Advanced Analysis, as their Beltway front was known, he would immediately be recalled to active duty. But technically, at least, he was a civilian right now, wasn't he?

Technically.

So how did Tombstone figure he was entitled to tell Jeremy who he could and couldn't talk to? Pamela Drake—of course, he knew who she was. And he knew her history with Tombstone as well. It wasn't like he had a romantic interest in her, was it? Hell no. But that chick he'd seen with Drake in the terminal, now that was a different matter. Maybe her secretary or something. He'd find out once they got on the boat. There were no secrets there.

"Pre-fight complete," Tombstone announced.

"Complete," Jeremy agreed.

Tombstone started the Tomcat's engines, increasing power as they rumbled to life. Inside the cockpit, Jeremy felt the familiar vibrations of a Tomcat on the ground radiate through the fuselage, up the frame of his seat, and resonate in his bones. It was a warm, welcoming sound, as though the aircraft had missed them and was eager to be airborne.

"Tower, 101, ready to roll," Greene announced, taking over the communications. The tower granted them clearance ahead of the COD and they rolled out smoothly past her, paused for a moment at the beginning of the runway for final checks, and then began their final roll out. Tombstone applied power smoothly, quickly taking her up to speed, then rotated at slightly over the minimum distance. He put the Tomcat into a steep climb, carefully following the tower's vectors to clear the area. The area around San Diego was busy, and he was careful to stay out of commercial air control areas.

"Better than the COD," Greene said. "Although I'm not sure why we needed a full weapon loadout."

"Always take weapons if they're offered," Tombstone said. "Besides, you never know when you'll need them."

"Are we? Likely to need them right away, I mean."

Tombstone didn't answer.

So this is just a routine mission to ferry a new aircraft out to the squadron, is it? Bullshit. There's more to this whole incident than meets the eye. Tombstone's acting like we're flying into a hostile area. He's bound to know more about this than he's telling me. They always do.

It was a source of continuing frustration to Jeremy that Tombstone and his uncle played their cards close to their respective chests.

"Okay, just so I know to stay awake," Jeremy said. Not like he could sleep in the back of a Tomcat, anyway. Not after what happened last time he'd dozed off. He slept through an engagement, and it had taken Tombstone shouting at him to wake him up.

"There's no specific threat to know about, Jeremy," Tombstone said, evidently reading his backseater's mind. "But it just makes sense to be heads up. You can't believe everything you read in the newspapers or hear on the air. Particularly not," he continued, animosity in his voice, "when Pamela Drake is involved. Just keep that in mind."

"I will. But once we get closer to the carrier—"

"Some fighters from *Jefferson* will meet us," Tombstone said. "And tanker support. I'm not anticipating any problems, but you never know."

"You never know," Jeremy echoed. He glanced down at his radarscope. "Looks like they're airborne. Where do you want to stay?"

"High and forwards," Tombstone said promptly, evidently

having already considered the issue. "We'll be in the data link, but I want my own radar taking a look ahead as well. Just in case."

Jeremy sighed. "I have a feeling I'm going to get real tired of hearing that phrase."

Greyhound 601
2120 local (GMT-9)

Pamela had sneaked a seat next to one of the four windows, and the light streaming in through the scratched and scarred plastic provided enough illumination for her to read her book as they flew. Winston had not been quite as quick to grab a seat, nor had the cameraman bothered to save one for her as he had for Pamela, and she was relegated to the back part of the plane, with the tail ramp in full view. The rear, Pamela had discovered early on, was also the most turbulent part of the COD, although none of it could be called particularly smooth. And other than in the few seats near the windows, there was not enough light to read. Not that Winston had brought a book anyway.

Beside her, the cameraman was asleep. He was an old hand at this and, although she had never told him so, Pamela's favorite to work with. Jeff possessed an unusually placid, level-headed manner, and even her worst temper tantrums seemed to pass right over him. Additionally, although she'd never told him this either, he was by far in her mind the most bloodthirsty of the cameramen. Given a chance between reaching out to try to save Drake from falling off a cliff and getting a good shot of the look of terror on her face, she suspected he would instinctively choose the latter. Maybe his even temper wasn't so much a good disposition as a lack of connection on some basic level with other people.

But she'd take good work over friendliness any day, and that was why he was here.

Finally, she fell asleep as well, and the hours passed quickly.

NINE

The admiral's conference room was packed with his staff and representatives from the ship's company. Despite the early morning hour, no one looked tired or sleepy, though more than one face showed purple bruises under the eyes. No one had slept much, Coyote included.

"Listen up, people. It's going to get worse before it gets better. We've got a COD inbound as well as message traffic five feet deep. For the time being, I want us all focused on self-protection and preventing another tragedy. I want a full CAP complement up, twenty-four seven. No chances—not until we figure out what's going on here. That clear?" Coyote scanned the faces of the staff seated around the table.

Lab Rat cleared his throat. "Admiral, could we get a clarification on ROE for the pilots?"

Coyote stared at him for a long, hard moment. "You got something on your mind, mister?"

For a moment Lab Rat wondered if he'd overstepped the bounds of propriety. But dammit, he was the admiral's intelligence officer—he got paid to point out problems, not to suck up like a yes man. "Yes, Admiral, I do," Lab Rat continued, unfazed by the scrutiny. "INCOS isn't holding up under these conditions and I don't think we can count on what the aircrew remember about it. This could get out of hand very quickly."

Coyote looked away. Lab Rat could see him arrive at a decision. "I'll brief all squadron commanders in one hour," the admiral said finally. "And I expect the word to get out to all aircrews. Now, how are we coming on the survivors?"

"Captain Gaspert says he's got a complete and accurate count," the operations officer answered. "Current muster was in the deck log, of course. So far, it looks like most of the fatalities are among his crew, especially the ones below the waterline. There just wasn't time for them to get out." He stopped, staring down at the list as though he could make the numbers change by sheer force of will. "Eighty-two missing, presumed dead. One hundred and twenty-eight wounded, sixteen of those critical."

The numbers sank in around the table, and few were unmoved. It was one thing, horrible though it was, to lose military members. Another thing entirely to kill civilians, as they all knew following the World Trade Center massacre.

"We're maintaining a full SAR," Ops continued. "The last rescue was two hours ago. Small boats and helos, with the S-3s as well. I think we'll find some more of them clinging to wreckage."

"Let's hope so." The admiral turned to the flag supply officer. "Any logistics problems I need to know about?"

"No, Admiral. We've outfitted the civilians with dungarees and T-shirts, basic toiletries, that sort of thing. We'll be fine until we can resupply."

"Okay, then. Anything else?"

Lab Rat cleared his throat. "Admiral, so far we're not certain who was at fault. The missile trajectories were almost exactly reciprocal. We had a near miss, or we had a hit. It's going to take more information from national sensors before we can be sure of what happened."

It was not what they wanted to hear. No one could bear the thought that the *Jefferson* might have been responsible for so many deaths.

But Coyote hadn't risen to command of a battle group by

being afraid to face facts. His face was somber as he said, "We'll see."

As the staff meeting broke up, Strike caught Lab Rat outside in the passageway leading back to their offices. "You got it in for pilots in particular for some reason?" he asked.

Lab Rat shook his head. "We put up CAP, they put up CAP. A lot of metal in a finite amount of airspace, with pilots on both sides truly pissed. You slam the ROE down their throats and I'll make sure it's in the pre-mission briefs. The last thing we need is a couple of hotheads banging wingtips with one of the Russians."

"Pilots will be pilots."

Lab Rat felt a surge of anger. "Weren't you listening? We don't know whose fault it was yet."

"The pilots know."

"They *think* they know. They don't. And I don't want anyone assuming an aggressive posture in the air until we do."

Strike shrugged. "It's inbred in a pilot. What are you going to do about it?"

Lab Rat's anger boiled over. "You remind them of what they were before they were pilots."

"What, civilians?"

"No. Officers. They follow orders and avoid confrontations with the Russians or I'll prefer court-martial charges myself. We clear on that?"

Strike stepped back a bit, surprised at the intelligence officer's rage. "Yeah, clear."

As Lab Rat watched him go, he struggled to rein his temper in. It would do no good to give in to the anger, no good at all. There would be enough posturing and storming from the line officers. His job was to keep it under control, to force them to face facts.

Once they knew what the facts were. And then, God help them all if *Jefferson* was at fault.

Forger 202
0210 local (GMT-9)

Mikhail Gromko put his nimble jet into a hard turn, letting
the g-forces wash over him like a wave. He fought off the
familiar drag, tensing his muscles just a bit, letting it toy with
him. It was like surfing, the ebb and the flow of gravity, an
ocean of speed and blue. That he was flying a real combat
mission made it all the more exhilarating.

In theory, Gromko knew he could die. He'd seen class-
mates auger in during Basic, and more screw up during the
advanced platform training. He'd attended the funerals, comforted the widows, and rewritten the flight schedules to cover
the empty crew slots. There was nothing theoretical about
what could happen to you when you flew Russia's most advanced fighter into harm's way.

Except that none of it applied to him. Gromko knew, felt
it in his Cossack bones, that he was invulnerable. The mistakes and equipment failures that had claimed his peers were
impossible for him. He was too smart, too fast, too *everything*
to let them happen. The options others failed to see would
be clear to him. The faulty reflexes that had betrayed them—
well, that was simply a matter of training and willpower, and
Gromko had more of both than most.

Even the two blips homing in on him on his radar screen
meant nothing to him. No, that wasn't exactly true—they
represented a challenge, an opportunity. He would show
them—in ways that only another pilot would understand—
that he was the better pilot. No need to even fire missiles for
that. He would show them and let their despair lead them
into mistakes.

Hornets—big deal. They might as well have been mos-
quitoes for all he cared.

Hornet 107
0215 local (GMT-9)

Thor could feel his wingman sliding out of position. It was
a sixth sense, one that did not require a radarscope or a visual

confirmation, as if somehow his own nerves ran the length of the swept-back wings. Some might say it was just experience, some unconscious perception of how the airstream around his own aircraft changed as his wingman changed position, but Thor knew better.

Without even glancing at the HUD, he keyed his mike. "Badger, tighten up."

"Roger." Thor could almost hear an audible *thunk* as the Marine Corps captain off his starboard wing slid his Hornet back into position.

"Antsy little bastard, isn't he?" Thor commented, now concentrating on his HUD. The Russian fighter that they'd been assigned to cover was jittering around in the sky, making a series of sharp turns and abrupt changes in altitude for no purpose that Thor could discern. His sixth sense extended only to his own wingman.

Suddenly, as the Forger completed a snap roll, Thor understood. He chuckled, then keyed his mike again. "Little asshole is trying to impress us. He's a hot shot, don't you know? Guess we're supposed to be crapping in our pants just watching him do some basic aerobatics."

"Well, gee. I'm impressed," the captain replied. "I haven't pulled some of those maneuvers since—oh, heck. Since Basic, I guess."

"Yeah. Let's just sit back a bit and watch. I don't like the way he's moving." Thor studied the gyrations the other aircraft was executing, almost immediately discerning a pattern. The pilot wasn't bad—in fact, he wasn't bad at all—but he had some bad habits that were already evident to the more experienced Marine Corps pilot. Like a tendency to go right, right, then left. Like two increases in altitude followed by a roll. Like a little sloppiness in hard left turns. All in all, not fatal flaws in the other aviator's skills, but little weaknesses that would get him killed.

If it came down to it. And it wasn't supposed to, not on this flight.

"Maybe I ought to show him how it's really done," the captain off Thor's wing mused.

"Yeah, right," Thor said. That was just what they'd been briefed to avoid. No horsing around this time, their squadron

CO had warned. Sure, show the Russian some fancy moves—entirely inconsistent with every warning they'd had *not* to provoke an incident. *Not.*

"Okay, then!" The captain's Hornet peeled away and headed for the Forger.

Admiral Kurashov
0225 local (GMT-9)

The general watched the Russian and American fighters clutter the radarscope, hating the ship more with every passing moment. It was unnatural to breathe stale air, barricaded from the sky and the earth. Men should not die like this, blasted to atoms in the sky or entombed in ships. No, if they had to die, let it be on the ground where they could return dust to dust and ashes to ashes, not suspended in emptiness to drift around the globe forever.

Finally, when he could stand it no longer, he left the dark cave of the ship and made his way to the flight deck. He forced himself to walk slowly and purposefully, aware that even sailors drew confidence and courage from the way he held himself, the confidence on his face. But every second he could feel the fear—no, to be accurate, the terror—beating louder and louder in his veins, insisting that he was about to be trapped forever in this cave of steel, that he would be trapped and drown.

The air, blessed even though redolent with jet fuel fumes and the scorched taste of rubber and metal, blasted him as he opened the hatch to the flight deck. Just a few moments, he promised his pride, aware that any longer away from Combat might be taken as him having something he wanted to hide. *Just a few moments to reorient myself, to know the time of day and what the weather's like. Then we'll get back to the business at hand.*

The moments stretched into minutes. Finally, he forced himself to clang the hatch shut, take a deep breath, and begin the descent back down to Combat. The scent of the outside clung to him down several decks.

"Status," he demanded crisply as he reentered Combat. The men manning the consoles were pale, colors never seen on a soldier's face. The officers were pale, too.

"Two Hornets launched for each of our fighters," the action officer replied. "Standard operating procedures—we have warned all flights to be careful not to provoke an incident."

"Very well." The general studied the large screen in front of him, aware of how his eyes were already accustomed to translating the unfamiliar symbols and lines into a tactical picture.

The fighters were ringing the transport, each orbiting close to a symbol marking their assigned station. Arrowing in from the direction of the carrier were five aircraft—no, he corrected, five *pairs* of aircraft, some of them already closing and beginning to circle around to reach the farthermost Russian fighters. They were all a safe distance away from the transport, if anything less than a thousand miles could even be called safe in the modern world.

"Two zero two," the watch officer said, a trace of worry in his voice. "Interrogative your intentions. You are not maintaining assigned station."

"Roger. I am just demonstrating the capabilities of the aircraft for our friends," the pilot's voice came back, amused and confident.

"That is not your mission," the watch officer snapped. "Maintain flight discipline."

The general felt a deep twinge of worry. This was not his environment; these pale strangers were not his troops. But the instincts born of countless conflicts evidently recognized something in this situation that was very dangerous.

Hornet 107
0226 local (GMT-9)

"Badger, get your ass back here!" Thor shouted.

"Hey, you said okay," the captain protested, already starting a turn in toward the Forger.

"Watch out!" Thor screamed. He could see the geometries closing, his own wingman's bad habits juxtaposed against the Forger pilot's, the inevitable approaching too quickly to stop. "Break hard right!"

"Sorry, I just—*shit!*" The captain's situational awareness was two seconds slower than Thor's, and those two seconds proved deadly. As he tried to tighten up his right turn to move back toward Thor, the Forger pilot snapped a roll, decreasing airspeed slightly as he did so. The change in airspeed was just enough to settle him a bit lower in the air—and wingtip to wingtip with the captain.

The captain screamed, wrenching the Hornet way past the normal flight envelope, and for a moment Thor felt an insane surge of hope that he might make it, even as one part of his mind coldly informed him otherwise. Thor's hand was already moving over to his IFF readout, flicking the code switches to radiate a distress signal. Just as he keyed in the last digit, the Forger's right wingtip brushed against the captain's canopy.

It looked like a gentle caress, no more that the lightest stroke of metal on metal, but the effect was instantaneous and disastrous. A spray of sparkling light trailed after the Forger's wingtip as the Hornet's canopy disintegrated.

Admiral Kurasov
0227 local (GMT-9)

"Get him back on deck. *Now,*" Gorshenko ordered, not waiting for a naval officer to speak.

There was a moment of hesitation—a moment too long. Before Rotenyo decided to obey the ground officer's command, one of the pair of Hornets split into two distinct radar blips, one of which headed directly for the Russian fighter.

Stupid young man. Your ego and your insolence are more dangerous here than even on the ground. "Withdraw—now!"

The Russian aircraft started to turn. The blip labeled as an American Hornet shivered on the screen as though it, too, were turning.

Too little too late. The general knew what was already inevitable.

The blips merged briefly, then separated. At the same moment there was a blast of ungodly noise over the aviation circuits. The green radar trace that was the Russian aircraft broke into four smaller blips that blossomed and merged into a cloud of noise in the sky.

Bolshovich arrived and absorbed the tactical situation in a glance. "Launch four more Forgers," he ordered. "Vector toward the American fighters. They're not going to get away with this!"

Gorshenko felt the crew respond to their captain's leadership. He turned back to stare at the radar screen again, a sinking feeling in his gut.

Hornet 107
0228 local (GMT-9)

"Badger!" Thor shouted. "Answer me!"

"Huh?" The captain's voice was woozy but audible. "I'm bleeding." There was a note of wonder in his voice.

"Badger, listen to me. Are you hurt? Can you fly?"

"I'm *bleeding*." A note of panic now as the pilot regained situational awareness. "The canopy."

"You had a brush with the Forger—can you fly? Are you getting a Master Caution light? Report status," Thor said, keeping his voice level.

"No. Two hydraulics, the cabin pressure alarm. That's all. Over temp on right engine." The pilot's voice steadied up as his training kicked in.

Thor snapped open his own emergency checklist and began reading down the action items. His wingman's responses came more and more slowly, his words slurred even over the static.

"Hornet 102, you are cleared priority for green deck," the air boss said. "Badger, can you get her down?"

"Yeah. Maybe." The pilot sounded as though it didn't make much difference one way or the other to him.

Thor keyed his mike reluctantly. "Boss, 103. Sir, recommend 102 eject rather than risk recovery on deck." He watched as the other Hornet rolled inverted, then sluggishly regained level flight. "He's losing flight controls, sir." *And it's only a matter of time before he loses consciousness, too. God help us if he blacks out on the way down to the deck.*

"Roger. Wait. Out." There was silence on the circuit.

As the silence stretched on, Thor watched as his wingman's aircraft became more and more unstable. Hydraulic fluid was streaming out behind it, some of it perilously close to the engine air intake. Any second now—

The air boss returned. "Roger, 103, concur with recommendations. One zero two, descend to angels fourteen and initiate ejection. SAR will be standing by."

There was no answer.

"One zero two, do you copy?"

"Badger! Eject, eject!" Thor shouted, hoping his familiar voice would penetrate the fog now descending on his wingman. "Punch out, Badger. Punch out!"

As if in response, the other Hornet banked sharply to the right. It began descending, and for a moment Thor had hope that his wingman had heard him and was descending in response to the air boss's orders. His hopes were dashed when the Hornet's angle of attack steepened and its nose drifting down and down and down until it was in a vertical dive.

"Badger! *Eject!*" Thor flashed out an urgent prayer to someone, anyone, who might have some degree of control over the universe: "Eject!"

Thor followed the Hornet down, shouting and praying, ignoring the equally urgent pleas coming from the air boss. Finally, at seven thousand feet, the last shards of the canopy peeled back from the aircraft. There was a flash of fire, then a long streamer of white parachute slashing across the sky.

"Chute! I have one chute!" Thor shouted.

"Roger, copy, SAR inbound!" The relief in the air boss's voice was palpable. "Stay with him, Thor, mark on top. They'll have a man in the water with him before his life jacket fully inflates."

"Roger." Thor moved out a bit, watching the parachute billow from a safe distance. It jerked his wingman up in the air as the Hornet continued its final descent. Oddly, a sardonic definition of a successful aviator from Flight Basic came to mind: number of takeoffs should equal number of controlled landings.

Well, Badger might not be a success according to that definition, but Thor would take what the universe offered up. If his wingman was still alive, if they pulled him out before he drowned, if he had survived the ejection without serious injury, then that would be enough.

Finally, after what seemed like hours, the chute and its cargo reached the surface of the ocean. Thor watched the improbably small splash, then moved away to allow the helo to descend.

Admiral Kurashov
0229 local (GMT-9)

"We've lost him," Rotenyo said, his voice unbelieving. "That bastard shot our fighter down." Without asking permission, his hand went to the switch that controlled the shipboard alarm system. The hard, insistent gong of general quarters pulsed in the general's bones.

"No," the general said. "It was not an attack. It was an accident."

But Rotenyo was no longer inclined to listen to him. It was too late to stop what one Russian pilot had begun.

TEN

As Tombstone escorted the COD out to the carrier, the hours of boredom passed, broken only by moments of sheer terror during tanking. Tombstone stayed well ahead of the COD, scanning the sky looking for any problems. Behind him, Greene monitored the radar. There was nothing to see.

They refueled for the final time six hundred miles from the carrier, and Tombstone was carefully watching the COD's position the entire time. Finally, when they had taken on enough fuel, Tombstone disengaged and turned back toward the carrier.

"Stony, this is Home Plate. Be advised four playmates inbound your position. You should hold them shortly." The operations specialist's voice was calm and professional. There was nothing in it to indicate that dispatching four fighters to escort an unarmed COD and a fighter flown by a civilian was anything out the ordinary.

"Roger, copy four," Jeremy responded. He glanced back down at his scope and sure enough, four new contacts positioned directly over the aircraft carrier had just appeared. "I hold our playmates now."

"Roger. Anticipate COD on deck in four zero mikes. The

tanker will top you off, then we'll bring you in after the COD and the playmates."

"What's going on, Home Plate? Why the playmates?" Tombstone queried. There was a moment of silence, static hissing over the secure circuit. Tombstone felt that uneasy twitch in his gut that always seemed to presage trouble.

"Be advised, Stony, that there was an INCOS incident approximately thirty mikes ago. SAR is currently on station. Possibility that there are two casualties."

"INCOS?" Tombstone said incredulously. "What the hell happened?"

"I'll brief you when you get down here, Tombstone," a new voice said, and Tombstone recognized Coyote's accent. "For now, just hold on to that Greyhound until your playmates get in position. We'll bring the Greyhound in first, then the playmates, then you. You got enough fuel?"

"Roger, plenty of fuel, Admiral."

"What the hell?" Greene muttered.

Tombstone said over ICS, "That's in case I create a flaming datum on their deck. They'll get the COD and their own aircraft on board and out of the way in case the old guy screws up."

"Like that's going to happen."

"Not everyone has your confidence in me," Tombstone pointed out.

Suddenly, Greene's screen flashed bright green. He lost all contacts, even the COD, as the noise blanked out every other signal. "Jamming!" he snapped, and immediately began to try to filter it out. He was able to reduce it to four broad noise spikes, but couldn't get the screen completely clear.

"All units, Home Plate," a new voice said over tactical. "Be advised we have airborne and surface jamming, two Mainstays and the Russian cruiser. Attempting to reach the Russian commander for clarification at this time. Set general quarters. Hold fire."

"Hold fire!" Jeremy swore. "Jamming! That's a hostile act by definition." A hostile act was considered an act of war and allowed for immediate retaliation.

"Right. Not our game, though," Tombstone snapped, although Jeremy could tell he was deeply disturbed. Adrenaline was dumping into his system, and the hair on the back of his neck bristled. Flying through jamming was like flying blind. He had no idea what was in the air in front of him outside visual range.

"I'm closing on the COD. Put our playmates between the cruiser and the COD."

Twisting around, Jeremy could see the COD now in visual range. He gave the other four Tomcats vectors to take station on the COD to avoid mutual interference.

"All units, all airborne units, set EMCON Alfa. Receive only on link. We have a clear picture, and will control targeting from here," the carrier TAO ordered.

While the Tomcat was capable of firing any of its weapons on targeting data provided by another platform, no fighter pilot liked to hand over control to someone else. But there was no other choice right now. The cruiser and the carrier, working together, had managed to blank out most of the interference and were transmitting a solid tactical picture. Once Tombstone and Jeremy shut down their own radar, they would have a good picture not broken by noise.

"Stony, Greyhound One. Be advised I am turning north to come within the cruiser's missile engagement zone." The voice of the female pilot flying the COD was higher than normal. She was well aware of her own complete lack of defenses.

"Roger, Greyhound One. We'll see you on deck." Tombstone put the Tomcat into a hard turn, moving away from the COD. Inside the cruiser's missile engagement zone, the COD stood a far better chance than under the protection of the Tomcat. While shooting down a missile with another missile was a particularly tricky evolution for a Tomcat, the cruiser's Aegis system had proved itself up to the challenge many times before.

"Stony, One, be advised that the Russian carrier is launching its fighters. Condition red, weapons tight." The admiral's voice was calm and confident. His orders told each aircraft to be prepared to fire at a moment's notice, and to maintain a continual tracking solution in all contacts, but not to release weapons unless attacked.

"Great," Greene muttered, his head now buried in the hard

plastic screen around his radarscope. This was what he hated
most about flying in the backseat, having his attention confined to the radarscope and ESM gear and his actions limited
to green pixels on-screen.

On his screen, there were ten symbols indicating hostile
air contacts. They formed up just off the Russian carrier's
starboard beam, then turned as one toward the COD scam-
pering for the carrier.

"No," Jeremy said, not believing what he was seeing.
"What the hell is going on?"

"I don't know." The tactical circuit was now a continuous
stream of reports, commands, and information, as every ship
in the battle group set general quarters and prepared for what
looked like the beginning of a Russian attack. But it made
no sense, did it? This was not the Russian way, to attack
with just ten aircraft. There should have been waves of aircraft inbound, supported by land-based missiles. Not ten aircraft that stood no chance against the heavily armed battle
group and airwing, none at all.

"Targeting radar," Jeremy snapped, as the ESM warning
device at his side began howling. "Tombstone, it's got a lock
on us!"

"Wait one," Tombstone said, although he was clearly no
happier about it than Jeremy was. "Where's the COD?"

"On final," Jeremy said, as he watched the symbol for the
Greyhound One turn in toward the aircraft carrier.

"Launch indications, launch indications—we have a
launch!" For the first time, the air traffic controller's voice
ratcheted slightly higher.

"Weapons free, all Russian platforms," the admiral
snapped immediately over the same circuit.

Four new symbols, each with an impossibly long speed
leader, popped into being on Tombstone's HUD and on Jeremy's screen. Missiles, launched by the Russian fighters—
and all targeted on the helpless Greyhound.

Greyhound 601
0310 local (GMT-9)

Pamela's eyes snapped open at the change in the aircraft's vibration. The pressure of the straps against her chest told her they were in a hard turn, far too hard for normal maneuvers. "What's going on?" she asked, speaking loudly to be heard over the noise inside the aircraft.

"They didn't say," Jeff answered, his voice placid. "No announcements." Not that they could have heard them anyway, given the noise level.

"They're kicking her in the ass, aren't they?" Pamela said. She leaned forward to see outside the window. It was still light outside, although she could see the first beginnings of sunset behind them. Off in the distance, sun glinted off metal. Their escort—probably Tombstone himself, she mused. And what the hell was going on, anyway?

She started to get up and step into the aisle, but Jeff grabbed her arm, holding her down in her seat. He gave her a measured look, and with a sigh, she sank back into her seat. There was really no point in trying to find out what was going on. If they preferred criminal charges against her for being out of her seat during the flight, she could kiss any more COD flights goodbye. Besides, whatever was going on, there was nothing she could do about it anyway.

Off in the distance, she saw the Tomcat peel off and vanish from view as it went toward their stern. The vibration inside the COD increased, as did the roar of the engines. Everything started rattling, and it felt like things were coming apart.

She kept her attention on the window, suddenly scared. Then she saw it, coming up on them from the back. It was a slender white speck against the sky, growing rapidly larger. The sun glinted off it, making it unbearably bright at times, transforming it into a swath of light.

"A missile," she said, horror in her voice. Unbelievable—who would fire on a COD in the middle of the battle group? But a missile it was, there was no doubt about it.

Jeff had his head turned away from her and his eyes were shut. Surely he wasn't going to sleep now, of all times? Now, that didn't make sense—and then she saw it, a small plastic

unit pressed between his ear and the hard foam back of the
seat. She jabbed him in the side, then grabbed it before he
could protest.

"Hey," he said. "Get your own."

She pressed it to her ear and listened. "Entering the
cruiser's missile engagement zone," she heard, as well as a
flurry of other reports.

"It's like a police scanner," Jeff said, no trace of apology
in his voice. "Rigged it up myself. You can only listen to
the unclassified conversations—that squeal, it means a circuit
is encrypted. But even the unclassified circuit is more than
they're telling us anyway, isn't it? Like things are really going to shit out there."

"Weapons free. Break, JPJ engage incoming."

"Roger, birds away, birds away."

"Lead, break right! I got him."

"Fox two, Fox two!"

The chatter on the circuit was heart-stoppingly familiar.
Jeff leaned over, cracked his head against hers, then pulled
the scanner between them so they could both listen. Pamela
turned her neck uncomfortably, trying to simultaneously keep
her ear next to the scanner while she watched the air through
the battered window.

Far below them, the ocean was a dark, smooth surface,
unusually calm even for this time of year. A few distant
whitecaps broke the surface, but there were long stretches of
almost mirrorlike swells. She saw three new missiles arrow
up from the direction of the cruiser, head straight up, and
turn slightly toward the missile behind them. As she watched,
the distance decreased between them at an alarming rate.

There was no use in denying it. She was terrified. But there
was no way she was going to show it, not now. No one else
in the aircraft, aside from perhaps the aircrew, knew what
was going on. As far as they knew, the COD was simply
making a particularly ragged approach on the carrier. If the
cruiser missiles did not intercept the ones launched by the
Russian cruiser, they would die with no more than a microsecond of warning before the aircraft was ripped apart.

Would she see it coming? Would there be a moment when
she stared out at a blue sky, saw metal shredded, saw the

fireball race through the aircraft's fuselage? For just a moment, she envied Winston's complete ignorance.

Tomcat 201
0314 local (GMT-9)

The four Russian Forgers split apart into two fighting pairs. They achieved horizontal separation while maintaining the same altitude, and turned to each point directly at the hapless COD. But just as the COD entered the cruiser's missile engagement zone, they broke off suddenly, as though they were listening to other communications. They wheeled west, ascended, and turned toward Tombstone and the four other Tomcats.

"What the hell are they doing?" Jeremy shouted. "Your dot, Tombstone," he said, indicating that he'd selected a target and Tombstone was cleared to fire at will.

"Roger. Fox two, fox two," Tombstone said as he toggled off the AMRAAM.

The AMRAAM was a fire-and-forget weapon, one that could be targeted directly from the Tomcat radar or from any other source. In this instance, the carrier's targeting data, stripped of the jamming, was fed directly into that missile's tiny brain. Once it was free of the Tomcat's wing, it activated its own small radar and maintained an active track on the assigned target. Capable of achieving speeds greater than Mach 4, the AMRAAM could catch anything it was sent after. Other missiles proved more difficult targets than aircraft, not only because of their increased speed, but because the stealth technology resulted in an exceptionally small radar return. That, coupled with the sheer size considerations of the smaller target, made exploding rod or fuel-cloud warheads more effective than a simple explosive warhead. However, in this case, Tombstone's Tomcat carried only standard anti-air explosive warheads.

"He sees it," Jeremy said. "It's got a lock, he's got a lock—shit, they've launched! Incoming, Tombstone!"

"I got it," Tombstone said as the symbol popped into being

on his display. "Activating countermeasures—hold on, Jeremy."

Tombstone put the Tomcat into a hard climb, rocketing up at nearly a completely vertical angle. The g-forces slammed Jeremy back into his seat, sitting on his chest like a five-hundred-pound tiger. He grunted, tensing all his muscles, forcing oxygen to his brain to prevent gray out. Just when he thought he would lose the battle, even with his anti-G suit, Tombstone pulled the Tomcat out of the climb and into level flight.

"It's still on us," Jeremy shouted as his vision cleared enough for him to make out the radar screen. "More countermeasures!" He popped off chaff and flares from the undercarriage of the aircraft. The bright hot spots and confusing metal strips would create additional targets for the missile, be it heat-seeking or radar. "Commencing spoofing." The test electronics built into the new model of Tomcat enabled it to intercept radar signals and to feed back, with a split-second difference, an identical pulse to the original sender. The transmissions from the Tomcat would look like returns from the missile's own radar. This would confuse it, causing it to reposition and chase the false target. The false radar returns had to be just right, not so strong that they were immediately obvious as a countermeasure, yet solid enough to override the real returns from the radar's own signal generator.

This particular Tomcat possessed one of the most advanced spoofing sets ever designed. Tombstone's uncle had a close relationship with a contractor, the result of all of his years as chief of naval operations, and quietly, without informing anyone else, he had loaded the latest electronics along with signal generators into this particular bird. The problem in using them lay in the fact that they would confuse the carrier as well, who was not expecting to see that particular signal radiating from a Tomcat.

"Got it!" Jeremy crowed as the missile turned hard to the right and was lost in the midst of the flares. "Not sure which one worked, maybe all of them. More incoming!"

On tactical, the other Tomcats were calling out their shots as well, firing the preferred AMRAAM and following it up with heat seekers. The orderly arrangement of Tomcats and

Forgers was now a furball of launches, missiles, and countermeasures. The confusion was made worse by the fact that they were all working off the carrier's targeting data, and the carrier was still having a problem dealing with Tombstone's Tomcat's spoofing.

"Jamming is secured," a surprised voice said over tactical. "Turn on your own radars—stand by for synchronization."

Jeremy flipped a switch. His radar had been placed in standby rather than completely secured—standard procedure—and was already warmed up and ready to transmit. In moments, their own picture was back on the screen.

Below them and off to their right, a fireball exploded in the air. It was a hard yellow and orange, so bright that it hurt to look at it. Black smoke boiled out immediately, and encompassed the entire area until it looked like a thundercloud with a fire inside.

"Bears," Jeremy said, noting that all the Tomcats were still present. "And another!" A second fireball, slightly higher than the first one, tore through the sky.

"Stony, Home Plate," a voice said, and Jeremy recognized it as the admiral. "Change of plans—you're first on deck. I'm turning you over to the TAO for further instructions, but I want to see you as soon as possible."

"They're running," Jeremy said. The two symbols representing the remaining Forgers had turned away from the port fireball and were going on afterburner toward their own carrier. "Coming to their senses or working off orders?"

"Maybe they finally got it straightened out," Tombstone said. "It still doesn't make sense that they went after the COD. Especially not after what happened."

"Maybe they were trying to retaliate."

"Maybe." But Jeremy could tell that Tombstone wasn't convinced. To tell the truth, neither was he.

Greyhound 601
0316 local (GMT-9)

Beside her, Jeff was swearing quietly. They could both see the fireballs high in the air, as could a few of the other passengers. Even with the noise in the passenger compartment, she could hear voices raised, and feel the uneasiness crescendoing to fear running through the aircraft.

Suddenly, they smashed into the deck, the motion throwing them all forward hard against their restraining harnesses. After the roller-coaster motion in the roiled air astern of the carrier, it felt like they had crashed.

Someone near the tail of the aircraft screamed, a high-pitched voice clearly well advanced into terror. Drake smiled. "Welcome to the fleet, Winston." Beside her, Jeff nodded.

Tomcat 201
0330 local (GMT-9)

"One zero one, call the ball," the tower said, indicating that Tombstone should sing out when he located the Fresnel lens on the stern of the carrier. From that point on, his flight would be controlled by the landing signals officer, or LSO, who would have visual contact on him and his position relative to the carrier's deck.

"Ball, 101," Tombstone said, his voice calm but tense.

"Roger, 101, I have you, sir," came the voice of the LSO. "One zero one, say needles." This was a request that Tombstone report on the readings of his automatic glide path indicators. If they agreed with the LSO's assessment of Tombstone's position on the required flight path, Tombstone would be told to fly needles, meaning that he could rely on them in making corrections to his flight path. More often than not, the LSO was not satisfied with the needles picture and would proceed to guide the aircraft in by himself.

"Needles high and right," Tombstone said. That assessment disagreed with his own assessment of where they were, and it was no surprise when the LSO said, "One zero one, disregard needles. I hold you on path, no corrections."

"Roger, concur."

In the backseat, Jeremy was silent. Aside from tanking at night and landing on the carrier at night, every landing was a special situation. It required the utmost concentration by the pilot. The backseater's only role at this point was to avoid distracting the pilot and to keep an eye on altitude and the area around them. Deconflicting the airspace was the carrier's responsibility, but aviators never liked to rely on anyone else to do that.

"Like riding a bicycle," Tombstone said, his voice tight. He eased back slightly on the power, letting the Tomcat sink gently down through the turbulent air. "A beer says I nail the three wire." There were four arresting wires stretched across the deck rapidly rising under them. Intercepting the three wire with the tail hook was considered the optimum landing.

"No bet," Jeremy said. "I always lose."

Tombstone chuckled slightly. "Okay, then, we'll bet on your next landing. I got a beer that says you can't nail the three wire."

"Stony, watch your attitude," the LSO said, unaware of the conversation taking place inside the cockpit, but referring to the angle of the Tomcat in the air. "Drop your nose a bit—yeah, that's it, looking good, looking good," the LSO continued, following their progress toward the deck.

"Come on," Tombstone said as the Tomcat slammed to the deck. "Bet me!"

"Three wire," the LSO said, confirming Tombstone's judgment. "Good one, sir."

As they hit, Tombstone slammed the throttles forward to full military power. There was a remote chance that something would go wrong between the tail hook and the restraining wire, and until the moment that a plane captain was willing to step in front of the aircraft to confirm that he was safely on deck, standard procedure required staying at full power for another takeoff. Jeremy had seen the consequences of ignoring the rule once. A new Tomcat pilot, overconfident after successfully qualifying, cut power immediately after snagging the one wire. The Tomcat tail hook had "kiddy hopped," or bounced away from the wire, and the Tomcat had started a rollout, but with insufficient power to get airborne. The pilot had not been able to brake in time, and the Tomcat had skidded across the deck, then over the edge. The pilot and his NFO had managed to eject safely but the aircraft was a complete loss. Had it been at full military power when the tail hook failed, the pilot would have been able to take off again and come around for another try.

"There's our COD," Jeremy said. The Greyhound had pulled forward into a spot and was in the process of shutting down. The ramp had dropped and passengers were starting to disembark. Two efficient white shirts and a few plane captains were herding them into the ship.

A plane captain stepped in front of Tombstone's aircraft and calmly held up his fists, indicating that Tombstone should reduce power. He then made the hand signal for retracting the tail hook. Tombstone did so, and the noise inside the cockpit dropped considerably. Then, following hand signals from the plain captain, he taxied the Tomcat to a spot across the deck. When given the engine shutdown signal, he shut it down, and they both pulled out checklists to begin the post-shutdown checks.

Jeremy glanced over at the passengers heading into the ship. One had stopped and was resisting efforts to drag her. She waved, making sure he saw her, and headed back into the ship.

"Yep, that's our COD," Jeremy said.

ELEVEN

Admiral Kurashov
0310 local (GMT-9)

The general listened to the captain of the ship rage on and on. If you listened to Bolshovich long enough, you started to believe that the ship was invincible, the American battle group a mere technical problem, and the glory and rewards that the crew would reap inevitable. Yes, it all sounded very fine indeed. As the general studied the faces around him, he could see that they were buying it.

Fine, unless you'd led a company on the ground in Afghanistan, the same assurances of glory ringing in your ears. Fine, until you heard the first bark of heavy artillery, saw the shadows in the mountains that moved closer. Fine, until the shooting started and your men coughed blood and scrambled frantically for cover, not finding it except behind the bodies of others.

It was a lesson he'd learned the hard way: the enemy can never be trusted to cooperate with your most brilliant plan. He wondered if the captain had ever learned it.

Probably not. Russia and the Soviet Union fought ground wars. Until recent decades, the purpose of the navy had been homeland defense, and that mind-set had never entirely left its officers. The scars of Afghanistan were on the hides of her army officers.

Maybe that's why I'm here. A sanity check, balance. Somebody who has lived in the fog of war, not just read about it at the staff college.

If that was the reason, he'd best start speaking up now. Throw some cold, hard reality on the cheerleading, make them know what it was to go into combat.

"Captain," the general said, his voice courteous yet commanding. "It is a good plan, a fine plan."

"Thank you, General. As you can see—" the captain continued, trying to override the general.

I was right. The general felt that intuition that had kicked in before the disastrous midair incident, and he continued as though the captain had not interrupted him. He had more experience dealing with officers headed for trouble than the captain, and there was the deference due his rank as well. "However," he said, "I question the wisdom"—*better take a hard line right from the beginning; he's not listening to suggestions*—"of challenging the American battle group head on. That was not in our mission statement. We are here simply to monitor their laser experiments and validate our own capabilities. We must not lose sight of that." He let his last sentence carry a harsh tone of rebuke.

The captain reddened. The general could tell that he was weighing the odds. At sea, the captain was the absolute commander of his ship and his people, subject only to orders from his fleet commander. The general was not in his chain of command, and the orders that had accompanied the general to the ship simply "suggested" that the captain give consideration to the general's advice and requirements. Not an order handing over command of any operational capabilities or even requiring the captain to do any more than consult with the general on issues regarding the laser, on the theory that the equipment would eventually be used in support of the general's campaigns. All in all, there was no legal authority for requiring the captain to obey the general's suggestions.

Except for the fact that he was a general, and a decorated, well-known one at that. His reputation in the army had not been ignored by the navy, and among the younger officers and enlisted men he was regarded with a degree of respect bordering on awe. It was only from officers of the captain's grade, ambitious men snapping at the heels of his career, that he faced any challenge.

"Thank you for your comments," the captain said finally. "Advice," he corrected, as he glanced around the room and saw a few other officers nodding in agreement. "It is always helpful to have insights from those in other warfare specialties. Sometimes an outside opinion can bring insights."

Outsider. Nicely done. The general let no trace of his thoughts cross his face. *Give him a bit more rope, I think.*

"However," the captain continued, fatally emboldened by the general's lack of response, "I can assure you that our capabilities are more than a match for the Americans. Their attack on our forces constitutes an act of war and we will retaliate."

Enough of this. Suddenly, the general had no more patience for the posturing bantam rooster parading before him. He felt an old rage surge through him. "No," the general said. "There will be no retaliation. Not until the investigation into the sinking of the civilian ship is completed. I need not remind you that the evidence shows that we may have been at fault in that."

Complete silence. The general locked his gaze on the captain's face. No one dared move, as though any movement would topple the unprecedented confrontation one way or another.

Afghanistan. Angola. Chechnya. Weariness swept through the general. Why was there no other way to learn these lessons other than through hard experience?

"They will attack," the captain said finally.

"They will not. They have as much to lose as we do." *And I am willing to bet that the man calling the shots in the American battle group has much more in common with me than with this captain.*

"They will," the captain said again.

The general sensed the mood change within the room as the spell the captain had woven crumbled and then collapsed. "You will prepare for that remote possibility. In the meantime, I suggest you stand your forces down from general quarters. There is no point in muddying the waters further."

And now he understands what it means when orders from a senior officer use the word suggest. It is a polite, face-saving way of ordering him to obey me.

TWELVE

Captain Jack Phillips stood silently just inside the black curtain that protected the bridge from white light from the
corridor, waiting for his eyes to adapt to the night. Around
him, the quietly reassuring sounds of a normal watch. He
knew he didn't have to be up here. It wasn't achieving anything except making the OOD nervous. But, under the circumstances, what did they expect? The major incidents at
sea in two days—and how nice and sterile that sounded, the
attack on the COD, calling the destruction of *Montego Bay*
and the loss of a Hornet "incidents"—and paranoia was running rampant among the officers on board. And it wasn't like
he spent every hour up here, although he suspected that those
times that he was away the XO and the senior department
heads were covering the bridge. No, it was just that in some
way he felt his presence on the bridge prevented anything
bad from happening and was an encouragement to the rest
of them.

It wasn't, of course. Leaving them alone to stand their
watches in their usual ways would show that he had complete
faith and trust in his officers of the deck. And he did, of

course. Otherwise they wouldn't be OODs on *his* ship. It was just that—well—hell, under the circumstances, any CO would have spent a lot of time on the bridge.

But you're not just any CO, are you? Maybe you're more like everyone else than you like to think.

Maybe so. There was such a crushing sense of responsibility, commanding an aircraft carrier. And right now, right as things stood, he needed to be on the bridge. Had to be.

The Russian task group remained twenty miles to the east, carefully pacing the American carrier and her escorts. For a battle group supposedly on independent operations, she was spending an awful lot of time following the *Jefferson* around. Not that he could blame them. They'd probably claim that *Jeff* was following *them.*

So far, the coordinated search-and-rescue operations had gone fairly well. No further incidents, not even a near miss. It was bound to play well with the international community that this was a joint effort. It wouldn't make up for what happened earlier, but it was a historic effort, almost on par with seeing the Russian ships listed as friendly forces during Desert Storm.

Two helos were just returning from three hours of searching the ocean below them. There had been no signs, not even floating debris or an oil slick. And of everything that had happened, that just didn't make sense. They should have found something by now. The ocean wasn't so rough that it would have destroyed all the evidence. And it would be another five days at least before they could call off the search. They couldn't, no way, quit before the Russians did.

"Still nothing, sir?" he heard someone say quietly behind him. One of the new female officers, he supposed. Maybe that little redheaded one. Good sign that she was up here during her off-duty hours, keeping an eye on things, just like he was.

"No. And I doubt there will be. If we were going to find anything out there, we would have found it by now," he said, without turning around. "But we can't quit before the Russians do, you know. Not when it might be our fault. Until we know for sure—" He turned around to give the little redhead the benefit of his years of experience at sea, and saw

Cary Winston standing behind him. Her mouth was slightly open, her finger on the play button of a recorder. And just as he was realizing he had stepped on his dick in the biggest possible way in front of the worst possible person, she said, "Thank you, Captain. I appreciate the insight."

"That was off the record," he snapped.

She shook her head. "I don't think so. You didn't say we were."

"You ambushed me."

"I simply asked a question. And you answered."

"Dammit, you can't do this!"

She held up a small tape recorder. The reels were still spinning. Phillips snapped his mouth shut.

"I think what the captain meant to say," a confident voice said behind him, "was that we're currently engaged in some complicated search-and-rescue maneuvers. To ensure that there are no distractions and to maintain the safety of both the bridge watch and our aviators, the bridge is closed to all visitors. Thank you for your cooperation." The slim, regal form of Phillips's public affairs officer stepped forward. Lieutenant Commander Brian Frank walked toward them until Winston had no choice but to back up or be run over. Frank held his arms out to corral her and herded her toward the exit.

As they disappeared behind the black curtain, Phillips heard Frank saying, "I believe you heard in the briefing that it is customary to ask permission to enter the bridge, particularly during night operations."

Surely she couldn't use what he'd said! This was intolerable, the reporters and news media invading his ship like termites. If they could surprise him on the bridge like this, they might as well be in his stateroom hiding in the head, reporting on what he sang in the shower.

A few minutes later, Frank reappeared. He let out a sigh of frustration and said, "Sorry, sir. I think I put the kibosh on it. They do know better than to pull that crap. At least, the experienced ones do."

"No more reporters on the bridge. Or in any other area of the ship, other than their staterooms, the passageway, and mess." Phillips spoke firmly, keeping his temper under control. "You'll hold a daily press briefing for them. Twice a day, if you think it's necessary. Any request for interviews with anyone on this ship must go through me. Except, of course, the admiral and his staff, and I'll talk to him about dealing with his people. I'm going to put a stop to this right now."

"Captain, I have to say, that's not the best way to handle this."

"And what is?" Phillips exploded. "They can't get away with this, Frank. I can't have them taking every comment somebody makes out of context and making a big deal out of it. Under the circumstances, we have to be careful."

"Yes, sir, of course. But in the long run, it's better to have them on our side, working with us. That way you can present a balanced picture in the press."

"Stage a crucifixion, is more like it."

But Frank shook his head, a determined look on his face. "No, sir, I have to disagree. These people have a job to do, just like we do. Okay, something went wrong out here. There's no way you can keep that quiet. And if you alienate them, you'll just convince them that we're covering something up. Because that's the first thing that occurs to me immediately, that there's a cover-up. And there's nothing like a cover-up or a gag order from the senior officers to get them hot on the trail. We need to work with them, not against them."

"No more reporters on the bridge," Phillips said stubbornly. "Or on the flight deck. And no more special tours of CDC or other operational areas."

"Captain, perhaps if we could work out some way that—"

"You've got your orders, mister." Phillips turned his back on his public affairs officer and stared out at the sea. Behind him, he heard Frank say, "Aye-aye, Captain." There was a soft rustle as Frank parted the black curtains to leave the bridge.

Around him, the rest of the bridge watch team was deadly silent. They had all overheard the exchange—couldn't help but, with the confined spaces—and were being very very careful not to piss the captain off.

Phillips strode to the right forward corner and climbed into his captain's chair. It was elevated so he could see out over the flight deck, and the corner afforded him some degree of privacy if he wished it. Those who could gravitated toward the left side of the bridge, leaving him alone. Gradually, the normal comments and orders of the watch team began flowing around him again.

Phillips stared out at the ocean, thinking. First the collision and now this. How was he supposed to make it through this without falling on his sword, much less causing an international incident? It was like if they said anything, they would be admitting they were at fault or were trying to hide something. Everybody who worked in search and rescue knew that if they were going to find something, they would have found it by now. There was no point, other than political appearances, in continuing.

But like too many things, this was one instance where the truth simply could not be told. To the rest of the world, they had to maintain an optimistic front, continue to search, wasting man hours and fuel on what was surely a pipe dream. But it wasn't something you could say out loud.

The moon was almost full and seemed unusually bright tonight. The reflected light shone down on the waves, illuminating the shadows between the troughs and casting a silvery glow over the ocean. It should have been quiet, peaceful, calm. But to Jack Phillips, it was anything but.

USS Jefferson
Starboard Passageway
0410 local (GMT-9)

The cameraman could feel Winston's barely suppressed glee. He tried to ignore it. It wasn't really his job, was it? A cameraman shot when he was told to, got the best visuals he could, and tried to fit them to the story. It wasn't up to him to decide what the story was, or how to tell it.

Was it?

Winston should have known better. It was her first time on a ship—hell, her first time covering a major story—and now she was playing with the big boys. From what he'd seen so far, she didn't understand that the rules had changed.

And where was Drake? How come she hadn't taken the kid under her wing, set her straight on the way things were? Drake would have never pulled anything like that on the bridge. First off, she would *not* have ignored the requirement to ask permission to come on the bridge. And if Winston had done that, everyone would have known she was there. But instead they had crept on like thieves waiting to ambush somebody. And he'd let it happen, knowing it was wrong.

Even if Drake had sneaked onto the bridge and gotten Jack Phillips's comment, she would never, ever use it. Because even if what he said was true, even though no one had said the magic words "off the record," she would have known that to use that comment would be to permanently close off that source of information. And the truth was that although the stories changed, the players didn't.

This captain, for instance. If he played his cards right, he'd end up commander of a battle group, then maybe even higher than that. There'd be another time, another place, when he'd be at the center of the story. And if Winston used this ambush quote now, she could forget about ever being able to talk to him again. It was a question of long-term benefit vs. short-term.

It wasn't just about Winston's career, either. What she'd done reflected on all of them, ACN and all the networks. All of them. If she screwed the pooch on this one, they would all take the heat for it.

"Can you get an uplink?" she asked.

"Probably. The conditions look pretty clear."

"Good. Let's do it, then. Just a short update segment."

Jeff shifted uneasily. "What does Drake think about it?" he asked tentatively, knowing that Drake had no idea this was going on.

"There's no need to bother her about this," Winston said levelly. "It's just an update. Besides, it's not like they'll go live with it. If Control doesn't like it, they'll kill it."

Well, she was right about that. There were other controls

in place other than the good sense of a reporter. Still, he felt pretty uneasy with the idea of doing this without Drake knowing. They might be having their own pissing contest, but when it came down to it, they were all on the same side, weren't they?

"Come on," she said. She led the way down the passageway to a sponson, an open-air enclosed area low on the ship. "Power up."

Jeff positioned the satellite dish, clamped it down, and waited for the tone. It came quickly, indicating he had a solid lock on the satellite. "Don't know how long this will last. You'd better get it first take."

"In five, four . . ." He counted down the remaining three numbers with his fingers, and pointed at her. Winston instantly aimed an expression of measured intensity at the camera.

"This is Cary Winston, on board the USS *Jefferson*. We have just learned that the situation is by no means as straightforward as was originally briefed. The captain of this carrier has just admitted that the attack on the *Montego Bay* might have been the result of a mistake on the American battle group's part, not the Russians. This has a profound impact on the search-and-rescue efforts under way. Despite the public face of confidence that there are more observers to be found, the captain of the *Jefferson* expressed great doubts about the wisdom of continuing the search. He said," she consulted her notes, "that if anyone was out here, they would have found them by now. Continuing the search now is merely a political maneuver, since the United States cannot justify terminating search efforts before the Russians do, *particularly when the United States may be at fault.*" Winston paused for a moment to let her damning words sink in. "This concern over politics may lead some to wonder just how sincere the rescue efforts are. If survivors are found, will they tell a story markedly at odds with the official United States Navy version of what happened?" She shook her head, looking grave. "At this point, it is a question of whether politics can be put aside long enough to save lives. Cary Winston, on board the USS *Jefferson*."

She held her earnest expression a few seconds longer, until

she saw the red transmit light blink off on the camera, and
then relaxed. "How did I sound?"

"Pretty good." Jeff was feeling even more uneasy, but she
seemed to take the words as high praise. She smiled happily.

"That ought to shake things up a bit. Okay, let's get some
sleep. It's going to be a long day tomorrow." Looking satisfied with herself, Winston led the way back into the ship
and headed toward the stateroom she shared with Drake. Jeff
watched her go, a sick feeling starting in his gut.

USS **Jefferson** *Stateroom*
0445 local (GMT-9)

"Ouch!" Winston's voice snapped Drake awake. Unused to
maneuvering in cramped quarters in the dark, her roommate
had stumbled over a chair on the way to her bed.

"What are you doing?" Drake demanded, her voice still
heavy with sleep.

"Just went to the bathroom," Winston said. But the
younger reporter's voice was far too awake for that. Drake
snapped on the small reading lamp over her bed. Its illumination revealed that Winston was fully dressed, not in a bath-
robe, and carrying her recorder and notebook.

"Where have you been!" Drake was fully awake now and
swinging her feet out onto the cold tile floor. "I told you, no
solos."

"I wasn't alone. Jeff was with me."

"That's not what I meant and you know it."

"So be more specific next time. Now, if you don't mind,
I'm going to get some sleep." Winston quickly shucked her
clothes, flinging them over the chair she'd run into, and
climbed into the top bunk.

Drake stood, and as the younger woman settled down in
her rack, she grabbed her by her nightshirt and pulled her to
the edge of the bed. "Who did you talk to?"

Winston let out a yelp of protest. "Just getting some background information and update on the rescue attempts."

Drake took a deep breath and silently counted to ten.
When she spoke, her voice was a model of murderous rea-

sonability. "I am going to give you one more chance. Level with me now or I'll see you get your young ass packed off this ship as fast as possible."

"You can't do that!"

"Want to bet?"

There was a long moment of silence, then Winston spoke sullenly. "We went up to the bridge to watch the helicopters coming back. And while we were up there, I talked to the captain."

"And exactly what did the captain say?" Drake asked, horror starting to build.

"He said if there was anyone alive, they would have been found by now and there was no point in continuing the search." Drake could hear the satisfaction in Winston's voice.

"You can't use that," Drake said. "He didn't know you were there, did he?"

"I just asked him a question."

She would talk to Jeff, find out exactly what had happened. There was no way Philips would have said something like that to a reporter, no way at all. She had to have tricked him somehow, and Drake would find out the details. "Well, you can forget about using it," she said firmly. "Not unless the captain specifically okays it. That's taking him out of context."

"I think we'll let Control decide that," Winston said, letting out a huge yawn. "You're not the content editor."

"*You already sent it?*" Drake couldn't believe it.

"Yep. It was breaking news, so we sent it as an update."

Drake grabbed her cell phone, pulled on her clothes, and headed for the passageway.

"Where are you going?" Winston asked, her voice for the first time showing a trace of fear.

"To try to undo the damage you've done."

Alone on the sponson, Drake called ACN Control. She knew the editor on duty well, and he would put a stop to this once he understood how things were. When she got through to him, he said, after listening to her story, "Too late. I already ran it at the top-of-the-hour update."

"You didn't." Drake swore silently.

"Yes, I did. Pretty good work for a new kid, isn't it? Although, I have to say, it makes your evening update look pretty silly, Pamela. I have you standing there saying everything is going well and everybody's trying hard, and then the kid brings in the quote from the captain saying they're just going through the motions. If you were in my seat, which one would you run with? I have to say, it makes you look pretty stupid."

"I don't care about that." Although, of course, she did. But there were other issues at stake here. "Then pull the spot. She ambushed him. We'll never get another useful word out of him if you run it."

"You're a reporter, Drake," the producer snapped. "Or have you been covering the Navy for too many years? If you're willing to live with just what they tell you instead of going after the story, then it's time we had someone like Winston out there. Now, unless you've got something useful for me, I'm a little busy right now."

Drake charged back to her stateroom, her mind working furiously. She had no doubt that there were going to be major repercussions from this. The producer might understand what news was, but he had not a clue what it was like to work on board a ship, to try to get the story where every part of the story was classified. And when the captain and the admiral saw the story playing on ACN, she and every other reporter on board would be lucky if they were allowed to read press releases, much less report a story.

THIRTEEN

The president was just beginning his working day when the news began to break. His quarters were silent, save for the normal quiet movements of the staff and Secret Service. His wife, Nellie, was off on some junket or another. What was it this time? Something to do with farms, he thought. Or animals. If he really needed to know, he could check with her secretary or the Secret Service. He found it faintly tragic that they should know more about her comings and goings than he did.

His two oldest children were fraternal twins, a boy and a girl. He had made it a priority to try to let them have as normal a childhood as possible. "As possible" being the key qualification. At least the press had been fairly decent about that, he reflected. His kids were rarely in the news. Somehow, the Secret Service, long adept at dealing with children in the White House, had managed to work out a fairly normal schedule of activities and team sports. Their needs had changed rapidly over the last four years as they went from being winsome ten-year-olds to being teenagers, but the Secret Service had taken it a good deal more calmly then he and Nellie had.

Timothy, the youngest, was just barely out of diapers, or
so it seemed to the president. At five years old, he was a
powerhouse, and the president had more than once heard the
comparison made to John-John. There was something still
and quiet about Timothy, a sense of unexpected maturity.
The president wondered how many years in therapy the last
four years in the White House would earn him.

With a sigh, he relaxed and leaned back, elevating the leg
rest on his easy chair. In a few minutes, the steward would
bring in breakfast. Until then, he was free. •

He shut his eyes and reflected on the last four years. Some
successes, some failures. For the most part, he felt he had
been a good president, one who had grown into the office.
The prospect of another four years in the White House was
both exhilarating and daunting. Of all the men and women
around him, only Nellie knew the strain he was under. The
Secret Service and his staff knew from long experience in
general what he was going through, but the specifics were
left to him and his family.

"Mr. President?" a soft voice asked. Jim Arnot, one of the
more senior agents assigned to his detail. Arnot knew better
than to interrupt him during these precious quiet moments
unless it was absolutely necessary.

The president lowered his leg rest and brought the seat
into an upright position. "Come on in."

Arnot moved quickly to his side and held out a message.
The president glanced at it then and snapped, "Turn on CNN
and ACN." Arnot switched on the three televisions, each one
tuned to a different news station. The president wondered
when the last time had been that he'd watched television for
anything other than the news.

He focused on the report in progress on ACN. That new
anchor, what was her name? Winston, that was it. He stared
at her picture for a moment, watching the clear blue eyes
and the satisfaction behind her reporter's mark. That partic-
ular·look in a reporter's eyes never boded well for the White
House. He clicked up the volume.

"The main concern at this point is how long it will take
the United States military to admit their culpability in this

tragedy. Our sources tell us that most of this expensive search-and-rescue effort is merely a cover, an attempt to shift attention away from inquiries into the actual sequence of events. Apparently the data tapes from the USS *Jefferson*, the aircraft carrier on the scene, show that there's a significant probability that the *Montego Bay* was struck by an American missile, not a Russian one. If so, this could have significant repercussions for America's maritime interests. The *Montego Bay* was one of the few ships still flying the American flag. Others have fled to countries with less rigid inspection requirements and lighter tax burdens." Winston paused, a hard glitter in her eyes.

Her co-anchor chimed in just as he was supposed to. "Give us the bottom line, Cary. Are we talking about a cover-up?" He was as sleekly handsome as she was.

Winston nodded. "I'm afraid so, Mike. There's no other way to explain the lack of information being released from the American military authorities. The Russians, on the other hand, have issued an open invitation for the press to visit on board their flagship. They have promised to provide full data packages to the media."

It was her co-anchor's turn to don a grave, stern look. "What about the media pool on board the aircraft carrier? Why aren't they involved in this?"

"I can't answer for everyone, Mike. I do know that several of those reporters have built their careers around cooperation with the military authorities. Maybe we expect too much from them. Do we really expect them to alienate the people who provide most of their stories? Oh, I'm sure there'll be a major effort to characterize the silence as a matter of national security, but let's be brutally honest about it. They have simply lost their objectivity."

The expression on Winston's face could accurately be described as triumphant, the president thought. He keyed down her volume, catching CNN at the top of its story cycle to hear the details. They were clearly taken directly from Winston's broadcast earlier.

He turned to Arnot. "Get me the chairman and the national security adviser."

United Nations Party
2000 local (GMT-9)

Wexler surveyed the crowd. It seemed that every nation on earth had at least a small contingent here, with many of them garbed in native costumes. The more junior diplomatic staff sometimes affected Western dress, but she had noted an increasing trend among the very senior diplomats and representatives to celebrate their individuality.

And that was a good thing, wasn't it? Even though nationalism had raised its ugly head more than once in recent years, in general strong, cohesive cultures were more conducive to peace. She found it especially interesting that the preference for native dress was increasingly evident outside of the United Nations building itself. The trend had started there, of course, with some African nations making a statement by wearing traditional garb to the sessions. Later, the Middle East states followed suit. Now it seemed that Western business suits had been abandoned for social functions as well.

The crowd had already broken into clusters along traditional lines. Despite the best efforts of the hostess to keep everyone circulating, the normal divisions were clearly evident. The Middle Eastern states and their clients were clustered around the buffet table, which had been carefully planned so that no religious preferences were offended. There was even a section of it labeled "kosher."

The Europeans, on the other hand, had taken up their normal position near the bar. Good wine flowed freely, and there were more than enough discriminating palates to appreciate the hostess's choices. The Central and South American states were split almost equally between the two groups, although Peru had chosen a corner table with Russia and India.

She turned to T'ing, the ambassador from China. "We can't even choose a table without making a political statement, can we?"

T'ing smiled. "Some would say you already have," he murmured.

"How so?"

"You wear white," T'ing said. "White, the color of mourning."

"Of purity and virginity," she offered. T'ing was gentleman enough not to take advantage of the straight line.

"In some places," he answered instead.

She surveyed the crowd and said, "I was just remembering how dull everyone looked not so long ago. It's refreshing, isn't it, to see so many styles?"

"It is," he said. "And I appreciate the opportunity to have a choice." He had selected his own native dress for this evening, although she knew full well that he had a number of exquisitely tailored Western suits in his wardrobe.

"And are you making statement?" she asked.

"Perhaps. But only to those who would understand it." He shot her cryptic look. "And your choice of white—was that a statement?"

"Yes. Of a bold and daring nature. How many women do you know who would willingly choose white with a buffet dinner served? The opportunities for disaster are infinite. Do you know how hard it is to get red wine out of silk?"

He smoothed the fabric of his tunic, a delicately patterned red and gold. "As a matter of fact, I do."

T'ing led the way to the bar and ordered a glass of wine for each of them. "The usual," he said, as he passed her the drink.

At a far corner of the room, a small chamber orchestra was quietly tuning up. She recognized a few bars of a violin as Mozart, and nodded appreciatively. Perhaps this evening would be more entertaining than she had thought.

The social obligations of her position were entirely more onerous than her official duties. So many parties and receptions, so many opportunities to inadvertently create an impression or send a message that she had never intended. Like the business of wearing white, for instance. Of course she had known that, but she had elected to wear the suit anyway.

She was just leading the way over to a small table where the British ambassador was chatting with a member of his delegation when she saw her aide, Brad, slip into the room. She tensed. While Brad occasionally attended these functions, this one had not been on his schedule. It was, if she

recalled correctly, a reception to welcome the wife of the
ambassador from Uruguay. On the scale of social events, it
was one that required a brief appearance, a polite greeting,
and perhaps one drink before she could plead other engage-
ments. Her staff was not expected to appear at all.

Brad spotted her immediately and made his way across the
room. She sighed and said, "Excuse me, will you?" to T'ing.

"How soon can you get loose?" Brad asked quietly.
"There's a problem."

"I don't suppose you can give me any hint?"

Just then, there was a small flurry of noise coming from
the general vicinity of the Russian ambassador. She turned
to look and saw that his aide was whispering urgently in his
ear. His face was growing choleric and his eyes were scanning the room. He finally saw her. His thick eyebrows drew
down and met, deepening into a scowl.

Brad noticed as well and shrugged. "So they're not as
careful on security as we are."

"Meet me at the door," she said.

Wexler circled the room, greeting acquaintances and
friends. She thanked the hostess for a stunning party, wel-
comed the new diplomatic wife, and then, as gracefully as
she could, headed back toward the entrance. She veered off
for a moment to find T'ing and offer her apologies. He did
not bother asking what had happened. Soon enough, he
would find out from his own staff. And from the expression
on the Russian ambassador's face and Brad's urgency, she
suspected the whole world would know before long.

Outside, even in the evening, the air was thick and humid.
Her car was already in front of the building, but the twenty
steps between the house and the car were enough to leave
her sweating.

Inside the dark unmarked Mercedes sedan, the air would
be cool—chilly, even. And dry—yes, dry. She could already
imagine it surrounding her, soaking the sweat off her skin,
cooling the blood she felt pounding in her temples. Of all
the marvels of the modern world, air-conditioning had to be
at the top of the list.

Brad's security people already had the back door open.
The cool air was beckoning her along with the silence after

the chatter of so many voices in so many languages. Sometimes it seemed like her time in the car was the most peaceful in her day. Even when she was forced to discuss business—and Brad's security policies had put an end to most of that—nothing seemed quite as urgent.

"Madam!" The rough, deeply accented voice of the Russian ambassador made her pause. "Is there an explanation for this outrage?"

So close. Maybe he would get into her car and they could discuss it there. Not that there was anything to discuss yet, although he clearly had a better idea of what had happened than she did.

No. Russians were reflexively paranoid and he would suspect they were being monitored. Brad stepped between her and the Russian ambassador.

"It's all right." Brad stepped to the side but stayed close.

"I see you are leaving the party early," she said pleasantly. "A nice evening, isn't it?"

"As are you," he said, ignoring the pleasantry. "Do not trifle with me, Madam." Wexler noted that he had dropped the honorific. "I want to see your president at his very early convenience. Surely there is some explanation for this? There will be many in my country who will take it for deliberate provocation. I must warn you," he said, wagging a thick finger at her, "that I'm not sure I can restrain them. Not this time."

"I'm afraid you have the advantage of me," she said, her voice still neutral and polite. "Just what is it that has annoyed you?"

"Don't pretend you don't know!" The ambassador swore, then stepped toward her, prompting Brad and his security people to move in closer. He saw them, and his scowl deepened. "Surely you don't take me for a barbarian? Do you think you are in physical danger? That I would attack you, perhaps slap you around a bit to knock some sense into that pretty little head? Or maybe," he said, ignoring Brad and stepping closer again, "that I would assault you?"

"Don't be silly," she said crisply. "Brad, please wait in the car. I'm fine."

"But—" Brad started.

She cut him off with a sharp wave of her hand. "I'm fine. Go on."

She stared until he reluctantly moved away and back to the car. Regardless of her orders, he stood outside it. She turned back to the Russian ambassador. "Now, what is all this about?"

"Is it possible that you do not know?" Seeing the incomprehension on her face, he laughed, an unpleasant sound to his voice. "So, the vaunted freedom of the press doesn't make any difference if no one hears it, does it? You should listen to ACN, Madam."

"And if I did, what would I hear?" she snapped, losing patience with the entire charade and almost as furious at herself for being caught unawares.

"That your American officers believe that your country may have been the one that hit that cruise ship. Not Russian missiles. American ones."

"I don't believe it."

"Ask your gallant aide."

She turned to look at Brad, who nodded, reluctance on his face. "It's possible."

"You have always been a poor liar, Madam Ambassador. Always."

"Not always." She said nothing more, simply smiled, her point made. The Russian's face clouded over. She thought, *You didn't seem to think so when you fell for the cover story about the Patriot missiles.*

Earlier that year, in an effort to discover who had planted a listening device in her office, she had intentionally faked a top secret conference with Brad about shipping Patriot missiles to Taiwan. There had been no such plan, but when the Russians had tried to blackmail her with the information, their perfidy had been exposed.

The Russian stepped closer to her. She could smell him, the rank odor. Brad stepped closer also.

"You know so little about how the world works," the Russian said. "How your actions affect the rest of the world. How they think of you. Not everything in the world that you dislike can be vetoed, Madam. Sooner or later, you will face reality."

"We faced reality on September 11," she snapped. "Don't talk to me about not understanding the world. What you'd better worry about is whether the world understands *us*."

He drew back. "If the World Trade Center taught you anything, it should be that you are not unique. There are not separate rules for Americans. There never were. There never will be." Before she could frame a reply, the Russian Ambassador stalked off. She slid gratefully into the air-conditioned car.

The White House
2230 local (GMT-9)

Either traffic was exceptionally light or both men had been expecting trouble. Probably the latter. Even in the lightest Beltway traffic, it would have been almost impossible for them to arrive at the White House so quickly.

The president had long ago given up apologizing for ruining either man's evening. It was the price they paid for wielding power. And if you got right down to it, that's what holding public office was about. Neither the general nor the adviser's salary would have been sufficient to entice them into the hours they worked. No, it was the ability to control what was happening in the world, the feeling of power, and, in the best cases, the fervent belief that somehow one could make a difference in the world for the better.

"Good evening, Mr. President," both men murmured as the Secret Service showed them in. The president had elected to receive them in his private quarters, and shoved the dinner tray away. He pointed at the televisions, which were now providing updates on the *Montego Bay* situation.

"Tell me what I need to know," he said simply.

The two men had undoubtedly discussed it on their way here because neither bothered to glance at the other. The general began. "I spoke to the skipper of the carrier and the admiral of the battle group on the way over here, Mr. President," he said. "We were not on a secure line, but I made sure that they would be standing by one later for instructions.

From what they could tell me, the reporter—that Winston—ambushed the skipper on the bridge. Sure, maybe he said some things he shouldn't have, but he thought he was talking to one of his officers. He's read her the riot act."

"A woman scorned," the national security adviser said quietly.

The president shot him a disgusted look. "I don't care if she's female, male, or something in between. What matters right now is that the situation is a mess. I need some answers, gentlemen. And I need them now." He pointed at the general. "Get the facts. You can use the secure phone in the situation room. I want to know everything." He turned to the national security adviser. "Organize State and the embassies. I want it made clear to Russia right away that we are not certain what happened and intend to investigate fully. If they want to send an observer over, that's fine."

The general started to protest, and the president cut him off. "I know about the additional security precautions. I think your people can handle them, don't you? We don't admit we're testing the system, nothing like that."

"I was just going to suggest, Mr. President," the general said, "that we have an exchange of observers. Surely the Russian data systems also captured the incident. If they're coming over to take a look at our data, we should be taking a look at theirs. It seems only fair."

The president nodded his approval. "I like it. It also shows that we're not admitting culpability. Okay, let's make that happen." He turned back to the adviser. "Any other issues?"

"Just one," the security adviser said. "It is not too soon to be thinking about our position if we are at fault. Will there be reparations? Exactly how will we handle it? I don't think I have to tell you that the international repercussions will be severe and far-reaching."

"You're correct," the president said.

"Thank you, sir. I'll get my people started on—"

The president cut him off. "You are correct that you don't need to tell me about the international repercussions. For the record, sir, I have every confidence in our people, our training, and our equipment. We were not at fault in this. I don't know how, but I intend to find out." He turned to the general, and saw the merest trace of a grim smile on the man's face. "And pass that on to your people. This isn't a witch hunt. It's more like *Ghostbusters.* Okay, back here in ten minutes." He gestured at the half-finished sandwich. "I'm going to choke that down, and I'll meet you both in the situation room. Anybody hungry? Speak up if you are. It looks like it's going to be long night."

The ten minutes stretched into fifteen. Solar flare activity, the general said, had disrupted all communications. It took some time to get a clear line to *Jefferson,* and he'd had to resynch several times. In the end, he'd spoken to both the skipper and the admiral.

"It's just as you thought, sir," he said. "The admiral swears there's no way they're responsible. Yes, there was an anti-missile missile in the air, and yes, it overflew the *Montego Bay*. But there's no way it hit the *Montego Bay,* Mr. President. No way at all."

"The Russians aren't agreeing with that, of course," the security adviser said briskly. "They claim their data shows intentional targeting of the cruise ship."

"And do they have any explanation for why we would target an American-flagged ship?" the president demanded.

The national security adviser shook his head. "No. They hinted that they believe their ship was the real target, and malfunctions in our own targeting resulted in the incident. But for some reason, they're not screaming that at the top of their lungs—just whispering it."

"Why, I wonder?" the president mused. "Any ideas?"

Both men shook their heads. "I didn't think so," the president said.

The lighting in the situation room was slightly dimmed, a condition the president found conducive to better briefs. He closed his eyes now, letting the facts tumble through his mind. None of it made any sense, none of it. Why would anyone nail an innocent cruise liner? There was no upside to that.

Unless she's not an innocent cruise liner. Could there be something going on at JCS and NSA that I don't know about? Possible, I suppose. If there was, that would make sense. It's the only thing that does. So then the question is—why are they blowing smoke up my ass? Or do they really not know?

The president reached a decision. He opened his eyes and said, "I want everything we can get our hands on shipped to NSA for full analysis. General, order all forces to set DEFCON three. I want the Russians to know we're serious."

"But the escalation . . . ," the security adviser began, his tone incredulous. "Mr. President, if you do this, the Russians will go to a heightened state of readiness as well. This is how it starts, each side making a point, saving face until it all gets out of hand. We can't risk it, sir. Not until we successfully test the system."

The president fixed him with a cold glare. "It's not open for discussion. Now do it."

USS **Jefferson**
Flag Passageway
1800 local (GMT-9)

Drake was just rounding the corner when she saw Tombstone farther down the passageway. He was facing her, towering over Winston, who was blocking his way. Behind her, Jeff waited, his camera pointed at the deck.

"Why are you here?" Winston pressed as she stepped forward toward the former admiral. "Everyone knows you're the expert in the naval conflicts, Admiral. Are you here to give Admiral Grant advice? Or to get an expert opinion on the cause of this disaster?"

"No comment," Tombstone said, and stepped to the right. Winston matched his move, still blocking his way.

Drake could see Tombstone's face go cold and hard. Even his normally impassive expression was frightening.

"I said, no comment." Tombstone's voice held impatience and irritation, although Pamela knew him well enough to know that one of his icy rages was coming on. Even she quailed before those.

Time to break this up. She started down the passageway. Tombstone looked up at her, and she thought she saw a trace of relief on his face. Drake planted one hand firmly in the middle of Winston's collar, clamped her fingers down, and jerked back and to the right. Winston let out a howl of protest and tried to kick Drake. Drake held her at arm's length, fury lending her strength. "Thank you for your time, Admiral Magruder. I apologize for the inconvenience."

Tombstone regarded the two of them with something that looked like amusement. "Thank you, Miss Drake," he replied formally.

Just then, the door to the admiral's mess opened and Admiral Coyote Grant and Captain Jack Phillips walked out. Both were in a towering rage. They immediately spotted Pamela, who was still holding Winston against the bulkhead. Phillips nudged Coyote, who sighed. "Let her go, Pamela," Coyote said wearily. "I wish you'd done that a couple of hours ago."

"Believe me, so do I." She released Winston, who started to attack Drake. The cameraman caught the younger reporter by her elbow and shook his head warningly.

"Admiral, Captain—I had no part in this. I didn't even know she left the room. I tried to head off the report but they'd already run with it. My apologies."

There was no reaction from either man, and Drake knew the damage was already done. No doubt they had spent the morning fielding calls from their superiors, who would want to know why in the hell someone would make such a stupid comment to a reporter. Winston's impromptu update would have far more international repercussions than she could ever have guessed.

"There will be a briefing for all media at ten o'clock," Phillips said finally. "The dirty shirt mess. Which is, by the way, now where all the media will eat."

"I see." To be evicted from the flag mess was no great hardship, but it was a precursor of things to come. "And the flag mess?"

"Off limits," Coyote said immediately. "As is this passageway. As is the bridge, Combat, and the flight deck, unless you're accompanied by the public affairs officer."

"You're gagging us," Drake said, disbelievingly. She had known it would be bad, but not this bad.

"Of course not," Coyote said promptly. "We're simply trying to make more use of your valuable time. After all, there are many areas of the ship you would not normally visit that we'll arrange access to. The bakery, for instance. What a fascinating story, those bakers working through the night every night to produce all the ship's baked goods. Cinnamon rolls, bread, pizza crust—it's really quite impressive. And has there ever been a really good profile on garbage disposal at sea?" He turned to Phillips, as though directing the question at him.

Phillips tilted his head and looked thoughtful. "No, Admiral, I don't believe there has been. But what an excellent idea."

"I'll get her off the ship," Drake said, desperate to redeem herself and the rest of the media. "We know she was out of line—I've never done anything like that to you. Don't punish all of us for her screw-up."

The two senior officers regarded her blandly. "Punish? What an absurd idea," the admiral said fondly.

Both senior officers left, met up with Tombstone farther down the passageway, and then disappeared into the side passageway that housed the ladder leading up to the flight deck. Drake started to follow, but then stopped. It was no use. It would take months, maybe even years, before this could be repaired. She turned on Winston, intending to blast her, but instead of a cowed reporter she saw Winston's eyes gleaming again.

"Now *this* is a good story," Winston said. "We'll call it 'Censored!' "

FOURTEEN

Wexler noticed the difference the moment she entered the United Nations building. After seven years of service, sometimes it seemed as though her own nervous system was irreversibly hardwired to the mortar and bricks of the structure. It was not something she could define precisely, more a tingling along the periphery of her nerves, warning her of danger. Was it some intuitive deduction from the angle at which the members' cars were parked, indicating agitation. A sense of a few more guards on duty than normal? Something about the way people moved?

She didn't know. All she knew was that she could feel trouble brewing.

Her suspicions were confirmed as soon as she entered her suite of offices. The British ambassador was sitting in a chair, having tea and chatting with her receptionist.

After they exchanged their customary greetings, she said, "So what brings you here this early today?" Her British colleague was not known for keeping early hours.

He drained his cup of tea and set it gently on the table

before speaking. "Trouble, I'm afraid. From the usual sources."

"So what else is new," she said. "The president briefed me last night. I'm afraid the Russian ambassador saw me leaving the party early and drew his own conclusions."

"Yes, rather." For once, he seemed at a loss for words.

Wexler and the British ambassador had had an unusual relationship. He had originally been posted to the UN with instructions to get close to her and interrupt her growing friendship with the Chinese. He had played the fool for several months in an attempt to win her friendship. It was only after she had confronted him that he finally dropped his irritating mannerisms. Since then, they had become close friends.

"Out with it," she said, not unkindly. The British tendency to beat around the bush and cloak matters in polite circumvention she understood. Indeed, on many occasions she appreciated it, but this was not one of those times.

"There is some talk," he began slowly, "of the role the United States plays in the United Nations."

"Is it the world police bit again?"

He shook his head. "No, and it's a bit more than rhetoric this time. The issue is the status of the United States' payment of dues."

It was Wexler's turn to be reluctant to speak. Not because she did not know what to say—but because this issue had haunted her nightmares for longer than she cared to think.

America covered a large portion of the operating costs of the United Nations. Currently, she was eighty million dollars behind on her payments. The amount had been appropriated in Congress, but the necessary funding bill was constantly bogged down with other issues. Additionally, there were constant protests from right-wing "patriots" who suspected that the United Nations was in the forefront of a worldwide government, a pawn of the Russians, a front for a military-industrial international conspiracy, and just about any other conspiracy you cared to name. Crackpots, mostly, Wexler thought.

But those crackpots voted. And they were very vocal, communicating their displeasure to their elected representatives. Privately, she believed that they were probably just as suspicious of their elected representatives as they were of the United Nations.

"Who's behind it?" she asked.

"India, I think," he said, a thoughtful look on his face. "Although it's hard to be exactly sure."

"Why India?"

"Why not?" He shook his head impatiently. "It's not necessarily India's idea, you understand. She may be acting as a front."

"For whom?"

"It doesn't matter." He began to regard her with some degree of impatience. "What does matter is that my sources tell me a motion will be brought to remove the United States from the United Nations for nonpayment of dues."

"Right." She let the disbelief show in her voice. "It'll never pass the general assembly. We're in New York, for god's sake!"

She hoped she sounded confident. Because she wasn't. Not at all. She had brought this matter to the president several times, trying to persuade him that at the very minimum they needed a contingency plan. He had yet to give her a date on which the dues would be paid, or to provide her with some justification that would make sense to the rest of the general assembly.

And so it comes to this.

For a moment, she considered the possibility that the United States might well be better off withdrawing from the United Nations. Certainly it would provide some relief to her own military forces. They were stretched thin around the world, so thin. Calling the United States the world's 911 force was not much of an exaggeration. If they gave up a large part of their peacekeeping responsibilities around the world, then there might be more funds available for research and development. Certainly the military would be a more attractive career if troops spent more time with their families.

But what will the world look like if we cannot intervene? Who will stop the next Hitler or Bin Laden? Can we really let the rest of the world go to hell while we hide behind a missile defense shield?

She shook her head. There were no easy answers, not at all. Aloud, she said, "When is it going to happen?"

"I don't know. Before long, I suspect. Getting that particular ball in play before the issue of the *Montego Bay* comes up would be a smart move. Things might move very quickly from this point on down." He drained the last of his tea and carefully positioned the cup on its saucer, avoiding her eyes. "I would have a serious chat with your president. You must be prepared to move on this immediately, Sarah. Immediately."

"Have I any reason," she began slowly, "to doubt that Great Britain would tell me about any such measure?" She kept her gaze locked on him, willing for him to look up, praying she would not see the answer she dreaded in his eyes.

"It is India," he said simply. "You know our special relationship with that continent. And after the recent election, my own party is finding that there are far more compromises necessary than we would like."

"Compromises that include deserting us." She did not bother to keep the sharpness out of her voice.

"Compromises that are necessary for the well-being of my country," he countered. "Both the United States and India are former colonies. We have much more recent experience with India, and still have generations of Englishmen living there. Then again, there is that special relationship we have with the United States. On balance, I believe that our loyalty to you would win out over our ties to India. But it is not nearly so certain a thing as it has been in the past, Sarah. Not nearly so certain."

"Then we will veto it ourselves."

"You might not be able to," he said, and the last card was finally played face up on the table. "Not unless your dues are paid. You don't know the rules as well as you ought to."

Oh, but I know the rules all too well. And you're exactly right. They do allow us to be removed and prevent us from exercising our veto power if our dues are not paid.

"Thank you for the warning," she said finally. "And your candor." However much she might dislike what he had to say, she'd rather hear it now than on the floor. Unpleasant truths were still truths, and at least she now had time to prepare her response.

My response. Like what? Not my problem. The president and Congress have to deal with this one.

He unfolded himself from the chair, rising to loom over her. "I wish the news could be better. If you can find out what happened with that cruise liner, it might make things easier."

"If I knew that, none of this would be necessary." She walked him to the door, letting the conversation slide into polite chitchat. After he'd gone, she retreated to her office. She leaned back in her chair, shut her eyes, and let her mind roam free. What in the world could she possibly do?

She spent perhaps fifteen minutes examining the alternatives, and then picked up the phone. She dialed the number herself. When the president's chief of staff came on the line, she said, "I have to talk to him. Now."

USS Jefferson
0500 local (GMT-9)

Pamela Drake was delighted to learn that Cary Winston was truly ugly when she was angry. Something in the way her face flushed and changed coloration sufficiently to make her appear brittle and artificial. The darker skin color contrasted badly with her blond hair and turned her blue eyes from open and winning to feral and hungry. It was a shocking transformation.

Pamela noted that Jeff was staring at her with a tart expression of professional doubt. He caught Pamela's glance and shook his head almost imperceptibly. No, Winston would not come across well on the camera. No amount of filtering or soft lens could mask the character now shining out of her face.

It wasn't that a reporter had to be good-looking. At least, not anymore. Drake knew that now and, looking back over the last few days, felt a surge of quiet pride at her own conduct. Winston might be fifteen years her junior, but she was a century behind Drake in the things that really mattered.

"You can't get away with this," Winston stormed. "I won't let you. The world has a right to know."

"Not on my ship," Coyote said coldly.

"Freedom of the press," Winston began.

"Don't you talk to me about freedom of the press," Coyote shouted, pushed beyond all endurance. "It's your type the causes most of the problems of the world, Winston."

"You think you can do whatever you want to out here," Winston snapped, the color rising even more in her face. "But you can't. I won't let you."

Coyote took a step forward. "Why you little—" He cut himself off and stood rigid for a moment. Then he seemed to relax and regain that hard veneer of command. "You are quite mistaken," he said almost conversationally. "I'm not barring the press at all. Miss Drake is welcome to stay, along with anyone else she is willing to vouch for.

"You, however, are a danger. Not only to my people and my battle group, but to your colleagues as well. God forbid that they should all be tainted by your reputation."

Just then, Lab Rat's errant lieutenant stormed into the room waving a piece of paper. "Sir, look at this! I think it was our missile that—"

"Shut up," Lab Rat snapped, his voice as angry as Drake had ever heard it.

The lieutenant saw Winston then, and his face turned pale. "I thought she left on the COD! Sir, I wouldn't—" The lieutenant shut up before he could do any more harm.

"Miss Winston was just leaving," Coyote said, now fully in control of himself. "Now if you will all excuse me?"

The master at arms took Winston by the elbow. "Ma'am?" She struggled briefly and he jerked her out of the office.

Coyote waited until she was gone. "Okay, what have you got?"

"The initial analysis of the electromagnetic spectrum during the attack on *Montego Bay,*" the lieutenant said, his voice shaking as he realized the magnitude of his error. "Admiral, it looks like it could have been our missile that hit her."

"Are you certain?" Coyote asked, his voice cold.

Lab Rat took the reports from the lieutenant. "No, Admiral." He shot the lieutenant a stern look. "We are *not* certain, not until I have a chance to review the underlying data. You *never* get reports at this stage of the game. There are too many factors that go into validated conclusions."

"Conclusions may not matter," Drake said, with a perceptible trace of despair in her voice. "Not with Winston. As soon as she gets back to ACN, she'll be broadcasting an update based on what she heard. Oh, sure, there will be some disclaimers. But the damage will be done. Admiral, it might be advisable for you to have your own update ready to go. Beat her back to the ground, if you will."

"Or we could just have her arrested when she lands," Coyote said. "Not a bad idea."

"A very bad idea," Drake said, now on solid ground. "Sir, the second you have her put into custody you will have just insured that every news organization in the world will run that as their top story. Winston will be a hero. She won't be reporting the story anymore. She will *be* the story. And every civil rights organization in the country will get behind her."

Coyote looked like he was about to argue, but Lab Rat broke in. "You're right, of course, Miss Drake," he said. He turned to the admiral. "We should have our own story ready to go. Our own twist on it." He glanced up at the clock. "And we have about ninety minutes to get it figured out and on tape before she lands."

There was an odd silence in the room as the officers contemplated the possibility that Pamela Drake was on their side. They looked everywhere except at her, trying to figure out some way around it. Many of them, she suspected, would warmly welcome the idea of arresting Cary Winston. But if she knew anything about the First Amendment and about the news media, it was that arresting Winston would be like pouring gasoline on fire. The results would be immediate, and deadly.

"Work it out," Coyote said. "Twenty minutes—then brief me. Get moving, people. This is a different sort of war, but it is war nonetheless. Now move."

He stormed out of the room, slamming the door behind him. There was another moment of silence, and then Drake said briskly, "Well, you heard the man. Let's get to work."

The United Nations
0900 local (GMT-5)

The ambassador for Great Britain had not been wrong in his
estimation. By the time Wexler finally finished briefing the
president and obtaining his guidance, it was common knowledge within the corridors and foyers that the United States
would be on the firing line that afternoon.

The president's guidance had been less than helpful. Do
what you can, he had said. She'd try to extract promises or
commitments to pay the dues, but he was having none of it.
Never had she known him to be so evasive and noncommit-
tal.

As the delegates and ambassadors and their staff mean-
dered into the assembly room, she watched carefully, assessing their positions based on which aisles each chose to walk
down, whom they greeted along the way, and whether or not
they looked over to meet her eyes. Her heart sank as she
counted up the votes. Even those smaller nations she thought
might remember benefiting from American intervention were
questionable. Bangladesh, of course—she would not expect
them to stand up against India. But Israel? And Turkey?
American assistance in cash, trade, and military commitments played a large role in their economies. Could they
forget that so easily? Certainly the present administration had
been a supporter, if not always a strong one, of Israel. And
Turkey had been the largest recipient of American foreign
aid for decades. The American bases there were valuable
additions to their economy.

But neither Israel nor Turkey glanced her way as they
came in. Great Britain did, of course. But he was far too
much of a pro to let her divine his intentions.

As the delegates settled down, the secretary-general called
for attention. He looked out over the assembly, his expression
one of grave reluctance. After the opening formalities, he
said, "I am informed that the representative from Liberia
wishes to be heard."

Liberia? What the hell? She had unconsciously started to
turn toward India, and caught herself just in time. She twisted

the other way to see the ambassador from Liberia rising to
his feet.

The Liberian ambassador was relatively new. She had met
him twice, and each time he'd seemed a proud, somewhat
distant man. Today, he was dressed in traditional garb. The
lines were long and flowing, the colors vibrant in this somber, conservative setting.

Her earlier conversation with T'ing came back to her, and
the different interpretations of her white dress. What should
she divine from what the Liberian ambassador was wearing?
In his culture, would he be considered conservatively
dressed? Or were the colors somehow significant, intended
to remind other nations of Liberia's allegiances?

For just a moment, she felt hopelessly out of her depth.
There was so much subtext that she should understand and
didn't.

But she had been the representative of the United Nations
here for seven years. Seven years—long enough to understand that all nations had some basic goals on their minds.
Long enough to understand that people around the world,
despite their most profound cultural differences, all had certain things in common. And she had managed all right,
hadn't she? So why should she suspect now that she
wasn't—go ahead, say it—competent?

She wasn't. No more than the other nations were competent to judge America's resolve and intent. And, just in case
there was any chance of misunderstanding, she would make
certain that America's position was eminently clear.

But what was America's position? The president's guidance had consisted up telling her to do her best. She decided
that her duty now to her country was to use her best judgment, thinking on her feet and reacting immediately. Since
America had no way of completely screening out every missile, every terrorist with a shoe bomb, and every radical arms
militia with a small vial of deadly biological toxin, America's
best interest lay in a peaceful world. And, like it or not,
resolutions by the United Nations provided a legal basis for
America to intervene in most of the world.

Presumptuous? Quite possibly. America did not have answers for every part of the world. Indeed, if Wexler was

certain of one thing, it was this: that peace had to come from inside a nation. It could not be imposed from without. The answers for the Middle East would not be the same answers for the fragmented former Soviet Union states. All America could do was stop a conflict and allow calmer heads to prevail in a region.

She took a deep breath, a feeling of calm descending. Whatever the challenge was, she would meet it to the best of her ability.

"Mr. Secretary General," the Liberian began, speaking English with an odd overlay of French and British accents, "it is well known to us all that certain countries are not meeting their financial obligations to this body. I do not need to mention any names. There are several countries, for whatever reason, in this category."

Interesting approach. I wonder what is behind it? Surely he has been pressured to denounce the United States in particular. Is he crafting a defense just in case we win? Or is there another message in this?

"It is understood, by some of us more than others, that the ravages of war, famine, and civil unrest can wreak havoc on even the most stable economies. Allowances must be made, compassion extended. And yet, do not all nations benefit if we function as we should? Is not the United Nations the source of food, relief, and assistance in maintaining civil order? Yes, of course it is. All of us recognize that. And therefore, we must come to a balance between compassion and holding nations accountable. Therefore, I call on the Security Council to appoint a special committee to examine this issue."

Now, that's not so bad. A special committee—I can live with that.

"And, pending the resulting committee report," the Liberian continued inexorably, "I suggest—no, I move—that we suspend membership in United Nations for all those members which are delinquent on dues." As he delivered this coup de grâce, the Liberian turned to face Wexler.

Wexler resisted the impulse to bolt to her feet and begin protesting. Instead, she took a moment to confer with her staff, as though all this was entirely expected, and then rise to her feet in a dignified manner. "Mr. Secretary-General, I must admit that I believe my country will fall into this category." *Must admit, hell. Everyone knows we're behind.* "I will not presume to speak for the other nations that may or may not lack the capacity to meet their obligations. And in truth, I cannot stand here and assure you that promises have been made to rectify this unfortunate situation immediately."

A murmur of surprise swept through the room, followed by a few acerbic comments. Wexler ignored them and continued. "However, I must tell you that if the United States is restrained from participation in the United Nations' deliberations, then we would have few options in regards to continuing support on ongoing resolutions." She paused to let that sink in and continued, "Foreign aid. Military assistance. Peacekeeping forces. Humanitarian relief operations. Rescue-at-sea patrols. International research stations, and flights to and from them. These are but a few of the activities that would be under immediate scrutiny."

Now the comments were louder and angrier, and several delegates from strife-torn nations looked stricken. She felt a flash of pity for them. What she was threatening could bring their entire worlds crashing in on them. She tried to stay focused on what she needed to achieve.

"Is that a threat?" someone shouted. She turned to survey the crowd but could not determine who had said it.

"No threat," she said calmly. "Just the natural consequences of withdrawing from United Nations participation. Now," she said, spreading her hands apart, palms up, in a gesture of reconciliation, "I do acknowledge that these issues must be addressed. And immediately. I can pledge my best efforts toward resolving them. Because I agree with the ambassador from Liberia. We must find that balance. And, as one of the founding members and home country of this organization, my country must set an example for others."

"And why haven't you paid your dues?" the secretary-general asked.

"I don't know." The murmurs and comments stopped at her frank admission. "Most of you understand the bicameral nature of our political process. The budget bill necessary to bring our dues current has been passed. It has not yet been

funded. I cannot tell you when that will occur. You understand, of course, that I work for the executive branch. This
is in the hands of the legislative branch at the moment. I will
do everything in my power to see that this is resolved at the
earliest possible time, but our doctrine of separation of pow-
ers precludes direct interference."

The silence continued for several moments, and whispers
among ambassadors and their staffs began to crescendo.
Wexler remained standing a moment longer, then said,
"Thank you, Mr. Secretary-General. The United States, of
course, will vote against this motion, and we urge other
nations to do so as well."

*Now, put that in your pipe and smoke it. See how many
of your playmates are willing to give up their aid packages
from the United States to support your agenda.*

She glanced over at India, and caught the hard glare from
her ambassador. *So Britain was right—India is behind it. And
Liberia—*

Brad leaned forward to tap her on the shoulder. "Foreign-
flagged vessels," he murmured, and then leaned back, apparently confident she would understand.

She did. A large portion of the world's merchant navies
flew the flag of Liberia as a flag of convenience. Liberian
safety inspections, license fees, and other requirements were
much less onerous than those of other maritime nations, particularly the United States. Somewhere in the subterranean
political maneuverings, someone had pointed out to Liberia
that it was entirely possible that U.S.-flagged merchant ships
might be perceived as being at risk. This might afford Liberia
the opportunity to grab even more of the market share. For
a nation such as Liberia, those revenues might be sufficiently
tempting to risk losing foreign aid from the United States.

"A motion has been made. Second?" the secretary-general
asked.

India leaped to her feet. "Second," the ambassador snapped,
and subsided with an angry glare.

The secretary-general regarded the assembly for a moment
then said, "The motion has been made, and seconded. Given
the nature of the question, I suggest that thoughtful and significant debate is required prior to a vote. Therefore," he

continued, picking up his gavel, "we will continue this matter until tomorrow morning, allowing each of you to consult with your principals. This meeting is adjourned."

Nice move. I'll remember that. She shot a warm glance at the ambassador from the Bahamas. He was not looking in her direction, but she thought she saw the faintest trace of a smile on his face.

On the way out, Brad asked, "So what now?"

"I don't know. I just don't know," she answered. The only thing that was certain at this point was that her chances of getting a decent night's sleep were gone.

USS Jefferson
0900 local (GMT-9)

A good night's sleep and a hot meal had improved the *Montego Bay* captain's appearance considerably. But his eyes still had a drawn, haunted look to them, and it would take more than twenty-four hours to restore color to his face and diminish the harsh lines drawn into his cheeks and forehead. Looking at him, Coyote suspected that even after the external signs of trauma were long gone, the scars on his soul would remain.

"Is there anything else we can do for you?" Coyote asked, his voice gentle. "Anything?"

Gaspert shook his head. "No. Thank you. Your people have been more than gracious. The only thing I need now is information. I'm sure my company representatives will be out tomorrow to assist with the . . . the. . . ." Gaspert ran out of words, and his face twisted.

"The investigation and the arrangements," Coyote said, swearing silently as he did so. Hard, so hard—it was one thing for a member of the military to pay the ultimate price. It was something they volunteered for, knowing that even if the danger seemed slight, there was always the chance that they would be called on to risk their lives—and perhaps lose them.

That civilians—no, more than civilians, vacationers, who

had paid for luxury, comfort, and a complete escape from all cares, innocent men and women—and, dear god, children . . . Coyote could barely keep the pain off of his face. If what had happened to *Montego Bay* was overwhelming to him, then he could not imagine what the man sitting before him felt.

"Can you tell me, Admiral—I know much of it must be classified, but anything you can tell me would help—what happened? Why were we attacked?" Gaspert's eyes were haunted, seeing again the flames, the men and women running and screaming, the complete destruction of his ship. "I was in the Navy, sir—I know, I've already told you that—listen to me, I'm rambling—but anything you can tell me, Admiral, anything at all . . ." Gaspert seemed to deflate like a balloon losing its air.

Dear god, how am I suppose to bear this? I could invoke security classifications, keep him in the dark for twenty or thirty years. Leave him to pass the years wondering what he did wrong, wondering how he aroused the Russian's anger or what he stepped into the middle of. Can I do that?

With a sudden, crushing certainty, Coyote knew that Gaspert's chance of surviving the next year hung in the balance. Without irrefutable proof that he was not to blame, that there was nothing he could have done, Gaspert would not allow himself to live when so many others had died.

"You were a surface sailor in the Navy," Coyote said, uncertain how to begin but knowing that he must.

"Yes, Admiral. Destroyers."

"There are some things I can tell you. As you remember, there are certain routines associated with discussing classified material. The first is this—a disclosure form, and acknowledgment." Coyote slid a form across the desk to him. "Read it, and if you agree to all the provisions, sign and date it at the bottom."

Coyote watched as Gaspert read through it, his finger moving down the lines. The form had not changed in twenty years at least, so he was relatively sure that Gaspert understood what he was getting into. Basically, it said that Gaspert was about to receive certain classified information, the minimum classification with the top secret. By signing, Gaspert acknowledged that, agreed to debriefing before he left the ship, and acknowledged that disclosing this material to anyone not authorized could result in a prison term of thirty years, a fine of twenty thousand dollars, or both.

Will that hold him? It wouldn't me. Not if I knew I had the passengers' relatives to explain the deaths to. For a moment, Coyote considered soft-pedaling it and feeding Gaspert the cover story.

"As you've been told, we are out here conducting battle group operations," Coyote said, reaching the decision as he spoke. He would pay for this later, perhaps, but he was going to do it. "The classified part of this is that we are also testing various defensive systems." Briefly, Coyote outlined the capabilities of the missile defense system, concluding with "And of course, the Russians were keeping an eye on us as well. In fact . . ." For the first time, Coyote hesitated, aware that he was stepping over a line he could never withdraw from. "In fact, they were testing their own capabilities as well. Probably a laser defense system, perhaps targeting just missiles. Perhaps not."

Gaspert appeared to absorb the information impassively. "That was no laser that hit us."

"No, it wasn't. It was a missile. The question at this point is whether it was ours or theirs. Just prior to the attack on *Montego Bay,* approximately twelve hours earlier, certain agencies lost contact with a satellite in geosynchronous orbit over this part of the world. This satellite was in the process of downloading information, and later analysis revealed that prior to going off line, it detected a blue flash from this part of the ocean. Then, as it went off line, it transmitted another blue flash. We believe the Russians may have executed a soft kill on the satellite using their new laser-based system. That seems to correlate with what our lookouts and surveillance aircraft observed as well."

"And so what does this have to do with *Montego Bay?*" Gaspert asked, and Coyote saw a trace of suspicion in his eyes.

"At some point, the Russians were apparently convinced that a fire control radar had locked onto them. Under the circumstances, they believed that we were targeting them."

"And they launched a missile. And hit my ship." A little life crept into Gaspert's face, but it was ugly.

Stop right now. Let him believe that the Russians screwed up and attacked his ship. It's something he can live with, and as a veteran, it's something he can understand. No, he'll never live easily with the memory of those people he lost, but at least he'll know it was nothing he did.

"You were well outside the exercise area, way outside of it," Coyote continued. "There was no reason to suspect you would be in danger."

"I know that. I was on the bridge when it happened. We were opening the distance even more. But it sounds like a whole ocean wouldn't have been far enough."

"Once the Russians launched a missile at us, we activated our anti-air defense systems. The cruisers are quite different from the ones you remember. In full automatic mode, they can ripple off missiles almost as fast as you can fire a forty-five."

"So they fired, then you launched and brought their missile down. And—" Gaspert's voice broke off suddenly. The beginning of anger in his eyes was replaced by horror. "Oh dear god," he whispered. "That's it, isn't it? You're saying that it might be your missile that struck rather than theirs."

"It's a possibility," Coyote said gently. "And the reason that I'm telling you this is that the media will no doubt began to speculate on that. They have so many satellites of their own, so many. Weather satellites, communications—we aren't the only ones watching this part of the ocean. And the resolution of some of the civilian satellites is even superior to our earlier ones. We use their information part of the time instead of our own."

"And they'll have people that know how to read those photos, too."

Coyote nodded. "Exactly. So I wanted to talk to you before you began hearing about it on ACN."

Gaspert's face was blank. He sat impassively, not moving. His eyes were only half-open. Coyote considered calling Medical. Surely Gaspert had been under such a strain that he was beginning to crack.

Suddenly, Gaspert spoke. Fire blazed in his eyes. "You

attacked me." His voice was cold and implacable. "You killed my people, the passengers—you. You." He looked around the admiral's cabin as though he had forgotten where he was. Then he turned back to Coyote, and his voice cracked as he said, "I want my people off this ship. Now. I don't care when the company is coming out, I don't care about the investigation. I'll never go to sea again anyway. But if you don't arrange to get us off this ship within the next hour or two, what I agreed to on that piece of paper won't mean shit. I will not be responsible for my actions, do you hear? I will not." Gaspert's voice was rising now, his fury evident. For a moment, Coyote thought the admiral might come across the desk at him.

"Of course," Coyote said, making his voice brisk and professional. "Completely understandable. I will make the arrangements immediately. Now, is there anything else I can do for you or your passengers?"

Gaspert started for the door. He paused with his hand on the doorknob. "Yes. You can all go fuck yourselves."

Coyote stared at the door that Gaspert slammed behind him. There were moments when he felt the true, crushing weight of his responsibilities, and this was one of them. Men and women—*civilian* men and women—were dead. And there was a chance it was his fault.

No, dammit. It wasn't our fault. It can't be. And I'm going to prove it.

Coyote jabbed out the extension for CVIC. When a junior sailor answered, he said, "Tell Commander Busby I want to see him. Now."

Coyote leaned back in his chair and closed his eyes. There had to be an answer hidden somewhere in the mounds of data *Jefferson* collected. There had to be. And if anyone could find it, Lab Rat could.

FIFTEEN

Lab Rat and Lieutenant Strain divided up the data between them. Or, more correctly, they divided up the task of watching the experts, their enlisted people, go over the hours and hours of data. If the admiral was right, the answer to what had happened lay somewhere in the stream of raw data contained both on the disks and in the printouts.

The key, Coyote believed, was in the raw data. Not in the smooth tracks and histories displayed in Combat. Not in the correlation the computer assigned to a series of radar hits. Not in the final product displayed on the electronic warfare console. No, somewhere in the down and dirty was an anomaly, one that the computer had considered and then either discarded or merged with the wrong sequence of detections. It had to be that way, Coyote insisted, if one started with the premise that the American combat systems were inherently superior to the Russian ones. And nobody wanted to dispute that with him, did they?

Lab Rat's leading chief petty, Chief Abbyssian, Senior

Chief Armstrong's replacement, had assigned his two best people to lead the reviews. The new chief had already gotten a good feel for his people's capabilities. He gave a thick sheaf of computer printouts to one petty officer, and the analog records to another. Then, with a couple of quiet suggestions, he arranged for Strain to work with the digital data and his commander to review the analog data. His reasoning was that he paired each officer's strength with the weakness of his technician. Then, the chief suggested, after each team had completed its review, they would swap data. The chief himself would review a CD that ran a scroll of numerical data next to its analog equivalent.

"I'm not sure what we're looking for," the chief said.

"Neither am I," Lab Rat answered. "But there's got to be something there—something. We don't know what happened out there, but whatever it was, it left traces in the electromagnetic spectrum. We've got gear sensitive enough to record the noise a gnat makes farting a hundred miles away. Whatever happened, we've got a record of it."

"That's the thing, sir," the chief said. "We've got too much data—tons of it. Pulling out the significant events from all the noise is going to take some time. Not to say we can't do it," he added, seeing Lab Rat's expression cloud up. "But you know what I mean."

Lab Rat sighed. He did, indeed. That was the problem with recording absolutely everything that happened at every frequency. It was not recorded as a set of discrete frequencies. This backup record was raw data, a complex waveform that would have to be broken down by the computer into its component frequencies. Okay, sure, it went pretty quickly. And in reality, there was only about five minutes of data that they needed to focus on.

But the broader question was what had led up to the fatal exchange of missiles. Why had the Russians fired? What had they seen in the hours preceding the launch that had convinced them they were under attack?

And finally, whose missile was where? The signal data would have to be matched with the radar pictures, another task that the computers could handle but one that introduced considerable ambiguity. The computer program had para-

meters for sampling data, smoothing it to discard erroneous
detections and then integrating it with a recursive formula.
While it was normally reliable and accurate, everyone understood that the process could introduce errors, false interpretations, and incorrect correlation of contacts that could
easily provide widely different results. So they were going
back to the raw data, to the individual radar hits, and per-
forming their own correlation as well.

"Of course, as soon as we get the data to NSA, they will
run it as well." The chief shook his head admiringly. "The
power they've got in their system—well, we don't even
come close."

"I know." Lab Rat had been on several tours of the NSA
facilities himself. "But we've got something they don't—
motivation. It's our asses that are on the line."

They pored over the data for hours, comparing notes as
digital and analog pictures revealed amplitude peaks that
might or might not be significant. As their eyes grew
strained, the pictures and the columns of numbers began to
blur. Finally, the chief suggested that they call a halt to it, at
least for a couple of hours.

"Everybody, get something to eat," Lab Rat ordered. "Be
back here in an hour. I think we're closing in on it."

And indeed he did. The Russians claimed that a fire control
radar had illuminated them. Under the current rules of engagement, that was strictly forbidden by the INCOS agreement. Additionally, under most circumstances, training fire
control radar on another military unit was considered a hostile act, an act of war. Immediate and appropriate response
was clearly authorized. Waiting to demand an explanation or
file protests meant taking the chance that you would be hit
by missile.

"If the Russians are telling the truth, we're at least partially
responsible for this," the chief said after the other sailors left
the compartment.

"I know, I know. But we've got to know what really happened," Lab Rat answered. "Everybody knows better than to
illuminate the Russians with fire control radar."

A strangely uneasy expression crossed the chief's face. He
looked away as though engrossed in studying imperfections

in the paint job on a nearby bulkhead. Without looking at Lab Rat, he said, "Yes, sir. Everybody on the ship knows better than to spike the Russians with fire control radar. But there were a lot of people on the cruiser, sir. Contractors, technicians—"

Lab Rat interrupted him. "They all know better, too. They build the damn stuff."

"—and the VIPs, sir," the chief continued. "They were in Combat when this happened." The chief nodded as he saw the look of horror on Lab Rat's face. "Yes, sir. I checked. There were ten civilians in Combat at the time. Two of them were sitting at data consoles, getting a full brief by the watchstanders."

"Live consoles?" Lab Rat asked, horror in his voice.

"They weren't supposed to be," the chief said. "But maybe somebody screwed up. Maybe one of them was capable of transmitting that fire control radar pulse."

Lieutenant Strain broke in with "Yes, sir, but is that really going to be an issue? I mean," he added hastily, "there's no excuse for it, of course. If we provoked them somehow, we provoked them. But what's *really* going to matter is who hit *Montego Bay*. Once that's decided, everything else just falls by the wayside, doesn't it?"

Lab Rat grunted. The lieutenant had a point. The cruiser may have inadvertently provoked the Russians. But no matter what had gone wrong, the Russians had targeted the cruise ship. As ghoulish as it might seem, that's what they now had to focus on.

"Okay, back at it in an hour," Lab Rat said. "In the meantime, we'll let the computer run its correlation and analysis on its own for a while. Compare that with what we come up with and see if there are any clues."

Just then, they heard, "Flight quarters, flight quarters. Now set flight quarters. Reason for flight quarters: launch of Greyhound COD."

Lab Rat breathed a sigh of relief. Everyone would be a lot happier with Cary Winston off the ship. Maybe now they could get some work done without looking over their collective shoulders.

Lab Rat shuffled hastily through his in box. There were

several CDs, each in its own jewel case, a computer label with date and time stuck in the middle of the lid. He collected them by the simple expedient of holding up the papers and letting the heavier CDs fall to his desk. He stacked them together, then began leafing through them to find the one he wanted. The disk covering the time and date in question was the third one down.

Lab Rat pulled it out, popped it open, and went to his CD drive. His computer was already running the data analysis program. He slid the CD into the drive holder, then shot that home.

The usual noises accompanied the drive pulling up the information. Lab Rat waited, growing more anxious by the moment. Finally, the screen displayed the data selection prompt. Lab Rat typed in a span of twelve minutes covering the missile launches and the beginning of the end for *Montego Bay*. Moments later, columns of numbers scrolled down the screen.

"Yell if you see something," he said. He hit the printout button and simultaneously began scanning the data. It was detailed and rich. Every signal that pulsed through the electromagnetic spectrum was captured, recorded, broken down into its constituent parts, and then analyzed for threat characteristics. A minimum number of hits by the detector were required before the computer would decide that a signal was a valid waveform and not a bit of spurious noise. Only those signals meeting certain criteria were displayed. But this, the raw data, contained everything the sensors had seen during the time period, valid or not.

Coyote strode into the room, anger on his face. "Anything yet?"

Lab Rat glanced over at Lieutenant Strain, who shook his head. "No, Admiral. Not yet."

Coyote swore quietly. "I need to know what happened, and I need to know right now. I just got a call from Third Fleet. The shit's starting to roll downhill."

"Sir?" Lab Rat asked, his stomach tightening up. He'd seen Coyote like this before, and it was never good news.

"They're claiming we're at fault. They say they've got proof and they are inviting every reporter in the world on board to see it. And, unless we ante up with an apology, they're saying—I'm translating this from the diplomatic double talk—there's going to be hell to pay." Coyote looked suddenly weary. "We're on the verge of a full-out shooting war, Lab Rat, unless we can come up with proof that they're responsible. This has spun up some sort of internal Russian issue we don't understand all that well, and it's escalating faster than the diplomats can jaw it out.".

"The Russians have always seen this program as a threat," Strain said quietly. "So has a lot of Europe."

"I know, I know. But that's way above our paygrades—mine included," Coyote said. There were a few moments of silence, broken only by a slight click as the CD continued spilling its guts on Lab Rat's screen.

"Stop," the chief said suddenly. "Scroll back up, sir."

"What is it?" Coyote demanded.

"I don't know yet, Admiral," the chief said. "I thought I saw somthing."

Lab Rat scrolled up, going slowly line by line. He hadn't noticed anything out of the ordinary, but he wasn't the specialist. If the chief thought he saw something, then it was worth checking out.

"Right *there*," the chief said, pointing out a line on the screen. He swore quietly, ran out of the compartment, and returned moments later with a manual in his hand. "Line 870, Commander. No doubt about it. If I saw that, I'd panic, too."

"Talk," Coyote ordered.

"What is it?" Lab Rat demanded. "Was someone targeting the Russians?"

"Yes, sir," the chief said. A grim expression settled on his face. "*Lake Champlain* was."

SIXTEEN

Saturday, July 5
USS **Jefferson**
Flight Deck
0500 local (GMT-9)

Drake, along with the admiral and his chief of staff, stood next to the island, watching the COD launch. It wasn't until the COD was off the catapult and making her turn away from the carrier that the noise abated enough for them to talk.

"That's it, then," Coyote said. "Now at least we can concentrate on figuring out what happened." He turned to head back into the ship, then stopped. "You know you're still restricted," he said, his back still to Pamela. "I know you didn't have anything to do with this, but I can't take any chances right now. If their laser system is fully operational, then we're at a real disadvantage."

"Yes, Admiral. I understand. But I've got an idea," she answered. *And a way to redeem myself.*

"Right." The admiral undogged the hatch and pulled it open.

"Seriously. Just listen for a second. If it's insane, I'll spend the rest of my time happily pumping out human interest stories for my hometown newspaper. But if it's not, it might make a difference."

She studied the face of the men around her. Distrust, anger, even hatred. She wasn't sure she could blame them. "You need to know what's going on over there. And, to be frank, we owe you one. We've already done some damage. Now, let us do some good." She held up one hand to forestall comment. "I'm not asking you to trust me. That would be too much. But you know the Russians have issued an open invitation for the international press to come on board and see what they have to say about the incident. Just let me go over there—see what they have to say. I might hear or see something that could make a difference."

All the officers turned toward Coyote. He was silent for a long moment then said, "Even with the restrictions we have put on you *here,* you're bound to have overheard things that the Russians would find very interesting. How do I know you're not going to pass information to them that would be very dangerous to us?"

"Our business is gathering information, not spying," she said coldly. "Yes, there are two sides to every story, and we try to tell both. But even though we're an international news agency, I am an American. I'm not going to slant the story, but if I happen to overhear something that might be useful to you, I can include it in the story. Just like Winston did. But this time, it would cut the other way."

There was a longer moment of silence, then Coyote turned to Tombstone. "What you think?"

Tombstone studied her, as if trying to see if there was any difference between the woman in front of him now and the woman he had been engaged to marry. Evidently what he saw reassured him. He turned to Coyote and said, "I'm inclined to let her have a shot at it. Miss Drake," he said, turning back to her, "you are a royal pain in the ass. But you are *our* pain in the ass. Not theirs." Transferring his gaze back to Coyote, Tombstone continued, "I suggest you get Lab Rat to brief her on what we're looking for. That way if she stumbles across something, it may have significance for her that it wouldn't otherwise."

"Right," Coyote said. "Well, Drake, you've got your shot at it. Don't blow it."

Admiral Kurashov
0630 local (GMT-9)

The helicopters began arriving shortly after dawn. Many of them were rated for nighttime flights and could easily have arrived at the Russian transport within a few hours of the announcement. The Russians, however, saw no need to incur the risks inherent in nighttime operations simply to satisfy the world's curiosity a few hours earlier. They insisted that no one would be permitted on board until after first light. As a result, by the time the sun was rising, there had been two near misses between helicopters waiting just over the horizon to approach.

The Russian swore quietly as he surveyed the radar screen. At last count, there had been eight helicopters inbound, and the latest news from shore indicated that two more had just taken off. The flight deck was going to be far more crowded then he liked, but that couldn't be helped. They'd said they would accommodate everyone who wished to visit, and accommodate the reporters they would.

One helicopter was approaching from the direction of the American battle group. It was ACN, with the inestimable Miss Pamela Drake. He'd seen her work before, and followed her reports on the United States Navy. A team of analysts studied every one of her reports in fact, alert for any possible inadvertent disclosure of classified data. Most reporters assigned to military units tripped up sooner or later, and valuable technical details filtered into their reports. He'd watched with grim amusement as American efforts to insist on pre-recorded reports were shot down. America's vaunted freedom of the press was one of Russia's most viable intelligence resources.

But today he wasn't going to let the reporters turn the tables on him. He wasn't intending to brief any classified details, but that didn't mean he couldn't make a mistake. He made a mental note to remind everyone to be cautious about providing any information. Everything had to be cleared by the public affairs office, *everything*. The political officers were controlling the release of information, and the entire evolution had to be carefully stage-managed. The sailors to whom the reporters would talk would be intelligence officers posing as average sailors. The tours of the ship would be conducted through tortuous routes, with some passageways blocked off and every turn intended to disorient the reporters. Every moment would be carefully crafted to give the illusion of complete and open access to all areas of the ship. That could not have been further from the truth.

"Bring the ACN helicopter in first," the Russian said, acting on impulse. "This one." He jabbed a finger at the helicopter coming from the *Jefferson*.

"Yes, sir, and what about the other ACN helos?" the air traffic controller answered. Two more ACN helicopters were awaiting permission to land, carrying additional reporters and technical crews.

"Bring them in order with the rest," he said. Perhaps Miss Drake would take note of the fact that she would be the first one on board.

Admiral Kurashov
0645 local (GMT-9)

Drake leaned forward to stare down at the flight deck as the helicopter hovered, then slid slowly sideways, transitioning from forward flight to hovering over the steel deck. The downdraft from the rotors beat against the deck and ricocheted back up, introduced a roiling into the helicopter's stability. But the Seahawk pilot was an expert and carefully maneuvered the helicopter directly above the landing spot before lowering her gently down. She touched down with barely a jolt.

Even before the rotors began slowing, a group of Russian sailors formed up as an honor guard on either side of the hatch. They didn't wear hats, but other than that they were attired in their best dress uniform. The wind from the downdraft whipped their neckerchiefs and jumpers around, making them flutter.

"I'd appreciated it if they could have waited a couple of minutes," Drake's pilot grumbled. "Just what I need, a bunch of Russians to worry about during shutdown." He sighed and glanced over at his co-pilot. "Let's get this over with fast. You start." The two ran through the checklist in record time, and finally powered down the rotors. The noise level began dropping immediately, and the Russian sailors seemed more at ease. Finally, the crew chief unbuckled from his seat and stood, facing the passengers. "Okay, ladies and gentlemen. Just like we briefed. Everybody follow me and stay close. This isn't our ship, people. What you don't know can get you killed."

Drake unbuckled her harness and stood, stretching as she did. It had been a short flight, but the constant pounding vibration seemed to resonate in her bones still. Jeff groaned as he slung his gear over his shoulder, clearly feeling some of the same discomfort. Around them, the other passengers stretched as well.

"All right. Here we go. Look sharp, everybody." The crew chief plastered a smile on his face then pulled back the side door to the helicopter. Sunlight poured in.

He jumped down to the deck and Pamela could see through the window that he was talking with the Russians. Everything appeared to be agreeable, and he returned to the open hatch almost immediately and motioned to them to begin disembarking. Drake waited her turn, chaffing at the delays. Finally, her line reached the hatch. She jumped down the two feet to the deck, blinking in the sudden sunlight. The sailors rendered a sharp salute as she walked down the double lines, and she nodded politely in return. Surely they didn't expect a civilian to return their salutes, did they?

The chief was waiting for her at the end of the line, and a Russian stepped forward to greet her. "Welcome, Miss Drake. I am your escort. Please, allow me to conduct you to the briefing room." He offered her his arm in a courtly gesture out of place on the flight deck of a warship. For a moment, she debated asserting her independence, her liberation, and her general disdain for such courtesies. Then, thinking better of it, she laid her hand in the crook of his elbow and said, "Thank you very much." She glanced behind and saw her cameraman stifle a grin, and thought, *Honey, not vinegar. Now let's see what we catch.*

The flight deck looked pretty much like flight decks everywhere. The air had a slightly different odor to it, probably a combination of fuel burning and cooking. It was not unpleasant, just different. The vast expanse of non-skid, the deliberate, measured steps of the flight deck technician, the glints of sun off of steel fuselages—all were familiar, even to the heat radiating up through Pamela's boots. Form follows function, she supposed.

They entered the ship just as they would an American aircraft carrier through a hatch in the island. From there, she followed her escort down two decks, twisting through a maze of passageways until they ended up in a large compartment. A large buffet table was spread out before them, the food carefully arranged and beautifully presented.

I wonder how much it cost to fly all this out. It would be a shame for it to go to waste. Murmuring thanks to her escort, Pamela sampled the caviar and then the salmon. Both melted in her mouth like butter.

The clatter in the passageway told her that her fellow reporters were arriving. They soon swarmed in, laughing and talking, shaking off the adrenaline buzz from the flight over. Pamela selected two chairs and dropped her gear on them, assigning Jeff to guard them.

There was a flurry near the door and every military person in the room snapped to attention. A Russian command was barked out, and they relaxed, although not by much. Parting the reporters with his sheer presence, a large, very senior Russian officer made his way to the front of room, managing to smile and look serious at the same time. He stopped to shake a few hands along the way, including Pamela's, murmured a greeting in Russian, and then stepped to the podium in front.

"Welcome to my ship," he said, permitting himself a brief smile. "My English is so weak. If you need translation, ask, okay?" He surveyed the crowd to make sure he'd been understood, then nodded. "Well, we wish for happier circumstances," he said, his expression becoming somber. "It is a tragedy, yes? Not only for conflict between America and Russia, but especially for the loss of souls on *Montego Bay*." To the surprise of the audience, he crossed himself, going from right to left in the Greek Orthodox style. He continued with "We will show you everything—everything. We will tell you what we think it means. You can decide for yourself. You can decide, and tell the world." He paused momentarily to survey them, meeting each one's gaze directly. "After, there will be no question that we are not at fault."

He motioned to a junior officer standing behind him, and stepped aside to yield the podium. "Good morning, ladies and gentlemen. I am the public information officer and will be conducting the initial briefing. Later, the admiral will be available to answer all of your questions. I think you'll find us all remarkably forthcoming." His English was smooth and unaccented. Seeing the brief looks of surprise on their faces, he smiled quickly. "Ph.D. in economics, Harvard," he said by way of explanation.

"First slide," he said, looking to the back of the room. The overhead lights were doused and a brightly colored graphic flashed onto the white screen at the front of the room.

Slick, very slick. Not like anything I've seen from them before—I wonder if it's just him or indicative of a broader trend in the Russian navy. Drake jotted down a note then transferred her gaze to the slide in front of her.

The symbology was all too familiar. No matter what they used in their own combat systems, the Russians had translated everything into American terminology to make it easier for their viewers to understand. And, judging from the slides, this would be a very simple, yet complete explanation.

The first slide showed both Russian and American battle groups, with a line drawn between them showing the distance between the two. As the officer spoke, he clicked the display into motion, and the two groups of ships crept slowly toward each other. When they were separated by approximately ten miles, the Russian group changed course to widen the distance between them. In the top, left-hand part of the display, a symbol crept onto the screen. It was labeled "Montego Bay."

"As you can see, we were observing the carrier's right-of-way as she was conducting flight operations. We had plans to launch ourselves, but decided it would be more prudent if we waited until we were farther away. Our own plans were postponed in order to ensure the safety of both groups." He looked at them to make sure they got the point.

Then he pointed at the *Montego Bay* symbol with his laser pointer. "And you'll notice she is also opening the distance, but in the opposite direction. I believe she intended to cut behind the aircraft carrier, retracing her steps slightly in order to maneuver around the carrier." He fell silent for a moment, and the seconds ticked by as the symbols marched inevitably toward their destinies.

He clicked another key, and said, "I am slowing the action now so that you can observe exactly what happened. The first evidence of problems came when we detected an American fire control radar targeting our vessel." As he spoke, a notation to that effect appeared on a screen. The action stopped. "As you can see, we are at a safe distance at this point and increasing the distance between us. There was nothing to provoke a hostile action from the aircraft carrier."

The contacts began moving again, and the scale of the display expanded. "At this point, our lookout observed a beam of light coming from somewhere near the carrier. You may confirm this when you return to *Jefferson*."

"I can try," Drake said, letting her tone of voice imply that she was not all that confident of the results.

"There are some limitations to your First Amendment freedom of speech, are there not?" he observed. He let that sink in for a moment, and continued with "At any rate, I am sure our information can be confirmed by other sources. There are many commercial satellites observing this area as well. The light was most distinctive and not likely to be mistaken for anything other than what it was—a laser."

"A laser?" Drake asked. "Were they testing a new weapons systems? What can you tell us about it?"

"We do suspect it is a new weapon system, possibly with an anti-satellite kill capability," the admiral answered, interrupting the public information officer. "More than that, we cannot say. To do so would reveal our own sources of information."

"Spies?" another reporter asked.

The admiral shook his head. "If you must know, the magazine *Scientific American*. That and *Popular Mechanics* contain a great deal of useful information." He winked and shook a finger at them, looking remarkably like a Santa Claus. "I am divulging state secrets by telling you this."

"If we can assume for a moment that it was indeed a laser, perhaps we can continue," the public information officer said. He clicked his controller again, and the picture changed, zooming in on the three ships. "I have eliminated the escorts for clarity's sake. This is the point at which the Americans launched their weapon. This occurred approximately ninety seconds after we were targeted by the fire control radar. The missile appeared to be headed in our direction, as you can see." He fell silent while the missile symbol inched its way across the screen, apparently headed directly for the Russian amphibious transport. "Immediately following the launch of the missile, we retaliated." The graphics showed a missile launching from his ship, targeted on the American vessel. "As you can see, there is little doubt of the sequence of events."

The room was utterly silent. It might be blue and red symbols projected onto a white screen, but every person in the room understood that they were about to watch the death of more than two hundred people.

As they watched, the American missile changed course slightly. It continued on, and then broke radically away from the Russian ship. "Dear god," Drake heard someone murmur. "No."

This isn't real time. It already happened. There's nothing you can do about it. Despite reminding herself of the unreality of it, Pamela felt a cold fear and an urgent need to do something, anything, surge through her. It was like a bad dream, running from a monster and feeling like you were running through molasses.

Without fanfare, without additional graphics, the symbol for the American missile intercepted the symbol for *Montego Bay*. There was silence.

The Russian missile continued on, then disintegrated when it was halfway between the American ship and the Russian ship. "One of your Tomcats," the public information officer observed. "A very difficult target, yet he hit it. Under different circumstances, we would convey our compliments to the pilot."

"So you're saying it was an American missile that hit *Montego Bay* and a Tomcat took your own missile out," Pamela said. "But all the reports so far say that *Montego Bay* was hit from your side. How do explain the missile coming in on the right side when the carrier was to her left?"

"Missiles are very versatile, Miss Drake," he said. "Right or left—it makes no difference. With the re-targeting capability of some missiles, they can loiter overhead for hours, waiting for the perfect target angle. Based on the trajectory, it appears that there was a flaw in the American missile guidance system. It went into re-attack mode, and found *Montego Bay*."

"What sort of programming error?" someone behind Drake demanded.

The public information officer looked to the admiral, who shrugged. "It is speculation only, but the laser—perhaps it interfered with the missile. Such has been known to happen."

"And your own experiments?" Drake asked.

The admiral smiled briefly. "You'll understand if I do not answer in detail. But yes, it is well known that lasers and missiles do not mix. There can be mutual interference of this sort."

"I'm passing out briefing packages," the public information officer continued, after a nod from the admiral. "In those, you'll find all the supporting data, including printouts of all of the critical moments you have just seen in this presentation. Flight schedules, watch schedules—it is all there. We understand that your intelligence people will no doubt want copies of all of this and we encourage you to provide them. Once you have studied the data, you'll understand that there cannot be any other interpretation of what happened. The American cruiser committed a hostile act by targeting our ship with their fire control radar. When we responded, the cruiser launched the missile that hit the *Montego Bay*. America must take the responsibility for this unnecessary waste of life."

Silence, as the reporters digested the information. Pamela glanced around the room and could see the war taking place inside each one of them.

Yes, they were reporters, dedicated to uncovering facts and

breaking news. They saw themselves as hardheaded and un-
emotional, and above the political machinations of governments. Yet the vast majority of the reporters in that room
were American by birth, American by education, and
uniquely American in outlook. At some level, perhaps below
conscious thought, they were fiercely protective of their
country, and deeply resented the Russian's conclusion that
the Americans were at fault. But even as they dealt with that
resentment, they had to face the facts. If they did not report
the truth, the four European journalists would. And by not
reporting it, they would be subjected to allegations of a
cover-up.

"I will answer some questions," the admiral said, stepping
forward. "I remind you, if you need a translation, ask. I will
do the same if I do not understand your question."

"Admiral, could you compare to status of the Russian and
American laser defense systems? Do you think the Americans have moved too quickly, taking chances they shouldn't
that resulted in this tragedy?" one reporter asked.

The admiral appeared to consider this for a moment. "The
development, I cannot tell you. But moving too fast—yes, I
think that is the case. My own people assure me that there
is much benchmark testing and simulation prior to an actual
firing. We have devoted a great deal of time and effort to
studying the problem, and we are not yet ready to test our
system at sea. Now, you may have heard that our engineers
are simply not as good as the American engineers. This is
not true. But we're taking reasonable precautions to make
sure that our system is dependable and controllable prior to
deploying it at sea.

"Furthermore," he continued, his accent growing stronger,
"there are many who have doubts about your system. Some
believe deployment will destabilize the entire balance of
power between your country and mine. Again, we have not
undertaken this of our own, but simply respond to America's
actions."

Drake could hear the sincerity in his voice. The questions
around her became more insisted, more probing. More and
more often, the admiral sidestepped the question, citing security reasons. After ten minutes, the public information of-

ficer stepped to the podium and said, "Thank you, ladies and gentlemen. And thank you, Admiral. Now, if you'll follow your escort, there is time for a brief tour of our combat center and the flight deck before your return here for a meal and to meet some of our people. If you have any questions or any needs, please do not hesitate to ask."

The reporters, acting on reflex at the familiar cue, gathered up their gear. The Russian escorts promptly rounded up their charges and eased them out of the room, half of the group heading for Combat, the other half to the flight deck.

Pamela's own escort approached her and said, "Miss Drake, I suspect you have seen many combat centers and many flight decks. The admiral would like to provide a private tour for you—an exclusive, if you will." The public information officer appeared behind him, nodding. "If you would come this way."

"Thank you. Come on, Jeff," she said, motioning to her cameraman, who fell into step behind her. The public information officer held up one hand.

"No pictures without my express approval. Agreed?"

"Of course. We're used to covering military operations, Commander. We understand the game rules."

He smiled. "Not everyone does. Your Miss Winston, for instance. This is why you were selected, and not the others."

Does everybody in the world know about Cary Winston? What is he trying to tell me by letting me know they know about her?

Drake decided that discretion was the better part of valor. She smiled. "She is very young. With time, she may be all right."

"Perhaps. But she will not be here."

The two Russian officers led the way toward the stern of the ship, descending another two decks. Pamela followed, dividing her attention between the passageways and the complaints of Jeff behind her as he maneuvered his gear through tight openings.

Surprisingly, the passageways looked very much like they did on America's carrier. The markings on the bulkheads were in Cyrillic rather than English letters and the compartment numbering scheme appeared to be slightly different.

But there was the familiar sense of too many people crammed into too-small spaces and the odd combination smell of fuel and cooking that she'd noticed on the deck. They passed a few sailors, who pressed themselves against the bulkhead in order to let them pass, even though there was more than enough room. A few murmured polite greetings. All averted their eyes.

Finally, when Drake sensed that they must be near the stern, they went up three decks. They were just below the flight deck, and the motion of the ship was more pronounced than it had been amidships.

The public information officer tapped out the security code on a cipher lock, then stepped back to allow them to precede him into the room. Pamela walked in, and saw that the bulkhead was crammed with consoles. In the center of the room, a large, spotless steel-and-white setup extended through the ceiling overhead.

"A laser," she said softly. She turned to face him, her excitement visible. "This is *your* system, isn't it?"

"Yes. Tested extensively but not yet ready for live targets." He held up one hand as the cameraman fumbled with his gear. "I'm sorry. No pictures. Not yet."

"May I get a closer look?" she asked.

"Yes, of course."

She walked slowly around it, trying to memorize the details. There was a large, clear cylinder in the center, with a maze of wires and connections at either end. Steel struts marked with calibration figures ringed it, holding it so perfectly in alignment that it looked unnatural.

In truth, there was not much to see. It looked remarkably similar to the one on board *Jefferson.* But she studied anyway, trying to memorize the details, counting the struts and supports with one part of her mind as the other worked out the wording she would use to describe it to her audience. "We are on the record?" she asked to confirm their status. "You know that term?"

"Yes. And I hope," he continued, with what was apparently a burst of candor, "that you will tell the Americans that we are quite far along in our own program. Should they decide to deploy their laser system, we will not be far behind.

Not far behind at all. However, I think that world opinion may have something to say about both systems. When the testing alone results in the deaths of innocent civilians, how much more dangerous would full-scale deployment be?"

"A very good question," she said. "And one that deserves an answer."

He smiled at her now, his expression relieved. "And the answers, as you must suspect, must come from your own people. We have shown you our system. Now ask them to show you theirs."

"I don't think they will." She shrugged. "You must know that I'm not in their good graces right now. Not after what Winston did."

"Yes, of course. That is the reason you are here. I think there can be little doubt that your network is willing to report stories that are not entirely flattering to your country."

"An understatement, but thank you for the compliment. It took a good deal of pressure for the admiral to allow me to come over here from the carrier, you know. They have tried to silence us, but it isn't working."

The Russian nodded sympathetically. "I must tell you, Miss Drake. I think the story you're after is not the one you'll eventually find. There has been a serious tragedy here, one that could have been avoided by honest communications between all parties. The responsibility for this lies with your— with the Americans."

"Please go on." Drake kept her expression neutral.

"Let me ask you this first," the Russian said. "Why exactly are the Americans here?"

"Routine operations, as I understand it."

The Russian looked her over carefully, as though trying to see into her mind. "And you believe that?"

"Well, I'm fairly familiar with normal carrier operations, and so far I have had no reason to doubt it. Should I?"

He laughed aloud. "Now I am certain that the story you will get is not the one you're expecting. Miss Drake, that battle group is not here on routine operations. They are testing an advanced weaponry system, one called theater ballistic missile defense, or TBMD. There are no laser communications, no oceanographic experiments. We are conducting a test of a new weapon, yes. And your Americans are conducting their own tests to counter it." He watched her closely for a moment, observing her reaction, then nodded in satisfaction. "I thought so. They did not tell you, did they?"

"What exactly does this TBMD do?" she asked, ignoring his question.

"It uses lasers to conduct a soft kill on a missile. It scrambles the electronics in the guidance system. Once that happens, it goes off course. Without guidance, the propulsion will cut out, and once inertia is overcome, it simply falls into the ocean."

"This all sounds very routine, then," Drake said, as though bored. "Surely this isn't the first time that you have conducted tests and the Americans have conducted tests of their countermeasures? It's very interesting, but not astounding."

"There's more. The Americans were not testing countermeasures. They were testing a laser system as well."

Drake didn't have to fake the surprise on her face. Yes, it all made sense. She had known from the beginning that Coyote and Tombstone were not being honest about *Jefferson*'s mission, and the Russian's report just confirmed it. And knowing that she did not know the truth, they had sent her here anyway, to find out how much the Russians knew. Surely they had known that the Russians would tell her what they suspected. They must have been counting on it, in fact. All that talk about a new weapon system, the radar she was to look for—just a cover story to sidetrack her. In reality, she should have been looking for that evidence on board *Jefferson* instead of on the Russian ship.

"What are your plans now?" she said, operating on automatic. "The search and rescue will continue, surely."

The Russian shrugged. "Your captain had it right. If there were more survivors from *Montego Bay*, we would have found them by now. We will continue to search for a few more days, but our hopes are dwindling quickly. I would be surprised if we find anything."

"Our sympathies to their families, of course," Drake murmured. Her mind was racing furiously as she tried to shape the new story in her mind. How much of it would she tell? How much secrecy was vital to national security, and how much was simply reflective of government secrecy?

"The reason I am showing you all this," the Russian continued after a moment, "is that you must find some way to convince the Americans how very serious the situation is. They tested their system, they caused the sinking of a civilian ship, then they tried to blame it on us. We view this as an act of aggression, an attempt to rally world opinion against us. We cannot allow this to continue. Unless there is a prompt admission of guilt and a complete apology—there were fifteen Russians on board *Montego Bay*—we will be forced to act to protect our own interests and to demonstrate the efficacy of our own system. It has been suggested that the USS *Jefferson* might be a suitable target."

"You'd attack the *Jefferson*?" Drake asked, her voice astonished. "Isn't that a little out of proportion?" She saw the look on his face, and waved her hand impatiently. "Yeah, yeah, the civilian ship and fifteen Russians. It's a tragedy—it bleeds, it leads in the news. But you're talking about *attacking* an American ship of war! Tell me why this makes sense!"

The Russian general regarded her gravely. "Talk to others on the staff here, Miss Drake. I think you will see that America committed two acts of aggression. First, by deploying this system despite the protests of the rest of the world. And second, by targeting our ship with fire control radar. You may not understand it, not as we do, but we consider ourselves already at war. You would be wise to remember that and to convey it to the battle group commander, Admiral Grant."

Drake spent the next five hours interviewing other members of the Russian staff, but as far as she was concerned, she got what she came for in the first interview. Later, as her helo lifted off to return to *Jefferson,* she stared back at the Russian ship. The real task now was sorting out the Russian manipulation from the American manipulation. For just a second, she wondered if Winston didn't have it right.

SEVENTEEN

The United Nations
0700 local (GMT-5)

Wexler could not recall a time when she had ever been quite so tired. Or so discouraged. Nothing in the world seemed to make any sense anymore, least of all what had happened at the United Nations in the last week. Beginning with the equivocation of Great Britain, proceeding to Liberia's motion as seconded by India, and finally to this—the complete and utter desertion of the United States by all her purported allies.

I will not look in the mirror. I will not. She did not need to see her reflection to know that her eyes were bleary and bloodshot, her face pale and drained. She could feel the results of too little sleep and too much caffeine in every inch of her body.

But what were the options? During a crisis, no one slept. *Forty-five minutes left. What will I tell them?*

The prospect of announcing to the world that the United States would not—*could not?*—pay its just obligations was simply unthinkable. So was the option of withdrawing from the United Nations. There had to be a middle ground—there had to be.

There was a knock on her door and Brad stepped in without waiting for an answer. If anything, he looked worse than she did. But there was a note of hope in his voice when he said, "Captain Hemingway to see you, Ambassador."

"I hope she brought her own tea leaves," Wexler answered, glancing at the antique can on her credenza. She'd run out of her favorite orange oolong three hours ago.

Captain Jane Hemingway stepped into the room. She held out a small brown paper bag. "As it happens, I do. We can drink it and then stare at the dregs and try to figure out what's going on."

"Divining answers from tea leaves requires a fresh pot, I think," Brad said. He plucked the bag out of her hand. "I'll take care of that."

He left, shutting the door behind him. Without waiting for an invitation, Captain Hemingway sank down on the comfortable couch. "Hell of a long week, isn't it?"

"For everyone, I suspect. Have you come to offer moral support, or just drop off a going away present?" Wexler could not keep the bitterness out of her voice.

Hemingway yawned and looked suspiciously, like she wanted to stretch out on the couch for nap. "Neither, really. Actually, you may consider me the cavalry."

"Want to explain that?"

Hemingway shook her head. "Nope. I mean, no, Madam Ambassador." Hemingway opened her briefcase, fumbling with the security latch for a moment and then extracting a sealed brown envelope. She raised it to her lips, kissed the seal, and passed it to Wexler.

Wexler felt an unreasoning flick of hope. She took the envelope, broke the security seal, and extracted the contents.

"Just read. Get all the way through it, and then I can answer any questions." Hemingway yawned again.

"Go ahead," Wexler murmured, already running her finger down the front page. "Crash out. I will wake you when I need you." Before she turned to the second page, Hemingway was asleep.

The first two sentences were sufficient to flush every trace of fatigue out of her body. It was the section entitled "Executive Summary," a quick overview intended to convince the reader to probe into the details.

Analysis of the electromagnetic spectrum during the attack

on the *Montego Bay* indicated the ship was destroyed by a Silkworm missile. Trajectory reconstruction indicated that the missile was fired from the Russian amphibious transport.

Wexler started to ask, "They can really prove this?" Instead, she glanced at the sleeping Navy captain and began to read the supporting documentation.

Minutes later, Brad reappeared with a fresh pot of tea. He took in the situation at a glance, quietly poured both women large mugs, avoiding the delicate teacups that Wexler favored, slipped a cozy over the pot, and withdrew without comment. Five minutes after that, Wexler said, "Jane."

Hemingway's eyes snapped opened. There was a microsecond of disorientation and then she was alert. She sat up, moving smoothly, and picked up the mug of tea. The fifteen-minute nap appeared to have worked magic.

"Cavalry, indeed," Wexler said. She tapped the sheaf of documents. "Since when did the cavalry carry dynamite?"

"There's more," Hemingway said. She yawned, then took another large gulp of the tea. "Don't ask me where I got this information from, okay? Just don't."

"Provisionally, I agree," Wexler said cautiously. "As long as there's nothing criminal about it."

Hemmingway shrugged. "Define criminal for me and I'll tell you. Just listen first, though."

She took a deep breath and shook off the last vestiges of sleep. "Has it occurred to you that damn little has been said about what started all this. That the Russians tested their TBMD system by taking out an American satellite? Doesn't it seem odd to you that nobody's screaming bloody murder about that, but they're up in arms about a fire control radar?"

"Yes, it does," Wexler said.

"What if I told you that the president told them they could take it out?"

"Impossible. What in the world would he gain by doing something like that?" Wexler asked.

"This." Hemmingway passed her another folder, this one containing a single sheet of paper.

Wexler looked at it, then felt her face turn pale. She stared at the information, just two short paragraphs and a photo.

"He traded the satellite for this information," she said slowly. It made complete sense to her now.

"Yeah. That's the way it looks. And I think we got the better end of the deal, don't you?"

Wexler snapped the folder shut. "I know who needs to see this."

"You can't tell them where you got it."

"I won't. They won't care. And," Wexler continued, her voice now grim, "it's going outside of the usual channels. It's going straight to the man who ought to have seen it first."

CVIC
0700 local (GMT-9)

Lab Rat ran his fingers over the folder again, feeling the rough surface of the coarse brown paper. It was an ordinary file folder, of the sort used in every part of the Navy for every conceivable purpose. Nothing at all to distinguish this one from those that contained everything from personnel transfers to plans for World War III.

Except there was something special about this particular folder. For the man who would eventually see it, it would be devastating.

But now Lab Rat had to find a way to approach the subject. It couldn't be gone into in front of everyone, no. That wouldn't be fair.

Tombstone strode into CVIC as though he were still in command of the battle group. It was as though he'd never left. How many times had Lab Rat seen him come in this way, wearing the same flight suit, or even occasionally khakis or a dress uniform?

Except for this. The informality. Even if we can't believe he's retired, he knows it. Tombstone stuck out his hand and said, "Lab Rat, good to see you again."

Lab Rat winced at the nickname. Of course he knew that's what everyone called him. It was even on his flight how much.

"I'm well, sir," he replied, silently swearing at himself for using such a formal tone of voice. Why couldn't he relax around Tombstone like everyone else? "And you?"

Tombstone shrugged his shoulders, his gun metal gray stare elsewhere. "Okay, I guess. You know what's up with all this?"

Lab Rat nodded. "Yes, sir. There are some changes in the composition of forces that you ought to know about." He extracted the first photograph from the folder and passed it to Tombstone. The former admiral glanced at it, then gave it to Jeremy Greene. Lab Rat fought to keep a look of concern off his face.

Tombstone keeps saying he's going to let the kid fly more missions, but he never does. I wonder if I ought to point that out to him. It's not really my place, but I don't know how many other people notice how unhappy the kid is. He's not a RIO and Tombstone should treat him like he is.

"So what are these?" Greene asked, his curiosity getting the better of his mood. "It looks like a landing craft."

"That's exactly what it is," Lab Rat said. "The latest and greatest in Russian landing craft. They're built like hydrofoils, but these guys have ours beat six ways to Sunday. Larger carrying capacity, more power, better sea-keeping ability. There's a retractable keel that stabilizes them up to sea state five. They're completely enclosed and carry a lot more firepower—they're armed, not just transports."

"That wouldn't be hard to do," Tombstone observed. "That's long been a problem with our landing forces."

Of course he knows about them. He had to when he commanded the battle group. Sure, the Marines had primary responsibility for the landing force, but he was in overall command until they made it to the beach. Aloud, he continued, "They've been developing these for use in the Black Sea and other littoral areas. A variant of these is used in commercial transport all over their waterways. They've got a lot of experience with them in the depot-level spare parts supply chain. It's not surprising that we're seeing them deployed in open ocean."

Green tossed the photo back on the table. "Sea state five is pretty impressive."

Lab Rat nodded. "And look at this." He turned the picture

so it was right side up to the two men. "Quad canisters. This may be a version of an anti-ship and anti-air missile they're testing. It's like a Stinger, we think. Range, probably ten miles. A rudimentary guidance system, and maybe—just maybe—a seeker head in the missile itself. Primary purpose self-defense but that covers a lot of offensive operations as well."

"Ten miles doesn't buy you much," Tombstone said.

"It might when I tell you the rest of it," Lab Rat countered. "Intelligence shows that the top speed of these babies is around sixty knots. *In sea state four.*" He saw the look of surprise cross both men's faces. "And they're maneuverable at that speed, sir. Yes, you can target them from further out, but don't count on them being where your missiles think they are by the time the missile gets there. Plus they carry countermeasures—lots of them. Small, tight electronics packages, and you know how small those are these days, along with the normal chaff and flares."

Tombstone glanced at Greene. The Tomcat they'd flown out to the carrier was equipped with the latest in spoofing gear as well. It could not only deceive incoming missiles and aircraft, but it could also project additional images to trick the radar into thinking there were twenty aircraft there instead of one. By manipulating the incoming radar signals, he could even give the impression that the twenty aircraft were maneuvering independently. Flying in a precision formation was an immediate dead giveaway.

Worst case, the additional images would make targeting difficult. And best case, the enemy would believe he faced a lot larger force.

"If they can do that, what else can they do?" Tombstone asked.

"That's what worries us. We don't know." Lab Rat extracted the next set of photographs and spread them out on the table in front of him. "The rest of it should be familiar territory. The Russian amphibious transport is the newest hull of its class. Packed with electronics, capable handling vertical takeoff fighters and helos. They've made some progress on deploying traditional catapults, but the word is that they're still pretty unreliable."

"Wonder why it's taking them so long to get ahead on that," Tombstone mused. "They've seen enough of our ships that they should have a good idea how it works."

"It's part of their mind-set," Lab Rat said. "Despite their power as a blue water navy, the Russians have always thought like brown water sailors. Coastal defense, supported by land-based aircraft. Amphibious forces—now, that's right up their alley. But a truly moderate floating aircraft fortress like ours? They can do it, technologically. But they don't have the fire in the belly for it the way we do."

Tombstone studied the last photo, worry evident on his face. "This part seems pretty routine, but those landing craft worry me now. We're going to have to get close enough in to use the guns on them."

"That's the recommendation from Top Gun," Lab Rat said.

"Okay, then." Tombstone yawned. "I'm going to go find my stateroom and rack out for a while. Jeremy, let's meet back here after evening chow, okay?"

As the two men started to leave, Lab Rat said, "Admiral? I wonder if I could speak to you privately for a moment?" He held his breath, hoping Greene would not cop an attitude. But the younger pilot simply flipped a hand at them. "You guys go ahead and catch up on the gossip. Me, I'm getting some sleep."

Tombstone turned back to face him. "So, what's up?" Clearly, the last thing the pilot wanted to do was sit down and talk.

"In my office, Admiral. Please."

Tombstone drew back slightly at Lab Rat's tone of voice, firm and professional. There was a spark of interest in his eyes, and some of the weariness seemed to drop away. "Like that, huh? Okay, you're on. Surprise me."

He just had to say that. Lab Rat led the way back to his office.

"Sit down, Admiral." Again, that odd tone of voice seemed to come out of him automatically. Now Tombstone's curiosity was definitely aroused.

"Spit it out, Commander." The shift to formal titles indicated that Tombstone understood this was not a routine matter. And yet Tombstone was no longer an admiral. He was a civilian and Lab Rat was the senior officer present. Some said that admirals never gave up their rank when they retired—with Tombstone, his command presence permeated every atom of his being. Try as he might, he would never be anything other than what he was.

"Sir, I have some news." Lab Rat groped for words for a moment then extracted a photograph and passed it to Tombstone. It had been digitally enhanced, and one corner held a blowup of a small section of the overall photo. Tombstone took it, smiling slightly, and then stared. The color drained from his face. For a moment, Lab Rat thought he would faint.

"When?" Tombstone asked, his voice hard and quiet. "When and where?"

"Yesterday morning," Lab Rat said gently. "And yes, that is the amphibious transport twenty miles off our beam."

Tombstone stared at the photo, his mouth working silently as he tried to force the words out through his throat. Finally, he simply looked up at Lab Rat with that cold, impassive face that had earned him his nickname.

"Yes, sir," Lab Rat said, answering the question he knew Tombstone wanted to ask. "We're certain. It's her."

Tombstone dropped his gaze down to the photo and held the picture with trembling fingers. "Tomboy," he said, his voice unbelievably steady. "You're alive."

Just then, the door opened. Pamela Drake, escorted by Chief Abbyssian, walked in. She held out a sheaf of papers with sketches on them, then a roll of film. "I think you're going to want to see this."

EIGHTEEN

Drake looked at the hastily constructed mock-up. Where the Russian laser had been all sleek lines and gleaming metal, this training model was composed of cardboard and tinfoil. It was a caricature of the deadly system she had seen.

"Over here," Lab Rat said, tapping on one end, "is the emitter. The crystal on the other end collects the light, focuses it into a coherent beam, and shoots it out. Everything else is just alignment and targeting. It's actually pretty simple."

"It's actually pretty ugly," Pamela observed.

Don't let my chief hear you say that. He'd be heartbroken." Lab Rat shot her one of his rare grins, and she was surprised to see how it transformed his face.

Commander Busby had been one of the most underestimated officers on board *Jefferson*. Physically, he was unimpressive, and his slight build encouraged people to dismiss him. But as she had learned in the past, there was nothing small about the intellect housed in that unimpressive body.

Perhaps to compensate for his physical shortcomings, Commander Busby had always adopted a stern, cool manner with her. Even after she had tumbled to the fact that he was deserving of a good deal of respect, she had never managed to penetrate his reserve. Long after the others had forgiven her for her conduct, Lab Rat remembered.

She studied him with renewed respect. *He holds a grudge, does he? But what about? I haven't offended him in particular, have I? No, no more than anyone else. Maybe it's because we're both in the same business—gathering information and getting it to the people who need it. But in my case, the people who need it are just average citizens. I wonder if you resent that, that your very best work will never be seen by anyone other than high-ranking officials and military personnel?*

"As you can see," Lab Rat continued, apparently oblivious to her scrutiny—but not, she suspected, as oblivious as he would like her to think—"getting the crystal out will be fairly easy. Once you have access and a little time, it should be a piece of cake." He shot her a sharp look, as though confirming that she understood these two qualifications.

"Access shouldn't be a problem," she said. "Based on what they showed me last time, I was right up next to it. It's the opportunity I'm worried about. I'm not sure about putting my cameraman in this position."

"We could substitute one of our people," Lab Rat offered.

She shook her head. "No, we've been over that again and again. Even if I can get one of your stiffs to relax enough to look like a civilian, the haircut would give him away immediately. They've seen my cameraman—they know what he looks like. And there's no way any of you could ever pass for him."

Her cameraman spoke up then, an annoyed tone in his voice. "What am I, chopped liver? I already told you I would do it, didn't I?"

Lab Rat turned his cool, analytical gaze on the cameraman. He studied him for a moment, his face expressionless. "Yes, my apologies. You did say you would do it, and I have no reason to doubt your capabilities. God knows you've probably been shot at more times than I have."

The cameraman seemed slightly taken back. "A few

times," he muttered, obviously a bit embarrassed. "It's a challenge, you know."

"I know." Lab Rat studied him for a moment longer, then turned back to Drake. "He'll be fine."

And just what does he see in my cameraman? What is it that I haven't noticed? If I had to, I'd say he's a good guy. We've been in some rough situations, and he's never backed down, but I wouldn't have thought he was the type to volunteer for something like this. Not as much trouble as I have getting him up in the morning.

The cameraman was shifting uncomfortably now. He evidently sensed the question in Drake's stare. He muttered a few words, then stopped.

"What was that?" she asked.

He sighed, now aggravated. "I know what you think of me. Especially after that stunt Winston pulled. I shouldn't have let her do it. I should have come to get you. But it was just like—I don't know, you're always ordering me around and acting like I don't exist sometimes."

Suddenly, with blinding clarity, Drake understood. She had treated him like a piece of equipment, like furniture to be moved around to suit her taste. All those times when he had captured pictures at some personal risk to himself, when he came back with the story against all odds—she hadn't really thought of him as part of the team, had she? He was just like—well, invisible.

He could have spoken up, one part of her mind argued. *Told me off sometime.*

No, he couldn't. Nobody does that to Pamela Drake. Not and gets away with it. What would you have done if he had objected? You would have shit-canned him and got another cameraman, wouldn't you?

Maybe. Or maybe not. I like to think I know a professional when I see one.

Then start treating him like one.

"I'm sorry," she said simply. It wasn't enough, not by a long shot. But for now it would have to do. She would find a way to make it up to him when they got back.

He was staring at the tile, scuffing his toe, looking for all the world like a ten-year-old caught with his hand in the cookie jar. "Doesn't matter. I just want everybody to know I can do my part." Finally, he looked a bit better. "I'm an American, too, you know."

"Have you thought about how to manage it?" Lab Rat asked, neatly cutting off the therapy session unfolding in front him.

The cameraman nodded. "I know exactly how I'm going to do it."

"How?" Drake asked.

He shook his head, and grinned. "Can't tell you. If you know it's coming, you won't look surprised and that will spoil everything."

"But surely we should go over this," Lab Rat said, tension creeping into his voice. "Two minds are better than one, you know."

"I know. And I'll tell you. But she," he said, indicating Drake, "has to stay out of it. That's the rule. If you tell her, I don't go through with it."

"Now, wait just a minute," Drake said hotly, her earlier regret for her conduct swept away in her impatience. "I'm not going unless I know what you're going to do."

Lab Rat held up one hand to cut the argument off. "Do you trust my judgment?"

She studied him for a moment, then nodded reluctantly. "Okay, then. He's going to tell me and I'll decide if it'll work. Then I will give you a go or no go. That'll have to be good enough," he finished.

Damn! They're double-teaming me. She gritted her teeth and glared at the two of them. "Okay. But when we get back—"

"If we get back," her cameraman corrected, "then I'll owe you an apology."

"Okay, okay," Lab Rat said. "If we can break up the mutual apology club here, we need to go over this again. Drake, it's going to take some neat sleight of hand to pull this off. You," he continued, pointing at the cameraman, "watch, to make sure you can buy us enough time for this. Now, do it again."

Again Drake practiced the motion of slipping back the housing, slipping her hand in, and quickly swapping the crys-

tal for the fake in her hand. She did it again and again, every
movement critiqued and analyzed by Lab Rat and her cameraman, until they were convinced she had it. By the time
they were finished, the muscles in her arm were trembling
with exhaustion.

"That will have to do it," Lab Rat said finally. He didn't
sound entirely satisfied, more resigned than anything. "Okay,
get a good night's sleep. Come back here before your helo
leaves and pick up the substitute. I'll be standing there when
you get back to take the real thing off your hands." He turned
away from them, dismissing them.

On the way back to her stateroom, Pamela couldn't help
thinking about her cameraman's choice of word. If. *He said
if we get back. What does he know that I don't?*

The cameraman stayed behind to explain his plan to Lab
Rat.

Admiral Kurashov
1500 local (GMT-9)

This time, as they approached the Russian ship, it looked
ominous. Perhaps it had been the company of the other news
helicopters waiting for their turn to land. Perhaps it had been
the warm welcome, or her anger against the Americans, that
had obscured the real situation. Now, flying in toward what
she had come to think of as the enemy, with her Trojan horse
in her pocket, Drake shivered.

The deck looked oddly silent. Perhaps the difference in
circumstances, but she wasn't so sure. The sailors looked
more—well—military, the uniforms more severe, their ex-
pressions more forbidding. The aircraft and helicopters were
lined up and tied down with a precision that bordered on
obsessive.

In the center of the deck stood a lone plane captain, his
hands held above his head. Everyone else was well away
from the center, clustered around the edges.

"I don't see our welcoming committee," the pilot said, his
voice betraying uneasiness. "You sure we're expected?"

"Absolutely." Drake tried to inject a note of confidence into her voice. "We're getting an exclusive on this one."

"Yes, well. In my line of business, an exclusive isn't always such a good deal," the pilot said. Drake saw him glance over at his co-pilot, and they exchanged a nod. "If it's all the same with you, we'll stay with our aircraft."

"You mean our getaway car?" Drake answered.

"Yeah. Maybe." The pilot fell silent except for some muttered self-encouragement as he approached the deck. He concentrated on his landing and brought them down as gently as he had before. As he opened his shutdown checklist, he turned back to look at her. Penetrating blue eyes stared out at her from under the decorated flight helmet. "You should know we don't fly suicide missions unless we're volunteers."

"Who said anything about a suicide mission?" she snapped. Beside her, the cameraman grunted.

"We never fly a mission that's not briefed. I mean *completely* briefed. Especially Intell. You get my drift?" His mouth hardened into a thin line.

So Lab Rat told him. That figures. It comes right down to it, that's the way they do it.

Drake wilted slightly under his glare. "I got it. And thanks."

He shook his head, dismissing her gratitude. "We all do our part, lady. So get in there and get back out. I want a nice quiet ride home, you hear? No cops and robbers."

Drake forced a grin. "Got it. Back in thirty mikes."

His eyebrows shot up at her use of military slang. "Don't get carried away with it. Be safe. If things fall apart, abort the mission."

"I know, I know. Lab Rat gave me the same lecture." She gathered up her gear, unfastened her harness, and got up to leave. Unexpectedly, the pilot stuck out his hand. "Names Dixon. Mike Dixon." He shook her hand solidly, and then shook hands with the cameraman. "Now go on, get out of here. The sooner you start, the sooner you're back."

The helicopter was shut down, but just barely. Drake knew from prior experience that he could be turning and at rotation speed in a matter of moments. She waved a casual goodbye and turned to face her Russian escort.

The public information officer was waiting for them. Although his face was professionally pleasant, there was none of the warm friendliness that she'd seen before. Were they suspicious? Maybe. But if they knew her, they knew enough to know that she would go after any story anywhere anytime. She was hoping her reputation would help her pull this off.

"Welcome back, Miss Drake," the public information officer said. "We're flattered at your interest in our ship."

He's not cool with this. Ill at ease.

"Thank you. It's nice to be back," she said casually. "I appreciate your hospitality. Perhaps if we can go inside, I can fill you in on what's happened so far."

The two officers glanced at each other, then the public information officer nodded. Not for the first time, Drake wondered who he really was.

He led the way back into the ship, and via a different route, to what was obviously a senior officers' mess. "A bit more privacy here," he explained when he saw her glance around. "I suspect not everyone should hear what you have to say."

Drake nodded. "You may have noticed that my last report got a lot of attention. High-level, too. The military and the politicians are crawling all over my boss's back. And this whole thing about the lasers—well, I don't have to tell you it's a political hot potato."

"So I have heard," the information officer responded. "I imagine that at some level, politicians are all the same."

"You got that right. Anyway, like I said, it's caused a real stir. From what I can tell, there's a lot of people rethinking their position. This laser stuff—yes, it sounds fine. But not if it puts us in another Cold War arms race, you know? The people that are in power now, they remember that. It wasn't so long ago that we were practicing air raid drills and building bomb shelters. And nowadays, when you've got laser-guided missiles and such, everybody feels pretty defenseless. I think, with a little pushing, that this can all go away and we can get down to the business of disarmament."

"And what would be your interest in this matter, Miss Drake?" he asked. "Simply that it is news?"

Drake looked down, feigning embarrassment. "There's that, of course. As you probably know, I've been around for a while. I've seen a lot of the world, and a lot of what happens when nations go to war." She looked up, and forced a fierce gleam in her eyes. "You may laugh, but what I've seen makes me believe that disarmament must start now. And start with us. The world is too small anymore. There's no room for nuclear weapons, not now that we know what they can do. The ozone layer, the potential for fallout—just look at Chernobyl. You people know better than I do what happens when nuclear power goes wrong."

"And what happened to your journalistic neutrality?" he asked.

"Who can be neutral in something like this?" she shot back. "When there's a chance that I can do something that will help stop this madness? No," she said, shaking her head, "maybe at one time I was. But now, after everything I've seen—well, it has to stop. And if reporting the stories the way they really are helps that, then all the better."

"An admirable sentiment," he murmured politely, and Drake could see that he wanted to believe her. "My family lived north of Chernobyl. Any shift in the wind and they would have been seriously at risk. But what can we do for you now?"

"The main thing we're missing right now is a hammer," she said bluntly. "Half the people I talk to don't believe your laser can possibly work. The other half are spread out across the spectrum. I need to crush this insane American superiority complex, show them that we're not the only nation in the world that can build a system that works. I'd like to get another look at the laser, and this time take some pictures. Any technical data you can release—" She held up one hand to forestall comment. "I'm not asking for military secrets. But if there's anything I can show them to prove that your laser works as advertised, maybe they'll believe we're headed for another Cold War arms race. Please," she put a note of pleading in her voice, "can't we just stop this madness?"

For some reason, Rodney King's anguished and oft-parodied plea ran through her mind: Can't we all just get along?

The two officers looked uncertain now, as though they

believed her but were not entirely sure of what to say. Or what they *could* say. Finally, the public information officer spoke. "I'll have to confer with the admiral, of course. But there's great merit in your arguments. We, too, would like a peaceful world." He stood, and smoothed out his tunic as he did. "Please wait here. We can provide refreshments while I talk to the admiral."

Intell. He's got to be—and a lot more senior than he lets on.

"Some coffee?" her escort asked. "Or perhaps a sandwich?"

"Tea would be fine," Pamela murmured, remembering the last cup of coffee she had on board a Russian ship.

"A sandwich sounds great," her cameraman said enthusiastically. He let his bags slump onto the couch and came forward eagerly.

A few minutes stretched into half an hour. They were fed, given freshly brewed tea, and the escort made polite conversation. She shifted the talk away from her to his family. He had a wife and two boys. His mother lived with them. Like most officers, he was worried about providing for his family, but was fiercely proud of the work he did.

Finally, the PIO returned, with the admiral following him. He stepped aside and allowed the admiral to approach Pamela.

The admiral studied her from under his bushy eyebrows. He was of a different generation than the other two officers, one who remembered the glories of the Soviet Union and the uncertainties of the Cold War. Her proposal would be tempting to him, but he would be even more deeply suspicious of her then the younger officers. "We provide you data. And you may take pictures," he said abruptly. "Some information we cannot tell. Pictures, basic information—yes. Take it to your people, the ones who do not believe that Russia is capable of this. Show them that if they continue this madness, we will match everything they do."

Unable to resist, Drake asked, "Admiral, you have been remarkably candid with us. How do you view the American development of this weapon?"

He glared at her. "It is an act of aggression," he snapped.

"The United States seeks to disrupt the balance that has kept the world stable. Once her missile shield is in place, what is to prevent her from attacking us first?"

"There are those who would say the U.S. will never fire the first shot," Drake said.

The admiral snorted. "The United States has used nuclear weapons before. Japan, yes? Russia has never done this. Only the United States. And I will—"

The PIO stepped forward smoothly, catching the admiral's attention. "The admiral has given me explicit instructions on what you may and may not see, Miss Drake. We hope that it will be sufficient to contribute to your efforts for peace. If you would come this way."

Arrogant—so arrogant. You would never see an American officer cutting off an admiral that way. She glanced back at the older man, and saw him deflate, a balloon from which the air had been let out. *Just who is this guy anyway?*

"Thank you," she said, suddenly just a little bit sorry for the admiral. He was a warrior, a military man, yet this weasely little politician had him under his thumb. He had not gone to confer with the admiral—he'd gone to the admiral as an equal.

"This way," the PIO said. He led them down the same passageways as before—or, at least Pamela thought he did. Some of it looked familiar, but she knew all too well how easy it was to get lost in the passageways on a large ship. She glanced back at her cameraman and saw him nod slightly. He was keeping track of where they were going, too.

And does he have a plan for getting us out of here? What am I supposed to do, drop some bread crumbs along the way?

They arrived at a hatch that they'd seen before, or at least it looked like the same one. She glanced at the marking above it and was relieved to see the numbers matched what she remembered. This time, however, a radiation trefoil had been added to the door.

Seeing her glance at it, the PIO smiled grimly. "Nothing to worry about. If you like, I can get you a dosimeter."

"How much radiation is there?" she asked.

"It's about like being on the beach on a sunny day." He waited patiently for her to make up her mind. Finally, she nodded.

He clicked in the numbers on the cipher lock and shoved the door open. There was no one inside the compartment. He stepped aside to let Pamela and her cameraman go in first, then followed. He turned and secured the door behind them.

It was just as she remembered it, sleek and deadly. The bright blue crystal at one end was dull. Lab Rat had explained that when the laser was operated, the crystal would glow. If it were in operation, she wouldn't be able to touch it.

"We'll shoot video from all angles," she said. "That way, we can cut in whichever views we need. And then some stills, both with me and without me." She glanced over at her cameraman. "Want to shoot an intro in front of it?"

"Yes, of course," he said impatiently. "Be great if we could get the admiral in, too. You mind asking him?" asked the PIO.

The officer paled a bit. "I do not think that would be possible. And as for me, I would prefer not to be in any photographs. I really have nothing to do with it other than providing briefings for visitors such as you."

That confirms it. A PIO who doesn't want his picture in the paper. Either they're a lot more shy than their American counterparts, or he's got other reasons for not wanting his face in the limelight, and I'm betting on the latter.

But then again, Pamela, you're not exactly what you appear to be either, are you?

She nodded sympatheticly. "Cause problems with your mates, would it?"

"They might think I was being—well—self-promoting, I think." He gave her a chuckle that sounded remarkably genuine. "And I'm not really sure how my wife would react to it. We're out at sea for a couple of months, then she sees a picture of me with a—well—I do hope I won't offend, Miss Drake, but my wife has a wide jealous streak."

Good move. Flattering me, are you? But you're a bit too young for me, sonny.

"I understand. But think about the positive side of it.

You'd become known as someone who contributed to world peace, you know. It could stand in good stead if you ever have a political career after the navy. That wouldn't be entirely bad, both in your country and in mine."

If I get home. She was certain that he did not want anyone in the United States studying his picture. *Particularly not anyone who might be associated with the CIA. Or the State Department.*

"Very kind," he murmured. "But I think not."

"Let me get to it," her cameraman said. He hoisted his camera to his shoulder. A red light came on. He moved slowly around the laser, shooting from every angle. As she watched, she could see the lens refocus slightly as he picked up the consoles along the bulkhead on one pass, the laser on the next. He moved in a slow, surefooted way, the camera remarkably steady. Then he shot from above, and from below, carefully traversing the entire length of the laser. She noticed that the PIO found reasons to move around the compartment, evading the camera's eye.

"That'll do it for now," the cameraman said finally. "Stills now. Color and black and white, you think?"

"Yep. Let's get everything we can," she answered. She moved over to stand behind the laser column and let her hands rest easily on it. "This okay?"

He studied his light meter for a moment, the shook his head. "Won't do. Hold on, I'll fix it." He dipped into his bag and extracted a small, powerful strobe. He mounted it high on the bulkhead with some temporary double-sided tape, and then ran the cord to his other hand. "Ready."

She pasted a bright smile on her face, then held her arms out to give some perspective to the length of the laser. "Serious face now," he ordered. He was in charge at this moment, not her. Drake obligingly assumed a serious expression. A suspicion started to grow in her mind and she could feel it reflected in her face.

"Good, good—look down, now. Like you're studying it. The look you used in Cuba, you know. That made some good shots, really good. That time when you were outside worked best, I thought." He was chatting now, unusual for him since his normal mode of communication was grunted commands and terse orders. She didn't have to ask. Now she was certain.

She tensed, ready. "Okay, here we go," he said. She dropped her hand down low on the laser, ready to move.

He glanced back at the political officer and said, "Now!" Her fingers shot into her pocket and she grabbed the fake crystal. At that moment, the light mounted on the bulkhead flashed in blinding light, so bright it seemed to burn through her closed eyelids and scorch her skin.

Intent on watching her, the information officer let out a sharp yelp. He spat out a few words that had to be curses. Then the light flashed again, and again, the strobe bursts coming so close together that it seemed to be one continuous blast of light.

Drake moved quickly, her nimble fingers flying over the laser, popping the catch, extracting the crystal, and slipping the other one into its place. Metal against metal as it slid home, a grating noise. She coughed to cover the noise.

She need not have bothered. Moving quickly, her cameraman jammed a cloth over the information officer's face. He went down almost immediately, dead weight. The cameraman lowered him easily to the floor. Then, extracting a roll of duct tape from his pack, he quickly bound the other man hand and foot, then slapped a strip of tape across his mouth. He dragged him into a corner and propped him up against a wall.

Drake watched, stunned. She could not believe what she was seeing. Who was this commando that looked like her cameraman?

He glanced up at her. "You okay?" She nodded dumbly. "Then let's get moving. We'll lock the hatch behind us and head for the flight deck. You remember the way?"

"I think so."

"Between the two of us, we can find it. Now move!"

He detached the light from the bulkhead and slipped it into his bag, then led the way out of the compartment. He waited until she had left, then pulled the door shut and spun the lock dial. He tried it and saw that it was locked. "Act confident."

They strode down the passageway, acting as though they

had every right in the world to be wandering around a Russian warship unescorted. Pamela greeted the few sailors who met her gaze as they made their way back to a ladder they both remembered. They went up and emerged onto the flight deck.

As soon as they stepped into view, their helicopter's rotors started turning. They moved across the deck purposefully, not running, but not loitering either. With any luck at all, it would take the Russians a few moments to tumble to what was happening.

"Let's get the hell out of here," Drake said, fastening her harness. She was surprised to see her fingers starting to shake. "The faster, the better."

Pamela Drake was no stranger to fear, but this was entirely different. There was nothing she could do, nowhere to run. The helo's top speed wouldn't have kept a fighter aircraft airborne, and the pilot couldn't even use that, for fear of generating suspicion.

So she was obliged to sit in the back and say nothing, sweating inside the harness that held her in her seat, the crystal, in her hand, in her front pocket. The forced inactivity made everything worse.

"Seahawk One, Home Plate," a voice said over her headset. She was tuned into the tactical chatter on the net. "Condition red—Russian cruiser has activated targeting radar. Be advised that all indications are that they are about to launch on you."

"They're what?" the pilot shouted in disbelief. "They can't do that."

"That's what we told them, Seahawk. But they seem to believe that you have something in your possession that belongs to them. Understand, we're transmitting on an unsecure circuit so they can hear your response. Now is the time to come clean, Seahawk. Tell us what's going on so we can make arrangements to work this out."

"Pamela, what the hell?" the pilot said.

"What?" she snapped. "You think I have something to do with this?"

The pilot made no response.

"Seahawk, hit the deck," a voice snapped. She recognized it as that of Tombstone Magruder.

"Roger," the pilot said even as he shoved the collective forward and headed for the surface of the ocean.

"What's going on?" Pamela asked, fear making her regret her earlier denial.

"We've got a chance down here. Keep one hand on your harness release latch, the other on your seat. If you see the side door open, get the hell out of Dodge. You got that?"

"Jump out of the helicopter?"

"Unless you want to be a welcoming committee of one for a missile, yes," the pilot said dryly. "You may not have noticed but we're a little short on countermeasures or electronics. This is a commercial helicopter, lady—not a military one. And short of simply trying to get lost in the haze—which, I might add, is a zero probability event—discretion is the better part of valor. I'll keep us as low as I can, but you be ready to move."

Pamela stared at the ocean, which had seemed closer just moments before. Now it looked dangerously distant. How far was it, anyway? Fifty feet? Thirty feet? She had no idea. Her fingers were already moving over her harness, making sure she could get it off quickly.

"Seahawk, incoming!" the circuit shouted.

"Now!" The pilot shoved the collective forward, dropping them down until the skids seemed like they must be cutting through the waves. He slammed the hatch open. "Go now!"

The brief maneuver had taken them measurably closer to the water. Pamela bolted out of her seat, stepped forward, and, without bothering to consider what might wait for her below, jumped. She cleared the skids by two feet, and the fall seemed to take no time at all. She plunged into the ocean, the impact driving the breath out of her lungs, as did the cold current below the surface.

For a moment, there was peace. Bubbles drifted past her, and the silence underwater was pure and clean after the noise inside the helicopter.

Almost immediately, her lungs started to hurt. She kicked hard, grabbing water with cupped hands and forcing herself back up to the surface.

The emergency inflation ring—where was it? Her already chilled fingers reached down the lanyard and yanked. Immediately, the gas canister expanded the life jacket around her. That done, she looked around for the helicopter. It was far above her, continuing to ascend. As she watched, there was a flash of silver in the air, heading straight for the helicopter. Then the explosion—deafening at this range, orange and yellow flames shooting through black smoke, an immediate vaporization of the aircraft. She let out an involuntary scream, and resisted the impulse to dive back into the cool, deep silence of the sea.

"Pamela! Over here." She barely heard the pilot's voice over the noise of the explosion. He was swimming toward her, cutting clean, short strokes through the sea, dragging a package behind him. Ten feet to his right, the co-pilot executed a smooth breast stroke. Once they got to her, they hooked a line on their air vests through a loop on hers, securing the three of them together. Then the pilot activated the auto-inflation lanyard of the package he'd been towing. There was a sharp hissing sound, and the package unfolded immediately and began assuming the shape of a life raft.

"What happened?" Pamela asked. It was a stupid question—what had happened was obvious. But the pilot knew what she meant.

"Once you were clear, I hauled back on the collective so she'd gain altitude and jammed the throttle open. Then we bailed down. We weren't much higher than you were, but it was still a long way down."

Drake choked as a small wave slapped her in the face. "We had a raft?"

"Complete emergency survival gear is required by both the FAA and the Navy for flights over water. I never thought we'd use it, though."

"There they are," the co-pilot said, speaking for the first time. He pointed to the horizon. Three small black specks just barely above the surface of the ocean were heading for them. "That's our ride home."

"If they can get here," the pilot said. There was a sudden blast of noise from overhead and two Forgers streaked by.

"It looks like the Russians may have some thoughts about that."

"They wouldn't strafe us," Pamela said. "Tell me they wouldn't."

Neither man answered her. She knew a moment of despair, then looked back at the helos.

Surely the *Jefferson* wouldn't—no, they wouldn't. Overhead, she saw Tomcats and Hornets forming a protective bubble around the rescue helicopters. Whatever else was going on, the cavalry had arrived.

USS **Jefferson**
1600 local (GMT-9)

Lab Rat raced across the flight deck as soon as the rescue helo touched down. Before the rotors had even come to a complete halt, he was standing by her hatch, waiting, a look of anticipation on his face. For a moment, Pamela felt a flash of irritation. Clearly, he had no concern about their helo, about the Russian missile shot, or about her own condition after jumping out of the helo. All he could think about was the government in her pocket.

Drake fumed. The plane captain finally approached, tapped Lab Rat politely on the shoulder, and motioned for him to move away. Lab Rat moved back just far enough to give the plane captain access to the hatch. Then, undaunted, Lab Rat leaped into the small passenger compartment as soon as the hatch was open.

Without a word, he held out his hand. As she fished around in her pocket, a smile broke out on his face. Finally, she withdrew the crystal and placed it carefully in his hand.

"Thanks," he shouted as he leaped out of the helicopter. "You have no idea what this means. None at all."

Oh, yes, I do. It's my ticket back into the inner circle.

Later, after she had been checked out by medical, had a long, hot shower, and changed into fresh clothes, she felt the weariness hit. It came on so suddenly she staggered, then stretched out on her rack. Waves of blackness swarmed over her, forcing her eyes shut. She was already dreaming when she heard a rap on the door.

For a moment, she considered pretending she wasn't there. Or shouting at them to go away. But that seemed like so very much trouble. Before she could decide what to do, the doorknob turned and the door opened. Tombstone stood framed as a dark figure against the red lights out in the passageway.

"Can I come in?" he asked.

With a groan, she shoved herself up on an elbow. Thank god she was still fully dressed. "Sure, OK. I'm not promising I can stay awake, though."

He pulled the metal chair away from the drop-down desk, turned it backwards, and straddled it. He crossed his arms on the back and rested his chin on his hands. "It's official. You're no longer in purgatory. You did a good thing today, Pamela. A very good thing."

"Thanks. I could have done without the part about the missile, though."

"Oh, I think that will play out all right, too."

"What's that supposed to mean?" She was unable to suppress a jaw-cracking yawn.

"You'll see." Tombstone fell silent, and Drake couldn't summon up the energy to engage in polite conversation. She felt herself drifting off, even sitting. She heard Tombstone stand up, the chair scraping across the tile.

"I'll go now. I just wanted to pass on my thanks. I know you'll hear it from the rest of the Navy later on—maybe not so much in public, because a lot of this will still be classified. But we remember who our friends are. You know how that works."

Suddenly, everything was all right. Tombstone, the Navy, her career—everything was just fine. She smiled up at him, then said, "We'll talk later when I'm awake. And thanks for coming by. That means a lot to me." She was asleep before the door shut behind him.

NINETEEN

Coyote watched as the messages scrolled across the screen.
Almost immediately, the data from National Assets began
merging with the tactical picture in TFCC until the area on
the screen between *Jefferson* and the Russian cruiser was
crowded with the symbols. It was a sight he hadn't seen since
the days of the Cold War when U.S. forces routinely war
gamed the possibility of a massive first strike from Russia.

Around him, there were muttered explanations as the
younger officers tried to cope with what they were seeing. It
seemed inconceivable, but their military experience was focused primarily around smaller conflicts, ones that involved
regions in the Middle East or isolated islands. Oh, sure, they
knew about the Cold War and they'd contemplated the possibility of large-scale conflicts with China or Korea. But
those were distant, theoretical scenarios, ones that they had
never even considered might really happen. Even Korea was
considered merely a regional conflict. But this, though—this
was worldwide devastation in the making, destruction on a
scale they had never contemplated.

"Focus, people," Coyote shouted, breaking the uneasy

mood. "Our attacks—how long until we have everything we've got in the air?"

His question seemed to snap his TAO out of his stunned trance. "Five minutes, Admiral," he said, his voice still slightly distant as he stared at the screen. Then, with the shake, he was back in the game. "A little less." His voice sounded more confident. "There is one tanker in the air already and we'll launch another as soon as the fighters clear the deck. Two SAR helos are airborne with three more on alert five."

"What about Air Force tanker assets?" Coyote asked.

"The Air Force has rogered up, sir," the TAO said. "They'll have gas in the air and on station in four hours."

Four hours, Coyote thought. *Too long from now to make much of a difference, unless this fight goes a lot more rounds than I think it will. There's too much offensive and defensive weaponry in this part of the world, and I just can't see it taking that long. Still, it's nice that they offered.*

"Wait," the TAO said, listening to a voice in his headset. "Correction, Admiral—the Air Force has one KC-135 en route to our location now. He's escorted by Air Force fighters, but they'd like to know if we can take over his defense once he's in the area."

"No," Coyote said. "Ask them if their fighters can remain on station for a few hours. We can send them back then, but I need every fighter on the front lines right now."

"Aye-aye, sir," the TAO said. Coyote turned back to the screen.

The front lines—and just where were those anymore? With the extended range capabilities of every ship, as well as global positioning and targeting programs, there was simply no part of the world that wasn't potentially on the front lines.

Another wave of Backfires appeared in the air. It looked like this flight would pass to the north of them. And where were they headed? The mainland U.S.? Apparently so.

"If they stick to their normal way of doing business, sir," a quiet voice said from beside him, "we can expect missiles launched from land-based ballistic missile sites when the Backfires are approximately one hour off the coast. They like to hit with overwhelming force, wave after wave of offensive weapons. There's nothing surgical about the classic Russian attack."

Coyote turned to look at Lab Rat, who was standing just to his right. "I know. That's what they're going to do, isn't it?"

Lab Rat nodded. "I'd be willing to bet on it. Unless we can find a way of unraveling this mess, Admiral, we're going to see a full-scale war between Russia and the U.S. And, unless our analysts are way off base, it will go nuclear very quickly." Lab Rat looked at the admiral, his eyes bleak. "There's no reason not to, is there? If they don't destroy our theater ballistic missile facilities, then mutually assured destruction no longer make sense. They have to take them out and take them out now. Before they are fully operational, before we can destabilize relations."

"First things first," Coyote said once again. "Our short-term objective is to stay alive. After that, we can worry about the rest of the free world. Now, how operational are all our theater ballistic missile defenses?"

"It's a close call," Lab Rat said wearily. "Sometimes they seem to work perfectly. Other times, they don't."

"Make this one of the times they do," Coyote said firmly. He turned back to the screen.

USS **Jefferson**
Flight Deck
1810 local (GMT-9)

Tombstone and Jeremy Greene were third in line behind the catapult. As they waited their turn, surrounded by the furor on the flight deck, Tombstone contemplated the odds. So far, it didn't look promising. This might be the last time he would be on this flight deck. Even if *Jefferson* managed to survive, the odds of Tombstone and Jeremy themselves returning from what was about to happen were small.

On one channel, a soft, flat voice rattled off the composition of the incoming forces. So far, the Russian strike consisted of three waves of Backfires, each carrying the Sunburn missile. The Sunburn anti-surface missile had a range of well

over three hundred nautical miles, and current intelligence
said there were versions designed for land attack that were
capable of well over one-thousand-mile ranges. The Sunburn
was loaded with nuclear warheads. And that, well—it
changed everything, didn't it?

There was no doubt that the Russians were prepared to use
nuclear weapons preemptively, at least according to their
doctrine. There had been rumors of nuclear and chemical
weapons used in Chechnya, but no one had been able to
confirm that. Even in Afghanistan—yes, if the Russians had
nuclear warheads on those Backfires, they had already made
the decision to use them.

"It's not supposed to be like this," Jeremy said suddenly.
"These days—this is all supposed to be over." There was a
lost, forlorn tone to Jeremy's voice. He was part of the generation that had grown up believing that the possibility of
nuclear war was something that belonged in the past. Ra-
tional people didn't behave like that, not knowing what nuclear weapons would do to the rest of the world. They just
didn't.

"Steady, now," Tombstone said, his voice reassuring. "One
step at a time. Let's get this turkey off the deck then get in
position to do some damage. They're still out of range. This
may be just a feint."

"Maybe." Jeremy was not convinced. For that matter, neither was Tombstone.

"How many false targets can we generate?" Tombstone
asked.

"Around fifty—and at that level, we start to get some over-
lap. No more than thirty if you want to be really convincing."

"Then here's what we'll do. We fly north, head off from
the rest of the fighters. As soon as all the fighters are off the
deck and headed for the Backfires, I want you to go active
with the spoofing. I want the Russians to see forty or fifty
fighters heading north, looking like they're going to come in
behind them and ambush him. That ought to draw off some
of the fighters from the main thrust and even up the odds for
Jefferson's fighters."

"If it works," Jeremy said. "It's a gamble."

"It will work," Tombstone said confidently.

It has to work, doesn't it? Because that's the only way I conceived of that we have any chance. We're way outnumbered, and if those Backfires get within range of the U.S., then there's no stopping them. No one has enough sense to back off and take a real look at what's going on. Not their people, not ours. And if there's a strike on the continental U.S., then there will be no stopping it. Not ever.

TWENTY

Hornet 102
1900 local (GMT-9)

Thor's Hornet smashed through the thin clouds like his namesake's hammer. The clouds streamed over the canopy, blinding him for a moment like a shroud. Then, as he continued to ascend, they peeled off in sheets and then thin strands that disappeared as he rose above him.

"One zero two, on station." Thor announced his arrival at the position indicated for the Hornet sponge, and waited. Every ten seconds, another Hornet was rippling off the deck below him, and the air would soon be thick with the small, nimble fighters. A quick tank, topping off his fuel, and then they would form up their wing and head out to meet the Russians.

That the odds were heavily stacked in the Russians' favor didn't bother him. Hell, they were used to being outnumbered, weren't they? If it had been a fair fight, the Navy could have handled it on their own.

The waves of Russian fighters and bombers showed on his HUD as small red symbols. They were still some distance out from the carrier, far enough not to be a problem. Then even as he watched, they edged closer, covering the airspace

at what seemed to be a snail's pace but was just a reflection
of the expanded range of the screen.

"One zero three, on station." A flurry of tail numbers followed, each pilot confirming as he joined on the sponge.
Thor listened with only half his attention as he maneuvered
his Hornet up behind the Air Force tanker, intent on topping
up his tanks. Soon the others would be taking their turns,
slipping in smoothly for a top up before they re-formed.

Finally, they were done. "Devil dogs, on me. Make every
shot count," Thor ordered. He peeled away from the sponge
formation, and Hornets lined up in ascending altitude behind
him, forming a classic attack V. Each one was locked in
place as though held there by an invisible ruler, the formation's impeccable precision a reflection of their skills. That
wouldn't last long.

"Okay, listen up," Thor ordered. "No plan survives first
contact with the enemy. Except this one. On my order, call
your target, break off, and take some Russians out. Simple
enough. You get low on fuel or Winchester, talk to the
Hawkeye and get a vector clear. Other than that, stay on them
until they're gone. By the time we leave, I want to see nice,
sweet clear blue sky with nothing in it but Hornets and Tomcats. Any questions?"

A chorus of yells and cheers, punctuated by the traditional
Ooooraaaah! answered him. The boys and girls were fired
up, the blood lust running hot in their veins, and just for a
moment, Thor pitied the Russians.

Tomcat 101
1905 local (GMT-9)

After the normal, heart-stopping moment when the Tomcat
seemed to hang in the air just forward of the carrier, they
were airborne. Tombstone poured the power on, ascending
rapidly, and headed for the Tomcat sponge. Fifteen Tomcats
were already there, with eleven more expected. But their
plans for the engagement weren't Tombstone's, and he intended to do all he could to even the odds. Tombstone headed
north.

"One zero one, interrogative your intentions," a puzzled voice said from the Hawkeye. "We seem to have a processing malfunction of some sort. I hold *two of you* airborne."

Tombstone cut him off by squelching the radio signal. "Roger, Hawkeye, I know what you're seeing. Guys, there's no reason for concern. Just keep track of us and our flight." Tombstone hoped desperately the Hawkeye understood what he was getting at. The communications circuits were supposedly secure, but the last thing he needed was some Russian with the daily codes who had enough smarts to figure out that everyone was seeing a damn sight more aircraft in the air than had actually launched. "We will *all* see you on the way back. How copy?"

There was a long silence on the net, and a few questions from the other fighters, which were quickly squelched by the flight leader. Some of them had tumbled to what was up and were making sure their slower shipmates did not queer the deal. Tombstone could imagine the discussion going on inside the Hawkeye, as forty aircraft appeared to be spaced evenly around what they had seen was one contact launching. But the Hawkeye's mission commanders were smart folks, and they would figure it out pretty quickly.

That was a bitch, wasn't it, he thought as he waited for the Hawkeye's response. You could no longer count on secure circuits being secure, not after Walker's treason had rocked the entire security establishment to its roots.

"Roger, one zero one. Understand your intentions for your flight. Good timing, Stony." The Hawkeye's voice was decidedly nonchalant, signaling that the mission commander had the picture now.

Good man. Quick on the uptake—hasn't said anything that would blow it.

"Roger, Hawkeye. Break, Stone flight, Stone leader. On me as lead." Tombstone immediately put his Tomcat into a hard turn to the north, easing out of it slowly as though giving the rest of his flight time to form up. All around him, the other Tomcats were watching, now well aware that what looked like forty aircraft on their radar was a single airframe.

"We have to stay out of visual range," Tombstone said to Jeremy. "If they get a visual honest, the game is up."

"Already on it," Jeremy said, his voice slightly ruffled. "There." With a click, he sent a copy of his recommended flight plan to Tombstone's HUD. "That should keep us well out of visual range and give us room to go buster if we have to get away from them."

"Looks good." Tombstone refrained from saying that his backseater was turning out to be a hell of a RIO. He knew quite well that Jeremy would not have taken it as a compliment. "I figure if we can draw them off at least one hundred and fifty miles to the north, the cruiser and the rest of the airwing can do some serious damage."

"Yeah, that should work," Jeremy said, his voice entirely neutral.

The entire point of the plan was to pull enough fighters out of the main formation to even the odds. But what neither one said, although both were thinking it, was that if the Russian Backfires caught up to them, they would have more problems than just blowing the deception. Because then the odds would be forty to one, and even Tombstone wasn't so sure he could handle those.

Tombstone caught a glint of sunlight on metal to the east. With a sinking heart, he realized that the game was up. If they could see the Backfires, then the Backfires could see them and they could see that instead of forty Tomcats crowded into this airspace, there was only one.

The high-pitched *deedle* of the ECM alert was coming faster now, more insistent. Then a second beat started, sounding counterpoint to the first. Then a third.

"Here come the players," Jeremy shouted.

"No, wait!" Tombstone ordered. "They're too far away— we don't have enough countermeasures to deal with them all. We'll have to wait until they all get closer, count on one massive clump of flares and chaff for all of them."

"Two more," Jeremy answered, his voice showing the first hint of fear. "Tombstone, that's five—no, six missiles inbound!"

Too many. There's no way we can take them on, even if there was a way to put enough chaff and flares in the air. Punch out now? We might have a shot at making it out.

Tombstone put the Tomcat nose over, heading for the ejection envelope. They were too high to survive punching out. As he descended, his thoughts raced. *Shit. Forty on one— what was I thinking? Yes, it worked. That's my only consolation.* Over tactical, he could hear the main body of Tomcats howling out in victory as their AMRAAMs dealt with the remaining fighters and then the bombers. The ones that survived were forced inside the cruiser's missile engagement zone and the cruiser made short work of them.

We did what we came to do. And that's the point, isn't it? You lose people all the time in this business. You get used to making the calls for the greater good.

But somehow, as many times as he had made this decision about aircraft and other crews, it was of no consolation when it was his own head on the block.

Tomboy. His thoughts lingered on her, a hard yearning flooding his body. How had he survived so long without her? Was that really her in the intell photos or was he just deceiving himself. And what would be the odds that he could go on without her? If she were truly gone, then there was precious little to hold him here, was there?

"We're in command eject," Jeremy said precisely, his voice now under control. "On your order, sir."

Sir. That's who I am when the chips are down. Not his buddy, not his friend—I'm "sir." None of us are ever really willing to die for the greater good, no matter what we tell ourselves. But we do it anyway, because of who we are. Jeremy is still young enough that he believes he's immortal. Oh, he knows he's not—but he doesn't believe he can die here and now.

He won't. I won't let it happen.

A fierce determination swept through him, a deadly fighting rage. He might be willing to eject and take his chances, looking forward to a reunion with Tomboy, but he wasn't willing for Jeremy to do the same. He was a youngster, still with his whole life ahead of him. They were going to make it out of this.

A plan occurred to him, one so ludicrous and dangerous that he immediately dismissed it. But the thought wouldn't go away, and all at once he could see how it might work. No, no guarantees—but it was their only chance.

"Hang on, Jeremy," Tombstone shouted, fury in his voice. "We're going to even the odds." Tombstone yanked back hard to put the Tomcat into a steep climb. He pitched her over slightly to the right, heading directly for the center of the Russian fighters.

"Mother of god," Jeremy breathed, as if to speak any louder would call the Forgers down on them. "Sharks—it's like swimming into a school of sharks."

"Heat seekers only, and guns," Tombstone snapped, too busy concentrating on flying to worry about the weapons. This would have to be Jeremy's show completely. Now that he knew what Tombstone had in mind, Tombstone had no doubt the Jeremy could finish the job.

All around them, the air was thick with Forgers. In aeronautical terms, with the aircraft maneuvering at around Mach 1, they were in each other's laps. There was no margin of error, no chance to recover from a mistake.

Already, the results of Tombstone's maneuver were having an effect. The AMRAAMs stayed locked on him, following him into the flight of Forgers. Tombstone punched up straight through them, his wing tips almost grazing them, then broke and came down behind them, temporarily shielding his aircraft from the missiles' radars by interposing the Forgers' fuselages.

The Russian anti-air missiles were fairly sophisticated, on par with the AMRAAM. But on final, their tiny radar control mechanisms locked onto his friends, they were unable to distinguish between Tombstone's Tomcat and the Forgers. Those few that did stayed locked on Tombstone considered transferring their intentions to the Forgers but were simply going too fast to make the turn. As nimble as they were, they were not as responsive as an aircraft.

"Two down!" Jeremy shouted, his voice starting to show hope. "It worked."

So far, so good. But we're not out of the woods yet.

As he swept back and behind the Forgers, Tombstone stabbed a quick burst from his gun, stitching a line across the vertical stabilizer of one Forger. For a moment, it seemed to have no effect, then fire and smoke billowed from the tail. *Probably nailed the hydraulic line.* The aircraft shuddered in the air and quickly dropped back, weaving across sky as though drunk.

"Fox one," Jeremy said, and Tomcat shivered as the heat seekers leaped off the wing. "Any second now, they're going to figure this out."

Tombstone could imagine what was going on in the other pilots' minds. They'd wasted precious minutes all trying to fire at once, crossing each other's fields of fire and turning their weapons on each other. He took advantage of their confusion to compound their problems, weaving around them, piercing the center of the formation several times and taking shots from his guns and with Jeremy's heat seekers when possible. In short order, ten Forgers were either seriously damaged and out of commission or destroyed.

"They've got it," Tombstone said. Sixteen of the remaining Forgers were withdrawing, taking the risk of exposing their tailpipes to him as they rapidly left the area. He took advantage of the negligence to pop off a couple more short bursts from his nose gun, and was rewarded with two more kills.

But the remaining four Forgers were a problem. Two on one—that was something they all knew how to do. The confusion factor was eliminated by removing the other aircraft from the area. Now that they knew of his ruse, they would no doubt turn south to provide reinforcement to the rapidly decimated flight under attack by the main body of Tomcats.

"We have problems," Jeremy announced. "Two chaff, two flares left."

"Roger," Tombstone said briskly. "I think it's time to get the hell out of Dodge." He toggled off their remaining AAM-RAAM, targeting the lead aircraft, then slammed the throttles into full afterburner. He dropped the nose down, letting gravity add to the aircraft's acceleration. Altitude was safety, but sometimes distance was even better.

"They're on us," Jeremy said. "Two high, two low."

"I know, I know," Tombstone said, his mind searching desperately for a way out. If he continued descending, he'd fall into perfect firing position for the two lower fighters. The higher two already had him targeted, and, secure in the knowledge that he could not escape, they were waiting for the perfect shot.

Suddenly, a voice came in over tactical. "One zero one, on my mark, break hard left and descend to five hundred feet, then clear the area for missile engagement, Stony."

"The cruiser," Jeremy shouted, joy in this voice.

"Five hundred feet, my ass," Tombstone said. "And how the hell am I suppose to manage that?"

"Quit whining and do it," Jeremy ordered, then sucked in a sharp breath as though surprised at his temerity. Tombstone cracked a grin.

Tombstone broke hard left, putting the Tomcat into a steep vertical dive. He waited for the precise moment, watching the geometry in this mind, then popped off the remaining flares and chaff. That was it. They were now out of countermeasures and weapons.

As he rocketed past, the two lower Forgers wheeled in concert to follow him. Just as they changed their angle of attack, they ran into the flares directly in their paths. Jeremy squirmed around to watch behind them and saw one Forger take a hit to the engine, followed shortly by an explosion as the turbine blades exploded off the rotor.

"One down," Jeremy said. "Now the last one—"

But the last Forger was proving tougher than his wingman. He maneuvered nimbly to avoid the cloud of chaff and flares, then continued descending, circling slightly to decrease his actual descent and remain in firing position behind the Tomcat. Once clear of the countermeasures, he would shoot, of that Tombstone was certain.

"Spoofing," Tombstone ordered. "One last time, Jeremy. And make it work."

"Roger." A second later, a flurry of contacts popped up around Tombstone on the screen. Invisible to normal eyes, but to the radar on the other aircraft, it must have seemed that the air was as cluttered as it had been earlier.

That took care of the radar seekers. But the heat seekers are still a problem. Without the flares, there are only a couple of decent heat sources, and that's our engines.

Tombstone broke hard to the left again, pulling out of the descent. The Tomcat complained, howling her protest as the g-forces built, stressing the aircraft past every design factor. She wasn't built to take this hard of a turn at this speed, but she was doing her best to comply.

"Stay with me, Jeremy," Tombstone shouted, fighting off the g-forces himself. "Stay with me." The maneuver was intended to shield his tailpipes from the heat seekers that would be fired at any moment. Sure, the rest of the aircraft had heat sources as well, but nothing as attractive as the fiery glow of the tailpipes.

But he had to ease up on the turn. There was no point to it if it resulted in both pilots blacking out and the aircraft departing controlled flight. Fighting off the blackness that threatened to overwhelm him, Tombstone slowed the turn and pulled up.

On his HUD, he saw six new targets with long speed leaders. The cruiser's missiles, headed now for the altitude he had just vacated, seeking out the remaining Forgers. Guided by the cruiser's deadly accurate Aegis radar and precision fire control equipment, the missiles were far more accurate than anything fired by an aircraft. At the very least, they would put the Forgers on the run.

Tombstone's problem was more immediate. The remaining Forger on his tail was not deterred and, having overcome his panic at the missile launch, was waiting for them.

The Forger was a heavy aircraft, on par with the Tomcat. This would be a knife fight, up close and personal, a fight in the vertical rather than horizontal. Neither had the edge in maneuverability or speed. It would come down to the skill of pilot vs. pilot.

At least fourteen minutes, that was all. Because Tombstone was all too aware that somewhere not too far off sixteen of the Forger's playmates were probably on their way in now to replace the ones the Aegis had taken out.

You don't know it, buddy, but you're dead meat. We already kicked your ass, taking out a bunch of your friends. Now there's just you left, and then I'm going to get the hell out of here before the rest of the gang shows up. So you just orbit off there, feeling oh so confident. You've got about fifty seconds to live.

Tombstone kicked the Tomcat into a hard climb, maxing

out his afterburners. Behind him, he heard Jeremy groan, but there was no time to think about his RIO. Not if he was going to keep them both alive.

The Tomcat shuddered, every joint and weld protesting this treatment. She was built tough, rugged, but the punishment Tombstone had been inflicting on her exceeded every design characteristic. They were so far out of the envelope now that Tombstone wasn't entirely sure what would happen.

Tomboy would have known. She flew out-of-envelope missions all the time as a test pilot. She always said there was a larger margin of safety built in than they'd ever tell us, just to keep us from being reckless.

The vibration inside the cockpit increased, the lower harmonics settling into Tombstone's bones like an old ache. For a moment, he wasn't sure he could take it. And then that magic happened again, the moment when he fused with his aircraft and became one with the metal. No longer were flesh and metal fighting alone to stay intact and conscious—they were fighting together. He felt her steel wrap around his muscles, her electronics settle into his brain. He held her together by sheer willpower. Together, no longer man and aircraft but one being, they were stronger than their individual parts. Tombstone had the fleeting suspicion that even if he lost consciousness, his mind would continue to reside in her computer, his eyes looking out of her radar, his fingers flipping the fire control switches automatically.

And as he thought about these moments later, he was never sure he remained conscious at all. Perhaps the fusion was more real than he thought. He had told only one or two people about these moments of fusion he had within the aircraft, and, except for Coyote, he had been met with polite but disbelieving looks.

The Tomcat rocketed up directly toward the remaining Forgers. She fought against gravity, eking out a few additional knots of airspeed.

About him, the Forgers opened up their turns, increasing the angle between their aircraft and Tombstone's, hoping to nail the perfect tailpipe shot.

Any second now, they're going to fire. Something, anything—just to put me on the defensive. I can't let them do that. I've got one shot at this before their friends show up.

Tombstone dropped the aircraft's nose down, breaking away from the straight vertical ascent. His mind was working at lightning speed, computing the exact angle he would need to intercept the Forgers. The master caution on his panel flashed intermittently, as though the aircraft were reluctant to admit she couldn't take it any longer. He ignored it, pressing her harder, demanding more of her—of himself—than anyone had ever asked before. And she rose to the occasion.

Time seemed to slow, almost stop. Around him, the Forgers were moving at a snail's pace. Tombstone could imagine the confusion in the other pilots' minds. It made no sense for the Tomcat to be screaming directly for him, not at all. Three additional Forgers were on their way back to wrap up the conflict, and sixteen more remained behind that. Now the Tomcat's only hope of survival was trying to run and relying on Lady Luck. Maybe the Tomcat could somehow evade the missile shot that would surely be coming. It was a pure crapshoot, relying on luck, but both the Forger's pilot and Tombstone knew it was the only logical thing to do.

To hell with luck and logic. I don't like the odds.

Then the Forger made his fatal mistake. He had felt secure in his tactical position, waiting for backup, comforted by the fact that a lone Tomcat could not take on the remaining sixteen Forgers by itself. Not now, not now that they knew what was going on.

Yet against all odds, the Tomcat was coming for him. It made no sense—and the Forger's pilot panicked. He did the one thing that he should not do, the one thing that Tombstone had been hoping and praying for. He turned to run.

Tombstone toggled off the remaining heat seeker, then rolled his Tomcat out of the hard climb. New stresses ran through the airframe as bolts and welds fought forces they were never designed to withstand. A barrel roll help bleed off altitude more quickly and, hopefully, confused the firing solution that the other Forgers were undoubtedly computing.

Then Tombstone settled into level flight, still at max afterburner, and started hauling ass. He descended slightly, letting gravity add airspeed.

Behind him, he heard a low moan as Jeremy regained consciousness.

TWENTY-ONE

USS **Lake Champlain**
1930 local (GMT-9)

The captain stared at the screen, his anger building. He'd told the pilot to break left and run—why the hell hadn't he complied? Sure, he killed some aircraft, but look at the situation he was in now. Running for his life, with sixteen Forgers on his ass.

"Is there enough separation?" he asked his TAO. "It doesn't look like it."

"At best, its marginal," the TAO said promptly, his cursor circling the lone blue symbol in front of a pack of red ones. "At worst, well . . ."

"It's too close," the captain said, his frustration building. The separation had been sufficient earlier, when he'd told the pilot to break, but now the geometry wasn't going to work. If they took the shot, they were just as likely to take the Tomcat out as they were the other aircraft.

"It is. But it's the only chance he's got," the TAO said firmly. "Captain, you have to take the shot."

The Aegis system had already assigned missiles to each of the enemy aircraft. The missiles were ready, waiting only for the TAO to release them. If the captain had not been present, the TAO had authority to release them on his own.

But with the captain present, everything depended on him.

For a second, the captain wanted to jump on the TAO and smash him into small pieces for such insubordination. Then he looked at the screen again and saw that the TAO was exactly right. It was a chance they would have to take, and one that he would answer for later if they were mistaken.

"Weapons free, target all Russian aircraft," the captain said immediately. No more than a microsecond had elapsed between the TAO's comment and his decision, but he knew the TAO had seen what his first impulse was.

Even before he finished speaking, the TAO had mashed a button down, clicking it firmly past the detente and sending the missiles on their way. The cruiser shook as the missiles rippled off at two-second intervals, a string of pearls stretching out from the ship into the clear blue sky. The forecastle was enveloped in a cloud of noxious fumes, the exhaust from the propellant. For a moment, it completely obscured their vision, as though they had just plunged into a heavy fog bank. Then it cleared, the wind whipping it past the bridge. In that few seconds, the missiles had virtually disappeared, and now only the best eyes could make them out as slivers of white against blue.

Once cleared of the ship, their courses changed slightly, each one heading for a different aircraft. They were still under the control of the Aegis computer, which was updating the target position data and feeding it in a constant stream to the missiles. The new course corrections were made as they bore in on the Forgers.

"Tomcat 101, incoming," the captain said into the mike. "Suggest you make best speed to be clear of the area."

Tomcat 101
1941 local (GMT-9)

"Clear the area, right," Tombstone muttered. "Just what the hell does he think I'm doing?" He tipped the nose of the Tomcat down another five degrees, now channeling his will into the skin of the aircraft, willing the air to slip over her skin with no friction.

"What?" Jeremy said, announcing his return to the world of the living.

"We're running from the Forgers," Tombstone said rapidly, his attention on the HUD. "Cruiser's trying to help us out, but it's going to be close. Watch for the missiles, Jeremy—I'm a little busy up here."

The last traces of blackness drained out of Jeremy's brain. He put his face down against the hard plastic mask around the radar screen. His heart sank when he saw the geometry. Sixteen Forgers chasing one Tomcat, and a ripple of long speed leaders aimed at the center of the pack. The cruiser missiles—yes, if it worked, it would save their ass, but there was an equal chance that they would be on the receiving end of the cruiser's volley of missiles.

A loud *beep beep* filled the cockpit. Jeremy tore his gaze away from the radar screen long enough to glance at the forward instrument panel. The master caution light burned steadily, its incessant tone announcing that there were serious problems with the Tomcat.

"Engine temp, right engine," Tombstone said. Jeremy looked right and saw flames coming out of the engine.

"Fire," he said.

"Initiating right engine fire suppression system," Tombstone announced, his hand slipping over the instrument panel with an ease born of experience, while not taking his gaze off of the HUD. "Flame out, right engine."

On the radar screen, the Forgers were now gaining rapidly as the Tomcat's speed peeled away. Reduced to one engine, they had lost not only speed but maneuverability as well. Tombstone was using the vertical control surfaces to maintain level flight, but the Tomcat wanted badly to roll to the right.

"We got problems," Jeremy announced. "They're closing too fast, they're too close. The missiles won't be able to distinguish between us. Tombstone, we have to punch out."

"No," Tombstone said, his voice low. "Hold on." Without warning, he slammed the Tomcat into a vertical dive, heading straight for the surface of the water.

As she departed level flight, the Tomcat began spinning. One engine, too fast, uncontrolled movement—even Tombstone couldn't pull them out of this one, Jeremy thought despairingly. And they couldn't eject, not with the spin on, not at this angle. Sure, airspeed was increasing sufficiently to widen the distance between the Forgers and the Tomcat, but what good was that if they augered into the surface of the ocean?

"Tomcat one zero one, interception in five seconds—four—three—two—contact!" the cruiser's TAO said, his voice tight. "Request you evaluate visually the damage."

We're trying to get out of his way and he wants to know if his missiles hit. If he hadn't been so frightened, Jeremy would have laughed.

Suddenly, the Tomcat broke hard to the right and her spin decreased markedly. The force threw Jeremy hard against his ejection harness. Then the Tomcat slowly rolled out of her spin, airspeed peeling off rapidly.

What the hell? He checked the instrument panel and saw that Tombstone had dropped both the landing gear and popped the speed brakes, giving him more control surfaces and decreasing her airspeed in order to regain control of the aircraft. *At that speed? She shouldn't have survived deploying landing gear.* For a moment, Jeremy contemplated saying that out loud, then he decided to keep quiet.

"Cruiser, one zero one," he heard himself say, although he had not the slightest idea how he was even functioning, much less alive. "Confirmed three—now four kills," his voice continued, and he realized that while some part of him was screaming in fear, another part was scanning the sky looking for fireballs. He relaxed and let himself function on automatic. "Eight now. And the remaining Forgers are getting the hell out of Dodge."

USS **Lake Champlain**
1943 local (GMT-9)

On board the cruiser, a cheer rippled through CDC. Not only was the Aegis computer assigning kills based on its assessment of the radar picture and a missile/target intercept picture, but the pilot of the Tomcat had confirmed eight of them

as well. In the next few moments, four more missiles went
down, bringing the total to twelve.

"They're turning," the TAO shouted, his gaze locked on
the screen. In front him, the speed leaders attached to the
enemy aircraft had shifted and were now pointed away from
Tomcat 101. "They're turning back!"

"I don't think it's us they're worried about," the captain
said. "It looks like the cavalry has just arrived." On the
screen, twenty small blue blips were just edging into view,
the contingent of Tomcats and Hornets from the main attack
party.

Tomcat 101
1945 local (GMT-9)

Red lights were rippling across the instrument panel, indicating cascading damage. Their problems had only begun
with the right engine fire, flameout, and shutdown. The hydraulic systems and electronics were following suit. The
Tomcat had fought bravely, but in the end, she had done
more than she was designed to, and the results were becoming obvious.

Tombstone let it all wash over him. Just for a moment, he
was going to concentrate on flying. Before long, he would
have to make the decision of whether to stay with her and
try to land, or whether to abandon her. But not right this
second. She was still flying.

Behind him, Jeremy was frantically popping circuit break-
ers, routing essential systems through backups, securing
those that were most damaged. The hydraulic leaks were the
most dangerous problem as the fluid was highly flammable.
If it came in contact with the searing white-hot engines, then
they were done for.

"Tomcat one zero one, Home Plate. Interrogative your
status?" the carrier asked.

"Request green deck and priority in the stack," Tombstone
said calmly, aware that he'd made his decision in that split
second. "I am declaring an in-flight emergency. Right engine

flameout, loss of two hydraulic systems. Operating on redundancy now, but we can get back on board."

"Say state," the carrier demanded.

Tombstone glanced at the fuel gauge and groaned. "Not good," he admitted. "I have enough for one pass, that's it."

"Can you take on some fuel?" a new voice asked, and Tombstone recognized it as Coyote's.

"I don't think so. She's about as maneuverable as a blimp right now, and I'm not sure the fuel probe is even intact."

A pause, then Coyote said, "I'm not sure about getting you back on board, Stony."

"I can make it," Tombstone insisted. He could. He knew it so deep in his bones that there was no denying it. "But we have to come on board now, Coyote. Give me a green deck?"

"All right." Tombstone could hear the doubt in his friend's voice. He knew what Coyote was thinking—the same thing he would have been worried about not so long ago. If Tombstone made a less than optimal landing—*come on, say it, if you crash, let's not bother with euphemisms*—then the remaining Tomcats and Hornets were stuck airborne until the carrier cleared the crash off the deck. Sure, they could orbit and tank, but from what he could tell, the battle wasn't over yet. Sooner or later, aircraft would start running out of weapons, and that was something that couldn't be taken care of with a tanker. They would have to get back on deck, have to re-arm. And if Tombstone's aircraft was a flaming mass, recovery or launch would be impossible for some time. And there was always the chance that a crash would cause enough damage to the deck or the arresting gear or the catapults—not to mention the island—to prevent any flight operations at all.

Maybe we should just punch out and take our chances. Tombstone considered it, even going so far as to raise one hand and close it around the red-and-white striped ejection handle. He could feel the tension on the cables holding it in place, feel the rocket underneath his seat poised and ready to fire.

No. We've come this far—I'm taking her home. Carefully, he pulled her into a slow turn, balancing out the thrust from one engine with her control surfaces.

"One zero one, come right to heading one two zero," the Hawkeye said, taking over the problem of directing the injured Tomcat to the carrier. "Glad to see you've taken care of that multiple personality problem, sir. It was getting a bit confusing up here."

"You should see the other guys," Tombstone joked.

"We did."

The Tomcat was responding well for an aircraft flying on one engine, a bit sluggish but responsive. As long as he could take it slow and careful, they should make it.

"One zero one, call the ball," the tower's voice said.

"Ball, one zero one," Tombstone said, the Fresnel lens now in view. "On final, no needles."

"Roger, sir. You're looking good, looking good." The LSO's voice was calm and confident, intended to reassure an uncertain or nervous pilot. No matter that Tombstone had more time in a carrier's chow line than the LSO had in the cockpit, the LSO was still in charge of the approach. "Come left a bit, sir. You're looking good."

The Tomcat balked at any attempt at fine-tuning the descent. Finally, Tombstone arrived at a compromise of staying roughly on course, reserving his strength and last-minute corrections for attitude and altitude adjustments.

"Three wire," Tombstone announced, his gaze now focused on the deck. The carrier was looming large, a massive and inhospitable steel cliff.

"You're on," Jeremy said.

"Altitude, altitude," the LSO barked, his voice now sharp. "Sir, you're too low!"

The roiling air astern of the carrier was taking its toll, as was the speed he was losing.

Should he correct, and risk overshooting if the carrier's stern dropped back down as he came over her? He didn't have enough fuel for another try—if he missed this one, she was going in the drink.

But if he didn't correct, if the carrier stayed stern high, riding up on the wave, there was every chance he'd smash into her ramp like a bug against a windshield. Maybe a compromise—he watched the stern, gauged its movements, and made his decision. He held his attitude and course.

"Oh Jesus," he heard Jeremy moan behind him. Tombstone ignored it, concentrating on willing the aircraft down onto the deck.

"Stay with her," Tombstone shouted. If Jeremy panicked and punched out now, there was every chance that Coyote's worst nightmare would come true, with an out-of-control Tomcat tumbling flaming across the deck. The only way out now was straight through it, bringing her down on deck in one piece. "I've got her, I've got her!"

Then, suddenly, they were over the deck. Instants later, they slammed down, the nose wheel taking more of the impact than it should, the tail following it. Tombstone knew a brief moment of panic as he waited for the tail hook to catch. The seconds dragged on as he skidded across the deck, still bouncing, waiting for the tail hook to intercept a wire and slam them to a stop.

Finally, it happened. The forward motion stopped abruptly, jolting them against their harnesses. Tombstone immediately increased power, in case of a bolter. All that that would accomplish would be to get them clear of the ship before they punched out.

Seconds ticked by. Finally, the plane captain stepped slowly in front of them and made the signal to reduce power. The fire-fighting team was assembled just outside the flight deck proper, waiting, hoses at the ready to dispense foam if necessary. The giant crane and the yellow gear were also manned, ready to push the Tomcat over the side if she caught fire.

Tombstone eased back on the throttle, reducing power on the remaining engine. The engine speed slowed, then it coughed and quit. The plane captain regarded him with a puzzled expression for a moment, then signaled to the yellow gear. The tow truck raced across the deck and came to a smart halt in front of them. Within moments, the hitch had been affixed to the nose wheel strut and the Tomcat was towed away from the arresting gear.

"I believe you owe me a beer," Jeremy said, his voice almost completely normal. "Nailed the one wire, didn't you? And about your attitude—well, the whole landing left a lot to be desired."

Tombstone laughed out loud. He twisted around to stare back at the younger pilot, who was making such a valiant effort at terminal cool. "You're some piece of work, Jeremy," he said.

"Am I? Well, you just wait until the first time our positions are reversed and you have to sit in the backseat during a landing like that."

TWENTY-TWO

Hornet 102
1946 local (GMT-9)

The incoming Forgers were still well outside range of the carrier when the Hornet sponge was finally filled. Thor, the flight leader for Packer flight, and his wingman split off from the pack. "Packer flight, we'll take the right side," Thor announced. There had been some discussion while on deck about whether the bomber/fighter composite squadron would maintain its current formation or whether it would split into two independent squadrons, one heading for the mainland and the other dealing with the carrier. So far, it looked like the Russians were electing to deal with one problem at a time.

A chorus of clicks greeted Thor's command, acknowledging the order. Packer flight peeled off from the sponge, Thor and his new wingman, Marine Captain Jim "Beetle" Bailey, in the lead, the rest spaced out at equal intervals behind them. Thor shoved his Hornet into afterburner, intent on closing the Forgers before the Backfires could come within range. His flight followed suit.

"Packer flight, break," Thor ordered as they drew within combat range of the enemy fighters. The Hornet fighting pairs immediately broke off, selecting their targets under the direction of the E-2 Hawkeye and boring in for the kill.

"Fox three," Thor said, toggling off an AMRAAM. They were at max range, but a few missiles inbound might serve to shake up the incoming aircraft. At the very least, they would break them off from their flight plan if they took defensive action, and a good offense was always the best defense. If you just counted numbers, the Hornets were slightly outnumbered, but that didn't tell the whole story. The training, the armament, and everything else made the odds more than equal.

"Beetle, let's take the one high. On me," Thor said, selecting the first victim. One Forger was at a slightly greater altitude than the others, apparently cruising alone. He would be no match for two Hornets.

"Roger," Beetle agreed. Beetle settled in above and behind Thor in the classic fighting pair formation. As they headed for the solo Forger, the other Forgers apparently noticed. Suddenly, the air around them was lousy with fighters.

"We have a winner," Thor announced. "This must be the flight leader."

"Coming around behind," Beetle announced, although there was no real need for him to tell Thor. He and Thor had worked together so often that his intent was immediately obvious to his lead.

"Let's keep them honest," Thor said, and toggled off another AAMRAM. To his left, he saw three Forgers approaching rapidly, almost within weapons range. His ESM warning gear began beeping rapidly.

Their target Forger broke right, descended rapidly, then wheeled back around to come in behind Beetle. But Beetle had anticipated this, and used his advantage of being in a smaller and more maneuverable aircraft to gain altitude, wing over, and dive back in behind the Forger. The Forger was trying to keep Beetle on the defensive, evading prime target position while waiting for the cavalry to arrive, but it wasn't going to work. He scraped past Beetle inverted, undercarriage to undercarriage, then rolled out and started hauling ass. Thor slid high and above them, waiting for them. "Fox one!" The heat seeker leaped off his wing, spitting fire out the back, hungry for the warm tailpipes just in front of it.

"Got one on me," Beetle announced, his voice calm. "You see him?"

"No, I—yeah, I got him." A Forger had descended from on high to slip in behind Beetle, and was following every move Beetle made as though being towed by an invisible wire. Beetle flipped his Hornet into a hard turn, trying to cut such a tight circle that the Forger couldn't get inside. For a moment, it looked like it would work, then another Forger arrived on the scene, certain that Beetle was too distracted with his target to notice him arriving.

"Fox two," Thor said, slamming off another missile at the newest arrival. He banked back around, then descended to fall into position behind the Forger chasing Beetle. "Beetle, break hard right!" As Beetled complied, Thor spit out a short round of fire from his cannon. The depleted uranium bullets bit into the Forger's engine, shattering it immediately. Thor was already turning hard to avoid the shrapnel and was well clear of it when the Forger exploded into flames.

"New target," the Hawkeye announced, "on your right, six o'clock low." Thor and Beetle both saw the contact immediately and, staying in their fighting positions, headed down to intercept him.

"Why does he have to send *us* down?" Thor muttered, unhappy with the choice. Sure, the Hornet was better able to handle changes in altitude, since it had a far higher power-to-wing ratio than the Tomcats did. The classic game for this situation, Hornet versus a heavier aircraft, was to force the fight into the vertical, taking advantage of the Hornet's greater maneuverability to entice the heavier aircraft into a mistake. It was different with a Tomcat, given its powerful engines, but all reports said the Forger didn't have nearly the horsepower the Tomcat did.

Around Thor, black smoke and flashes of fire littered the air. He broke hard to the right, avoiding the shrapnel then rolling over and descending toward the new target. It would be a bitch to survive enemy fire only to be nailed by FOD in his own engine.

"Nasty," Beetle said. The Forger had rolled inverted, winged over, and was trying to slip into position behind Beetle. But Beetle cut hard to the right then suddenly reversed the direction of his turn, forcing the Forger out into the open.

"Open range, Beetle," Thor said, suddenly realizing how close they were. "You're too close, you're too close!"

"I'm pulling out," Beetle said, his voice suddenly tight. He was still inverted, following the Forger down in the bottom half of a loop. He eased his Hornet out of the descent into level flight, now right side up, intending to clear the area for Thor's shot. But as he did so, the Forger seemed to stagger in the air and Beetle's Hornet clipped its tail assembly.

The Hornet immediately departed control flight, falling through the air like dead metal. Light, smoke, then black trailed from its tail. Thor was closer to the Forger but too close for a missile. He jammed the weapons selector to guns, and rattled off a long blast with his nose cannon. The Forger's canopy shattered, glass hanging in the air for a moment to catch the sun like a rainbow. There was a blast of white smoke, and debris streamed out of the cockpit. Smoke billowed from the Forger's right engine, followed shortly by a stream of liquid that burst into flames. Thor was already rolling out, moving away and hunting for Beetle when the Forger exploded.

"Beetle!" Thor shouted, scanning the air for the injured Hornet.

"Seven clock, low," the Hawkeye said, barely pausing as it rapped out orders to the remaining Hornets.

Thor saw him then, sunlight blinking off metal as the Hornet tumbled. "Beetle!" Thor shouted again, kicking in the afterburner to intercept his wingman. Was Beetle even alive? The impact should have been survivable. Beetle had hit the tail assembly, sure, but he hadn't hit the cockpit as far as Thor could tell. Had the g-forces gotten him?

Thor was on him now, following him down, screaming his name in the mike. He thought he heard a brief, clipped answer but he couldn't be sure. He could see inside the cockpit, but the Hornet's erratic movement made it hard to tell if Beetle was injured. If Beetle was still alive, his hands were glued to the controls and every ounce of his concentration would be focused on pulling out of the deadly spin.

Was it possible—was Beetle's Hornet pulling up? It

seemed to be, but the motion was still so severe that Thor could see no way to recover. If Beetle could just stabilize enough to punch out, that would be good enough. There was no way this aircraft was going to land, no way at all. It had no business being airborne. The best they could hope for was to save the pilot.

Unbelievable. The Hornet's motion was stabilizing. It was still in a steep dive, but the yaw was damping out. It still maintained a slow rotation around its longitude, but maybe, just maybe it was slow enough to let Beetle get out.

"Beetle, you got it—eject, eject!" Thor shouted, still not knowing whether his wingman could hear him.

His own ESM warning gear beep cut through the cockpit, demanding to be heard. Lock, missile lock—but where? Thor broke off from following Beetle's injured Hornet and searched the air around him.

At first he couldn't find it. Then it came out of the sun, headed directly for him, two Forgers with nose guns blazing. Thor dropped his Hornet's nose and shot under them, exposing his tailpipe for an instant but more willing to risk that than his undercarriage. The Forgers streamed past him, guns still firing, tracers blindingly white against a blue sky, searching for him. The Forgers started to turn back on him, but Thor was already back in position, his own gun firing now. Two could play this game.

The lead Forger turned away, tipped over into a steep dive, and headed for Beetle's injured Hornet. Thor swore. Surely the Forger pilot could tell that the Hornet wasn't quite flying anymore. What was the point in going after one that was already fatally injured?

Just then, the cockpit blew off Beetle's Hornet, followed shortly by a small, black figure. Beetle ejected at a forty-five-degree angle from the cockpit, fire blazing under the ejection seat as the rocket drove him through the air.

"He's clear, he's clear," Thor shouted, relief flooding him. For just a moment, he thought Beetle would make it. But then, just as his wingman was clearing the dying Hornet, the aircraft rolled again. The tail assembly smacked into his wingman, driving him sideways.

The Forgers, evidently having seen the ejection, tried to

break off. Thor was torn between keeping Beetle in view and pressing the attack on the Forgers. There was really no choice—he was in the air for one reason, and that was to kill Forgers.

"Chute, I have one chute," Thor shouted over tactical. "Beetle, immediately below my position. Requests SAR."

"Roger, Packer lead, we have him," the Hawkeye replied. "SAR is standing by."

Dammit, they're standing by until it's safe to come in. And it won't be, not until these Forgers are gone.

Thor wheeled his Hornet back and gave chase. The Forgers saw him immediately, and cut around, trying to throw him off, but Thor anticipated their maneuver, ascended, then dropped into perfect killing position. He toggled the weapons selector to Sparrows, then changed his mind and selected guns. He boosted into afterburner for a few seconds, closing the distance, the Forger gyrating through the air as it tried to shake him. Thor shot off a short blast, feeling an immense satisfaction as the tracers made their way through the Forger's skin. He pulled out, then dropped back down to get another visual on Beetle. He couldn't get too close, for fear that his jet wash would collapse Beetle's chute. From this range, he could not tell whether Beetle was conscious and had his hands on his risers or was simply riding the chute down.

He would be okay, Thor knew he would. Hell, it hadn't been that hard of a hit, had it? Marines survived far worse than that and came out okay, didn't they? Sure they did.

His ESM demanded attention. "Son of a bitch," Thor muttered, turning back to open sky to find the threat. It took him a moment, but then sunlight splashed on metal and he saw his new target coming at him out of the sun. No heat seekers, then—too dangerous. Too much danger that the missiles would take off after the sun instead of the aircraft, and Thor was getting low enough on weapons that he couldn't afford to waste a single one.

The Forger was above him, descending rapidly, and it wasn't alone. Slightly above and behind, a second one came, hoping to catch Thor as he broke for altitude to escape the lead aircraft. It would have been no problem with a wingman, since the wingman could have kept the higher aircraft distracted long enough for Thor to gain altitude, but it was slightly trickier now. The real problem was being low on weapons, especially in a two-on-one situation.

Thor punched into afterburner and pulled away from the two, briefly exposing his tailpipes before wheeling back in on them. His ESM was screaming now, warning that missile launch was imminent, that targeting radar had a lock on him. Thor ignored it. His eyes could tell him more than any electronics could right now.

A missile leaped off the lower aircraft's wing, heading for the Hornet's underbelly. Thor held steady for a moment, then ejected chaff and flares, winging over and descending, pulling up hard enough to come up on the other side of the aircraft. If the missile managed to follow the maneuver, there was at least a fighting chance that it would see its own aircraft as the target. Meanwhile, time to deal with the higher bird.

The other aircraft was waiting for him, standing off in the distance, evidently wary of the Hornet's maneuverability. But Thor was starting to run low on fuel, and the danger of a prolonged two-on-one fight was quickly becoming a problem.

Altitude, I need altitude. And a wingman. Thor boosted again, screaming to the air. The ESM screamed again, and he punched out another round of countermeasures, then pulled out of his climb and ejected more flares as a screen when he turned.

"Thor, I got the lower one—stay clear!" Fastball Morrow's voice said over tactical. "Fox one, Fox one." The heat seekers streaked across the air, nailing the Forger in the ass. Between ensuring that Beetle's aircraft was dead and trying to take on Thor, the Forger had lost the big picture, and Fastball was on it before it knew what happened.

"I'll get the other one," Thor said, grunting, as he pulled the Hornet in a tight turn. The higher Forger, watching the destruction of his wingman, had decided he didn't like the odds anymore. He had turned, intending to run back to the pack, when Thor caught him with a Sidewinder.

Man, I'm in the hurt locker, Thor thought, surveying his

fuel gauge and weapons status. One AMRAAM, two rounds of countermeasures, and just a little more than fumes in the tank. "Big Eye, Packer lead—Texaco."

"Roger, Packer lead, Texaco bears 304, range 20 from your position. Standing by, full-service and all lines open."

Twenty miles—can I make it? Sure—there's always a margin of error built into these things. Thor swore quietly, knowing he'd screwed up by not watching his fuel more carefully. No point in surviving a couple of Forgers if you dump your Hornet in the drink by running out of fuel.

Tomcat 201
1946 local (GMT-9)

"Isn't it a good day for flight?" Fastball crowed, snapping out of a fast barrel roll. In the backseat, Rat gritted her teeth. "The weather, the sunshine, and a bunch of stupid Russians— man, you have to love it!"

They were on the fringes of the Tomcat sponge, waiting for the rest of their flight to arrive. From the moment they'd started their pre-flight brief in the ready room, through the walk-around on deck, the launch and climbing to altitude, Fastball's mood had grated on her nerves.

Just what was there to be so happy about? Outnumbered, bombers in the center of the formation—no, she didn't really see a reason to be happy. Sure, it was the job, and it was— well, not a good thing, but certainly a gratifying challenge to go into combat. It wasn't something you were happy about, exactly. High on, maybe, more alive than you were at any other time. Every moment was precious, every sense heightened. Probably the result of adrenaline, she knew, but that didn't make it any less exhilarating.

But happy? No, she wasn't happy. The difference between her attitude and Fastball's was that she now knew she could die. Unconsciously, she ran her left hand down her right sleeve, felt the reassuring shape of her muscles under her fingertips. A few inches either way and her arm would have been blown off. Held as it was, she had been on the verge of bleeding to death in the cockpit before Fastball had gotten them back on the deck. It was only by sheer luck and good surgery that she retained complete use of her arm and was allowed to return to flight status. Sure, Fastball had been there, had seen the damage, had known how close she'd come to dying. Another foot or so and the shrapnel would've punched through his guts instead of her arm.

But until it happens to you, until you feel your own skin and flesh tearing, until you work through months of rehab and healing, you never really believe it. It always happens to someone else.

Well, she had been that someone else, and she knew it made a difference.

"Dolphin flight, on me." Bird Dog's voice rapped out over their flight circuit. "It's still one solid cluster fuck, boys and girls. The lightweights will take the right side and we'll head for the heavies on the left. Come in over the top and call your target on the E-2's mark. Any questions?"

Of course there weren't, other than whether the Hornets knew that Bird Dog was calling them lightweights. They had gone over this in the ready room, then again on the flight deck as a pre-flight. The Hawkeye had updated them while they were gathering at the sponge point, and they were about as up-to-date on the disposition of forces as anyone had any right to expect.

Rat stared down at the radar screen until goose bumps shivered on both arms. There was something evil about seeing Russian fighters and bombers in a formation they'd studied as history. This was back to the bad old days, the Cold War, when families were building bomb shelters in their backyards and the world was poised on the brink of nuclear war.

Stop it. It's just fighters. The bombers don't even count. They're too slow and heavy to make any difference at all, at least as far as our mission is concerned. A turkey shoot, once we get to the Forgers.

But the Forgers, those were a problem. The Tomcats were slightly heavier but more powerful. She ran through their performance characteristics in her mind again. Insert techno—

"Fastball, close up," Bird Dog ordered, his voice curt. Obediently, Fastball slipped into position tight on Bird Dog's right wing.

"What's the matter, you getting lonesome?" Fastball asked cheerily.

"Do you have to be like this?" she snapped, her nerves finally fraying.

"Like what?" he asked, sounding surprised.

"Like you're having fun! Fastball, get your head in the game. This isn't Top Gun School or a computer game."

"I know that," he said, sounding hurt.

"Yeah, right."

There was a long silence, and she immediately regretted her words. The fact that Fastball irritated her said more about her attitude than about his. Maybe they shouldn't have returned her to flight status. Maybe she'd lost her nerve.

"Okay, Rat," Fastball said, his voice not quite as obnoxious. "Sorry. I just thought—well—I thought it'd cheer you up."

"Fastball," she muttered, "just fly the aircraft, okay? When I need an amateur psychologist, I'll let you know."

Just then, her ESM gear bleated out a warning. She snapped her gaze back to the radar screen and saw that they were just crossing over and above a Russian flight. This was the single most dangerous part of the transit, when they were directly in front, although above, the Russian fighters. They presented an excellent target aspect, broadside to the radars then flashing their tailpipes.

"Afterburner," Bird Dog ordered. "Break formation." This, too, was exactly as planned, providing a more difficult problem for Russian targeting.

The punch of the afterburner shoved Rat back into her seat. For a few seconds, she was too busy trying to breathe and keep her attention on the scope to worry about Fastball and whether or not he thought she'd lost her nerve. Then, as the g-forces eased off, she saw they were across. The plan was to continue ten miles past the formation, then swing back and approach them on an angle. A few more minutes—now.

"Now!" she said, giving Fastball the signal. He had anticipated her command and was already pulling into a tight turn and heading back toward the Russians. Below them, Bird Dog was accelerating, pulling away and increasing the separation between his aircraft and theirs to standard distance.

Immediately, three Forgers rose up to meet them. All around them, as the fighting pairs broke formation and selected targets under the Hawkeye's direction, the Forgers split up to meet them.

The sheer numbers were overwhelming. Every fighting pair was facing four, if not six, aircraft. And still more were in formation, closing in tight on their Backfires, ready to take out anyone who got too close.

"Keep your distance," Bird Dog reminded everyone. "Fox three, fox three." An AMRAAM leaped off his wing, heading for the lead Russian. Bird Dog immediately broke off, accelerated, and ascended. The Russian he had targeted turned back into formation, panicked by the incoming missile and scattering the Backfires like marbles.

One part of Rat's mind applauded the performance. Another part was panicking. Bird Dog did realize, didn't he, that he couldn't shoot his whole load at first encounter? Sure, if you didn't get by the first missile, then there was no point in worrying about the next one, but you couldn't expend every countermeasure on the first shot at you. That was a lesson she'd learned early on.

Bird Dog evaded the countermeasures easily, swinging over the top of the second Forger then wheeling back around to take another shot. It was clear he believed there was nothing to worry about, that the Forger in front of him had his complete and total attention. Fastball was supposed to be watching to make sure of it.

The second Forger proved to have a steadier hand. It stood its ground as the missile approached, waiting until the last second then braking hard down in a nearly vertical descent. The missile almost had it, but then was unable to follow. Trying to turn, it lost itself in a compact burst of flares and detonated harmlessly. The Forger lost its tactical awareness, however, and as it turned back to face Bird Dog, it exposed itself vertically to a heat seeker. Fastball, never one to miss an opportunity, snapped, "Bird Dog, break right!" and, at the same second, toggled off a heat seeker. The Tomcat below maneuvered almost instantly, but had Bird Dog been a hair slower or taken time to question Fastball's command, it would have been a toss-up as to whether the missile took out the Forger or Fastball's lead.

"Nice shot, Fastball," Bird Dog said coolly over tactical. Rat cringed. By refusing to admit that he had been in danger, Bird Dog merely compounded the problems with Fastball. And once the two pilots had determined to out-cool each other, there was little a RIO could do to stop them.

The third Forger had not escaped their attention, either. Realizing that both of its companions had been lost, it fell back slightly, and waited for a second Forger to form on him. Then, moving a loose pattern that suggested a lot of experience, the two moved in.

"And here come the big dogs," Fastball shouted, evidently realizing the same thing. "Bring them on!"

The preferred tactic would be to take on one, then the other, but the Russians were not giving them that choice. The Forgers split apart almost immediately, each one gunning for an individual target.

"Fox one!" Fastball shouted, shooting an AMRAAM. Even as he did so, the ECM blared its warning.

"He's got us, Fastball," Rat shouted, her fingers flying over the controls as she pumped out chaff and flares. Not too much, not too little—just right. Her radarscope exploded with a buzz of static as the chaff spread.

The Forger was on them almost instantly, nimbly evading the chaff. He came in again, blasting off another missile then cutting away and circling back up under, like a shark after a swimmer. Rat saw tracers just off their right side, and realized that the Forger was hoping to trap them between the missile, the chaff, and its guns.

Fastball saw it coming, too. He tipped the Tomcat nose down, letting her drop like a rock, and then pulled back hard, kicking into afterburner in a display of raw power that the Forger could never match. In seconds, he was back at altitude, high in behind the Forger. The missile veered off, losing its lock and streaking off toward open sky.

The Forger, not to be outdone, seemed to leap through the air as it followed Fastball up. It couldn't manage the sheer power of the Tomcat in a climb, but it could cut well inside what its pilot thought was Fastball's turn. The Forger cut across the arc, intending to intercept them and drop into position behind, firing off the heat seeker to increase the distraction factor.

Fastball swore, and reversed his turn. He pulled up again, flashing the undercarriage of the jet at the Forger, then dove over to drop back in position. The Forger, not realizing what was coming, had once again turned in the vertical, intending to intercept, and had failed to allow for the change in altitude. Once he realized his error, the pilot began maneuvering radically across the sky, cutting a series of hard turns designed to exceed the Tomcat's envelope. But once again, Fastball saw it coming. He kicked afterburners back in and simply powered his way through a gut-wrenching ascending turn, coming back down behind the Forger again.

The ECM warning went off again, and Rat twisted in her harness, looking for the threat. Meanwhile, Fastball bore down on the helpless Forger, almost psychically guessing which way the other aircraft would turn. Finally, the Forger tried to run one too many times. Tracers streaked across it and seemed to disappear, harmlessly passing through its skin.

Rat knew that was impossible. Everything she knew about the Forger said that its underbelly had additional armor plating on it, enabling it to more effectively and safely support ground operations, but the rest of the fuselage was lightly armored in order not to weigh the aircraft down too much. Consequently, the rounds would do maximum damage.

Evidence to support her conclusion was not long in coming. The Forger twisted in the air, trying to evade the Tomcat. But just as it leveled out, it spun violently to the right, rolling so hard it was almost a blur.

Fastball pulled away hard, clearing the area. As he did, the Forger's wing snapped off, flying off at an acute angle to the fuselage. Other pieces of gear broke loose, peppering the sky with bits of metal, oil, and debris.

A few seconds later, the inevitable happened. Fuel hit hot metal, flashed past its ignition point, and the Forger exploded.

"Where's Bird Dog?" Fastball asked, trying to control his

voice but clearly breathing hard. Maybe she overestimated his cool, Rat thought, because he sure didn't sound like a guy who was really enjoying himself.

"Three clock, and low," she said instantly. One part of her mind was always fixed on lead, tracking his position and maintaining a running picture of where he was relative to Fastball. Not always a RIO's job, but that was the way it worked when she flew with Fastball.

"Okay." Fastball dropped the nose of the Tomcat down, then rolled over, searching the sky below them.

"There, just to the right," Rat said.

"Bird Dog, you okay?" Fastball asked.

It was Bird Dog's RIO who answered, saying, "Yes, we're fine, just about—there." A fireball in front of Bird Dog punctuated the RIO's self-satisfied pronouncement. "That's two."

Immediately, Bird Dog's Tomcat broke off and began ascending, coming up to meet them. As Bird Dog flashed past them, Fastball fell into position on his wing, following his lead. There was no need for conversation. Both pilots knew exactly what they were doing—picking out the next target.

This time, the Russians were taking fewer chances. Five Forgers broke off to meet them, settling into one group of three and a traditional fighting pair, a configuration that had Rat worried. Funny how your mind got used to seeing just pairs. Now, with one trio joining on them, it was too easy to lose track of one of the players. Not to mention the second pair.

"I'll take the three," Bird Dog said. But even as he spoke, the lower pair broke off and gave chase. Bird Dog had no choice but to react. "Stay loose, Fastball," Bird Dog snapped, a trace of worry in his voice. "I'll be right back."

"Not a problem, Dog," Fastball said. But even as he spoke, Rat could see that there was indeed a problem.

Fastball shoved the Tomcat into afterburner, shoving Rat back hard in her seat. "Ah," she grunted.

"Altitude," Fastball said, grunting as well. "Altitude. That's first."

"They're tracking us," Rat warned. One Forger was directly behind them, falling behind slightly but in perfect position. His playmates were on either side, offset by five thousand yards so that the formation of Tomcat and three-point Forgers looked like a trefoil.

"Sun," Fastball said, not deigning to explain any further. Not that it was necessary—Rat knew where he was heading. He turned hard and pointed the nose directly into the sun. It glared off the canopy, blinding her. Rat jammed her head down hard against the plastic to block out the light. Fastball probably had his eyes shut by now—the way he was today, she doubted he even needed his eyes in order to fly and fight the aircraft.

"They've got a lock," Rat warned, her fingers tweaking the picture into focus as the gear began its warning time. "Chaff—no flares, not at this angle."

"Roger. Hold on." Coming from Fastball, that could mean practically anything. Rat braced herself.

Fastball began a series of violent maneuvers, skipping across the sky like a pebble. The orderly formation of Forgers behind them broke apart slightly as they tried to anticipate his next move, each waiting for the perfect shot. But by forcing them to maneuver, he fouled their fields of fire. And there was one other problem—although she suspected the Forgers hadn't notice it yet, the Tomcat had slowed its violent maneuvers, and the net effect had been to decrease the distance between the Forgers and the Tomcat to within minimums. They were too close now to fire their missiles.

That didn't mean they were defenseless. All at once, the air around them was lousy with tracers. For a moment, Rat quailed. Then, seconds before he did it, Rat knew what Fastball intended. She started to object, to warn him not to, that it was too dangerous, but it wouldn't have done any good.

Just at the point the Forgers began to realize they had a problem, Fastball manually swept the wings forward, deploying his speed brakes and landing gear. The Tomcat reacted as though it had hit a solid object. Its speed slowed abruptly, peeling off knots so quickly that it was inside the stall envelope almost immediately. But as the Tomcat slowed, the Forgers shot past her. Forcing out another two seconds of maneuverability before the Tomcat became aerodynamically unstable, Fastball sprayed the three with gunfire, reversing their situation.

Smoke enveloped two Forgers immediately. The third was apparently untouched. It broke away from the others, afterburner glaring, then, from a safe distance, turned back in on them. Rat could almost sense the other pilot's fury and determination.

Meanwhile, Fastball was having to cope with the aftereffects of his daring maneuver. The Tomcat was no longer flying. It hung in the air for a second, then, as gravity began to assert its pull, the angle of attack deteriorated. Gravity won, as it always did, and the Tomcat began dropping like a stone, tail first.

Not good. Very not good. Rat wanted to scream, but it would have done no good.

Fastball swept back the control surfaces and punched the afterburner. The thrust was sufficient to rotate the Tomcat in the air, so instead of falling tail first, it was nose down to the ocean. The airframe picked up speed quickly, regaining lift as air flowed over the wings. Within moments, Fastball had built up sufficient airspeed to regain control of the Tomcat.

Too late! The other Forger was now on them, popping off missiles like fireworks. *Poor fire control,* one part of Rat's mind noted coolly. *Just as bad as the last Forger. Spend everything now, and nothing left for later if you need it.*

"Fastball, break right," Bird Dog's voice shouted. "I'm on him—break right, dammit!"

Fastball reacted as instinctively and quickly as Bird Dog had earlier, turning so hard that he shed precious airspeed. But stalls can be recovered from. Missile hits can't.

"Fox one," Bird Dog shouted. Rat twisted in her seat, staring back at their tail. She saw Bird Dog's missile coming in at right angles to them, but for a moment she thought it was headed straight for them. But no, Bird Dog had judged the angle quite accurately. The missile was not aimed at the Forger, it was aimed at where the Forger would be in three seconds, which was where Fastball was now. As the aircraft continued on their courses, it worked out just as Bird Dog had planned. The missile pierced the Forger's flank, and for a moment Rat thought she saw it sticking out from the side.

A microsecond later, the warhead detonated, destroying the Forger.

"Nice shot, Bird Dog," Fastball said, too, too cool.

"Not bad," Bird Dog acknowledged offhandedly. "Sorry I couldn't get here sooner."

"Not a problem," Fastball said. "We managed."

Rat wanted to scream.

Just then, the Hawkeye came over tactical. "Dolphin lead, assist Packer lead, bearing zero three zero, range ten."

"Thor? Where's his wingman?" Bird Dog asked.

"SAR operations under way," the Hawkeye replied calmly. "You want to discuss this now, or get your ass in gear?"

"I'm on it," Fastball said immediately.

"No, I'll—" Bird Dog began, only to be interrupted by the Hawkeye.

"Roger, Fastball. Dolphin lead, remain with flight." The Hawkeye continued with a rapid summary of the scenario— eleven kills for Dolphin flight, one Tomcat splashed. That left one without a wingman, and it was Bird Dog's duty to fill in.

"Acknowledged," Bird Dog said, already turning back toward the rest of his flight. "Fastball, take care of it, and get your ass back here."

And assist where fastball pulls doors but out of the bacon.

Tomcat 101
1950 local (GMT-9)

One bomber peeled way from the pack, evidently intending to make a run for it on its own. Tombstone changed course and headed directly for it. His blood was running hot, his anger concentrated into every cell. His entire life seemed to depend on killing Russians. Nothing else could ease the pain in his soul.

Suddenly, his international air distress frequency came alive. A low-pitched but definitely female voice snarled, "Damn you, all of you. I'm not going to do it—fuck you!" The transmission cut off as abruptly as it began.

Tombstone's blood seemed to freeze in his veins. The aircraft around him disappeared. It was as though he was in suspended animation, trapped lifeless between the ejection seat and the sky. The words pounded in his brain.

She always had a mouth on her. That's just what she would say. But what were they trying to make her do?

"Tombstone? You okay?" Greene snapped. "Get your head in the game, asshole."

Tombstone didn't answer. The voice obliterated his entire world, the words overwhelming them. No, not the words— the voice. Because he was as certain as life itself that Tomboy had been speaking.

"Stony?" the voice said. "I love you."

"Stony—oh, god. That's her, isn't it?" Greene said, his voice weak. "Tombstone, where is she?"

"I don't know," Tombstone said, his lips barely moving. He was cold, so cold. Sweat poured off his forehead and his palms were clammy. "She could be anywhere."

"Stony One, Hawkeye. Be advised that last transmission was from an aircraft. The line of bearing and track put it directly in front of you. Whoever that was, she's on that bomber."

I can't do it. No one would expect me to. I'm already dead—I won't kill her, too. The stream of consciousness flowed through Tombstone's mind, confusing him. He waited—for what, he wasn't certain.

"I won't do it!" Her voice again, howling her anger and outrage. It was just like her, that indomitable spirit even when confronted with the most unimaginable odds. "Let go of me, you can't—*there!*" If he thought he had been cold before, he was mistaken. The savage glee and victory in her cry of triumph froze his very soul.

The sky in front of him shattered into fragments of glass— no, it wasn't glass. The top of the bomber exploded, sheets of metal peeling back from the fuselage. Small black dots shot out at forty-five-degree angles to the aircraft. The bomber was still airborne, just barely, it's structural integrity assaulted by the violence of the ejections.

Was she strapped in? She was fighting with them—no, she wasn't.

Of course she was—Tomboy wouldn't be that stupid.

Or would she? Would she find a way to grab an ejection handle and yank down, knowing that it would eject everyone except her. Would she ride a dying aircraft down to the surface of the sea, sacrificing herself in order to destroy the aircraft?

"Tomboy!" The howl was ripped from deep inside of him, anguish and protest rolled into one. "No!"

There were eight chutes now, floating down in the air. The bomber itself was wobbling, trying to fly but not able to, its autopilot unable to keep up with the cascading damage and system failures.

"She punched out," Greene said. "Tombstone, she punched out, she punched out." Greene repeated the phrase like a mantra, trying to refocus the pilot's attention. Finally, in response to pleas and threats from his backseater and from the Hawkeye, Tombstone rallied.

"I'm okay."

"Stone One, you have priority in the pattern. Get your ass on deck." The stern voice of the admiral echoed over the airwaves. "Pull yourself together, partner. Get that aircraft back down here. Now! We have SAR en route the chutes."

"Come on, Tombstone," Jeremy said, his voice gentle but urgent. "Let's get back to the boat—come on, you can do this with your eyes closed."

Cold, so cold—dear god, I've been there, punched out, not knowing if I'd survive. They said they had eight chutes. She'll make it. I'm sure she will.

"Come right, course three two zero," Greene said, his voice firm. "Descend to ten thousand feet."

Mechanically, Tombstone flew the aircraft. He flew with precision, muscles and mind detached from his intellect and emotions, automatically taking the Tomcat around the marshal stack, lining up on the stern of the carrier, calling the ball, making the adjustments required, and taking his Tomcat in for a perfect three-wire trap. A perfectly executed approach and trap—all done by reflex.

At the moment the plane captain stepped in front of his aircraft and signaled him to reduce power, his world shattered into pieces. Instead of reducing power and taxiing to his spot, Tombstone eased the throttles back. The hard scream of the Tomcat died. The aircraft rolled backward slightly in response to the pull from the three-wire. Tombstone applied his nosewheel brake, waited for the tension to ease off, then retracted the tail hook and popped the canopy.

Tombstone reached down to safe his ejection seat, then stood. He swung one leg over the side of the aircraft, groping for the foothold, then descended to the deck.

There was a moment of confusion on the deck, then the yellow shirts stormed across nonskid and clambered up the boarding ladder. Jeremy unfastened his ejection harness and climbed into the front seat. He popped the brakes, taxiied to the spot, and ran through the shutdown checklists. There were still Tomcats in the air that needed to get down on deck, and they couldn't land until this aircraft moved.

Tombstone walked blindly across the deck, saying nothing. Her voice drowned out the rest of the world. Two white-shirt safety deck observers were shortly joined by Admiral Grant. A corpsman slipped in beside him, followed shortly by a doctor. The rest of the flight deck crew formed a protective circle around him.

Tombstone disappeared into the skin of the ship. Greene watched him go.

TWENTY-THREE

Monday, July 7
USS **Jefferson**
2000 local (GMT-9)

Pamela had just returned from the shower and was toweling off her wet hair when she heard the announcement over the 1MC. The ship had been at flight quarters for a couple of hours, but that was no big deal. After all, this *was* an aircraft carrier.

But the bongs from the ship's bell startled her. She glanced at her clock to see if they were chiming the hour for some reason, but it wasn't time for bells. The carrier had never used bells for hours regularly anyway.

And the bongs continued, on and on and on. She counted, stopping at eight.

Who the hell? Only top officials, up to and including the president, rated eight bells. She shoved her hair into some semblance of a style, grabbed her tape recorder and her sunglasses, and headed for the flight deck. Her cameraman was smart—Jeff would meet her there. He knew what eight bells meant.

There was a crowd of people heading for the flight deck and she went with the flow, up the ladders and then out the hatch into the bright sunshine. To her surprise, several hundred sailors already stood in formation in their white uniforms. The captain, executive officer, and the admiral stood at a microphone stand in front of them.

As she watched, the helicopter hatch opened. Two lines of sideboys formed up, all immaculate in dress whites. Bells, sideboys—who exactly was this?

Seconds later, she knew. Six men in dark jumpsuits wearing sunglasses and caps emerged, fanning out around the sideboys. They checked the crowd carefully, then one of them turned back to the helicopter.

A familiar figure—tall, dark hair with silver along the edges, and bright blue eyes—emerged. He seemed at home on the flight deck, entirely comfortable with the military honors being rendered, and returned the salutes tendered snappily.

The president. What was he doing here, so soon after the election? Shouldn't he be in Washington, attending parties? Then the scene became surreal in the extreme. The president walked toward Coyote and Captain Phillips, returned their salutes, and then accepted a small box and a padded certificate holder from the admiral. He looked around, as though puzzled.

An awards ceremony, then. So why wasn't it announced? And who was it for? A number of names came immediately to her mind, and she swore silently about the public affairs officer's failure to notify her about the ceremony. No, it wasn't hard news, but it was good human interest stuff.

Her cameraman had arrived and stood by her side. He was already rolling as the president emerged from his helicopter.

The admiral saw them, and to her amazement, the admiral and a president began walking toward her. She had a brief, irrational impulse to curtsy, which she suppressed immediately.

"Ms. Drake," the president said. "How are you feeling now?"

"Fine, Mr. President. None of us suffered any injuries."

"Well, fine. I'm afraid I have some bad news for you, Ms. Drake." The president's expression was somber. Pamela felt a flash of anger. Tombstone had promised she was out of purgatory. If the president thought he was going to get good press for this ceremony, he had another think coming.

"I'm sorry to hear that, Mr. President. Of course, the freedom of the press has always been something you've supported. If you intend to reinstate the admiral's policy of barring the press from significant events, then I'm afraid I will have to—"

"Ms. Drake, I think you want to shut up right now," Coyote said, a huge grin breaking out on his face. "The bad news is not that we're going to get rid of you. It's that for once in your life, perhaps the first and final time, you are the last one to know something."

"What?" Pamela searched for words, unable to figure out why both the president and the admiral were grinning at her. Then the admiral stepped to her side, offered her his arm, and said, "You are the guest of honor at this little ceremony, Ms. Drake. And I would be honored to escort you to the podium."

She turned to her cameraman and was not surprised to see him laughing at her, still taping. "You knew," she said accusingly.

"Listen to the admiral, Drake," Jeff said.

Five minutes later, Pamela Drake was sporting a defense metal on her lapel. And trying desperately to figure out how she was going to explain it to her boss.

GLOSSARY

0-3 LEVEL: The third deck above the main deck. Designations for decks above the main deck (also known as the damage control deck) begin with zero, e.g., 0-3. The zero is pronounced as "oh" in conversation. Decks below the main deck do not have the initial zero and are numbered down from the main deck, e.g., deck 11 is below deck 3. Deck 0-7 is above deck 0-3.

IMC: The general announcing system on a ship or submarine. Every ship has many different interior communications systems, most of them linking parts of the ship for a specific purpose. Most operate off sound-powered phones. The circuit designators consist of a number followed by two letters that indicate the specific purpose of the circuit. 2AS, for instance, might be an antisubmarine warfare circuit that connects the sonar supervisor, the USW watch officer, and the sailor at the torpedo launch.

AIR BOSS: A senior commander or captain assigned to the aircraft carrier, in charge of flight operations. The "boss" is assisted by the mini-boss in Pri-Fly, located in the tower on board the carrier. The air boss is always in the tower during flight operations, overseeing the launch and recovery cycles, declaring a green deck, and monitoring the safe approach of aircraft to the carrier.

AIR WING: Composed of the aircraft squadrons assigned to the battle group. The individual squadron commanding officers report to the air wing commander, who reports to the admiral.

AIRDALE: Slang for an officer or enlisted person in the aviation fields. Includes pilots, NFOs, aviation intelligence officers, maintenance officers, and the enlisted technicians who support aviation. The antithesis of an airdale is a "shoe."

AKULA: Late-model Russian-built attack nuclear submarine, an SSN. Fast, deadly, and deep diving.

ALR-67: Detects, analyzes, and evaluates electromagnetic signals, emits a warning signal if the parameters are compatible with an immediate threat to the aircraft, e.g., seeker head on an anti-air missile. Can also detect an enemy radar in either a search or a targeting mode.

ALTITUDE: is safety. With enough airspace under the wings, a pilot can solve any problem.

AMRAAM: Advanced medium-range anti-air missile.

ANGELS: Thousands of feet over ground. Angels twenty is twenty thousand feet. Cherubs indicates hundreds of feet, e.g., cherubs five = five hundred feet.

ASW: Anti-submarine warfare, recently renamed undersea warfare. For some reason.

AVIONICS: Black boxes and systems that comprise an aircraft's combat systems.

AW: Aviation anti-submarine warfare technician, the enlisted specialist flying in an S-3, P-3, or helo USW aircraft. As this book goes to press, there is discussion of renaming the specialty.

AWACS: An aircraft entirely too good for the Air Force, the advanced warning aviation control system. Long-range command-and-control and electronic-intercept bird with superb capabilities.

AWG-9: Pronounced "awg nine," the primary search and fire control radar on a Tomcat.

BACKSEATER: Also known as the GIB, the guy in back. Nonpilot aviator available in several flavors: BN (bombardier/navigator), RIO (radar intercept operator), and

TACCO (tactical control officer), among others. Usually wears glasses and is smart.

BEAR: Russian maritime patrol aircraft, the equivalent in rough terms of a U.S. P-3. Variants have primary missions in command and control, submarine hunting, and electronic intercepts. Big, slow, good targets.

BITCH BOX: One interior communications system on a ship. So named because it's normally used to bitch at another watch station.

BLUE ON BLUE: Fratricide. U.S. forces are normally indicated in blue on tactical displays, and this term refers to an attack on a friendly by another friendly.

BLUE WATER NAVY: Outside the unrefueled range of the air wing. When a carrier enters blue water ops, aircraft must get on board—i.e., land—and cannot divert to land if the pilot gets the shakes.

BOOMER: Slang for a ballistic missile submarine.

BOQ: Bachelor officer quarters—a Motel Six for single officers or those traveling without family. The Air Force also has VOQ, visiting officer quarters.

BUSTER: As fast as you can, i.e., bust yer ass getting here.

C-2 GREYHOUND: Also known as the COD, carrier onboard delivery. The COD carries cargo and passengers from shore to ship. It is capable of carrier landings. Sometimes assigned directly to the air wing, it also operates in coordination with CVBGs from a shore squadron.

CAG: Carrier air group commander, normally a senior Navy captain aviator. Technically, an obsolete term, since the air wing rather than an air group is now deployed on the carrier. However, everyone thought CAW sounded stupid, so CAG was retained as slang for the carrier air wing commander.

CAP: Combat air patrol, a mission executed by fighters to protect the carrier and battle group from enemy air and missiles.

CARRIER BATTLE GROUP: A combination of ships, air wing, and submarines assigned under the command of a one-star admiral.

CARRIER BATTLE GROUP 14: The battle group normally embarked on *Jefferson.*

CBG: *see* Carrier battle group

CDC: Combat direction center—in the modern era, replaced CIC, or combat information center, as the heart of a ship. All sensor information is fed into CDC, and the battle is coordinated by a tactical action officer on watch there.

CG: Abbreviation for a cruiser.

CHIEF: The backbone of the Navy. E-7, -8, and -9 enlisted paygrades, known as chief, senior chief, and master chief. The transition from petty officer ranks to the chief's mess is a major event in a sailor's career. On board ship, the chiefs have separate eating and berthing facilities. Chiefs wear khakis, as opposed to dungarees for the less senior enlisted ratings.

CHIEF OF STAFF: Not to be confused with a chief, the COS in a battle group staff is normally a senior Navy captain who acts as the admiral's XO and deputy.

CIA: Christians in Action. The civilian agency charged with intelligence operations outside the continental United States.

CIWS: Close-in weapons system, pronounced "see-whiz." Gattling gun with built-in radar that tracks and fires on inbound missiles. If you have to use it, you're dead.

COD: *see* C-2 Greyhound

COLLAR COUNT: Traditional method of determining the winner of a disagreement. A survey is taken of the opponents' collar devices. The senior person wins. Always.

COMMODORE: Formerly the junior-most admiral rank, now used to designate a senior Navy captain in charge of a bunch of like units. A destroyer commodore commands several destroyers, a sea control commodore the S-3 squadrons on that coast. Contrast with a CAG, who owns a number of dissimilar units, e.g., a couple of Tomcat squadrons, some Hornets, and some E-2s and helos.

COMPARTMENT: Navy talk for a room on a ship.

CONDITION TWO: One step down from general quarters,

which is Condition One. Condition Five is tied up at the pier in a friendly country.

CRYPTO: Short for some variation of cryptological, the magic set of codes that makes a circuit impossible for anyone else to understand.

CV, CVN: Abbreviation for an aircraft carrier, conventional and nuclear.

CVIC: Carrier intelligence center. Located down the passageway (the hall) from the flag spaces.

DATA LINK, THE LINK: The secure circuit that links all units in a battle group or in an area. Targets and contacts are transmitted over the LINK to all ships. The data is processed by the ship designated as Net Control, and common contacts are correlated. The system also transmits data from each ship and aircraft's weapons systems, e.g., a missile firing. All services use the LINK.

DDG: Guided missile destroyer.

DESK JOCKEY: Nonflyer, one who drives a computer instead of an aircraft.

DESRON: Destroyer commander.

DICASS: An active sonobuoy.

DICK STEPPING: Something to be avoided. While anatomically impossible in today's gender-integrated services, in an amazing display of good sense, it has been decided that women can do this as well.

DOPPLER: Acoustic phenomena caused by relative motion between a sound source and a receiver that results in an apparent change in frequency of the sound. The classic example is a train going past and the decrease in pitch of its whistle. When a submarine changes its course or speed in relation to a sonobuoy, the event shows up as a change in the frequency of the sound source.

DOUBLE NUTS: Zero zero on the tail of an aircraft.

E-2 HAWKEYE: Command and control and surveillance aircraft. Turboprop rather than jet, and unarmed. Smaller version of an AWACS, in practical terms, but carrier-based.

ELF: Extremely low frequency, a method of communicating with submarines at sea. Signals are transmitted via a miles-long antenna and are the only way of reaching a deeply submerged submarine.

ENVELOPE: What you're supposed to fly inside of if you want to take all the fun out of naval aviation.

EWs: Electronic warfare technicians, the enlisted sailors that man the gear that detects, analyzes, and displays electromagnetic signals. Highly classified stuff.

F/A-18 HORNETS: The inadequate, fuel-hungry intended replacement for the aging but still kick-your-ass-potent Tomcat. Flown by Marines and Navy.

FAMILYGRAM: Short messages from submarine sailors' families to their deployed sailors. Often the only contact with the outside world that a submarine sailor on deployment has.

FF/FFG: Abbreviation for a fast frigate (no, there aren't slow frigates) and a guided-missile fast frigate.

FLAG OFFICER: In the Navy and Coast Guard, an admiral. In the other services, a general.

FLAG PASSAGEWAY: The portion of the aircraft carrier that houses the admiral's staff working spaces. Includes the flag mess and the admiral's cabin. Normally separated from the rest of the ship by heavy plastic curtains, and designated by blue tile on the deck instead of white.

FLIGHT QUARTERS: A condition set on board a ship preparing to launch or recover aircraft. All unnecessary persons are required to stay inside the skin of the ship and remain clear of the flight deck area.

FLIGHT SUIT: The highest form of navy couture. The perfect choice of apparel for any occasion—indeed, the only uniform an aviator ought to be required to own.

FOD: Stands for foreign object damage, but the term is used to indicate any loose gear that could cause damage to an aircraft. During flight operations, aircraft generate a tremendous amount of air flowing across the deck. Loose objects—including people and nuts and bolts—can be sucked into the intake and discharged through the outlet of the jet engine. FOD damages the jet's impellers and doesn't do much for the people sucked in, either. FOD walkdown is conducted at least once a day on board an aircraft carrier. Everyone not otherwise engaged stands shoulder to shoulder on the flight deck and slowly walks from one end of the flight deck to the other, searching for FOD.

FOX: Tactical shorthand for a missile firing. Fox one indicates a heat-seeking missile, fox two an infrared missile, and fox three a radar-guided missile.

GCI: Ground control intercept, a procedure used in the Soviet air forces. Primary control for vectoring the aircraft in on enemy targets and other fighters is vested in a guy on the ground, rather than in the cockpit where it belongs.

GIB: *see* backseater

GMT: Greenwich mean time.

GREEN SHIRTS: *see* shirts

HANDLER: Officer located on the flight deck level responsible for ensuring that aircraft are correctly positioned—"spotted"—on the flight deck. Coordinates the movements of aircraft with yellow gear (small tractors that tow aircraft and other related gear) from maintenance areas to catapults, and from the flight deck to the hangar bar via the elevators. Speaks frequently with the air boss. *see also* bitch box

HARMS: Anti-radiation missiles that home in on radar sites.

HOME PLATE: Tactical call sign for *Jefferson.*

HOT: In reference to a sonobuoy, holding enemy contact.

HUFFER: Yellow gear located on the flight deck that generates compressed air to start jet engines. Most Navy aircraft do not need a huffer to start engines, but it can be used in emergencies or for maintenance.

HUNTER: Call sign for the S-3 squadron embarked on the *Jefferson.*

ICS: Interior communications system. The private link between a pilot and a RIO, or the telephone system internal to a ship.

INCHOPPED: Navy talk for a ship entering a defined area of water, e.g. inchopped the Med.

IR: Infrared, a method of missile homing.

ISOTHERMAL: A layer of water that has a constant temperature with increasing depth. Located below the thermocline, where increase in depth correlates to decrease in temperature. In the isothermal layer, the primary factor affecting the speed of sound in water is the increase in pressure with depth.

JBD: Jet blast deflector. Panels that pop up from the flight deck to block the exhaust emitted by aircraft.

USS JEFFERSON: The star nuclear aircraft carrier in the U.S. Navy.

LEADING PETTY OFFICER: The senior petty officer in a workcenter, division, or department, responsible to the leading chief petty officer for the performance of the rest of the group.

LINK: *see* data link

LOFARGRAM: Low-frequency analyzing and recording display. Consists of lines arrayed by frequency on the horizontal axis and time on the vertical axis. Displays sound signals in the water in a graphic fashion for analysis by ASW technicians.

LONG GREEN TABLE: A formal inquiry board. It's better to be judged by six than carried by six.

MACHINIST'S MATE: Enlisted technician that runs and repairs most engineering equipment on board a ship. Abbreviated as "MM," e.g., MM1 Sailor is a petty officer first class machinist's mate.

MDI: Mess decks intelligence. The heartbeat of the rumor mill on board a ship and the definitive source for all information.

MEZ: Missile engagement zone. Any hostile contacts that make it into the MEZ are engaged only with missiles. Friendly aircraft must stay clear in order to avoid a blue-on-blue engagement, i.e., fratricide.

MiG: A production line of aircraft manufactured by Mikoyan in Russia. MiG fighters are owned by many nations around the world.

MURPHY, LAW OF: The factor most often not considered sufficiently in military planning. If something can go wrong, it will. Naval corollary: shit happens.

NATIONAL ASSETS: Surveillance and reconnaissance resources of the most sensitive nature, e.g., satellites.

NATOPS: The bible for operating a particular aircraft. *see* envelopes

NFO: Naval flight officer.

NOBRAINER: Contrary to what copy editors believe, this is one word. Used to signify an evolution or decision that should require absolutely no significant intellectual capabilities beyond those of a paramecium.

NOMEX: Fire-resistant fabric used to make "shirts." *see* shirts

NSA: National Security Agency. Primarily responsible for evaluating electronic intercepts and sensitive intelligence.

OOD: Officer of the day, in charge of the safe handling and maneuvering of the ship. Supervises the conning officer and other under-way watchstanders. Ashore, the OOD may be responsible for a shore station after normal working hours.

OPERATIONS SPECIALIST: Formerly a radar operator, back in the old days. An enlisted technician who operates combat detection, tracking, and engagement systems, except for sonar. Abbreviated OS.

OTH: Over the horizon, usually used to refer to shooting something you can't see.

P-3S: Shore-based anti-submarine warfare and surface surveillance long-range aircraft. The closest you can get to being in the Air Force while still being in the Navy.

PHOENIX: Long range anti-air missile carried by U.S. fighters.

PIPELINE: Navy term used to describe a series of training commands, schools, or necessary education for a particular specialty. The fighter pipeline, for example, includes Basic Flight then fighter training at the RAG (Replacement Air Group), a training squadron.

PUNCHING OUT: Ejecting from an aircraft.

PURPLE SHIRTS: *see* shirts

PXO: Prospective executive officer. The officer ordered into a command as the relief for the current XO. In most squadrons, the XO eventually "fleets up" to become the commanding officer of the squadron, an excellent system that maintains continuity within an operational command—and a system the surface Navy does not use.

RACK: A bed. A rack-monster is a sailor who sports pillow burns and spends entirely too much time asleep while his or her shipmates are working.

RED SHIRTS: *see* shirts

RHIP: Rank hath its privileges. *see* collar count

RIO: Radar intercept officer. *see* NFO

RTB: Return to base.

S-3: Command and control aircraft sold to the Navy as an anti-submarine aircraft. Good at that, too. Within the last several years, redesignated as "sea control" aircraft, with individual squadrons referred to as torpedo-bombers. Ah, the search for a mission goes on. But still a damned fine aircraft.

SAM: Surface-to-air missile, e.g., the standard missile fired by most cruisers. Also indicates a land-based site.

SAR: Sea-air rescue.

SCIF: Specially compartmented information. On board a carrier, used to designate the highly classified compartment immediately next to TFCC.

SEAWOLF: Newest version of Navy fast-attack submarine.

SERE: Survival, Evasion, Rescue, Escape; required school in pipeline for aviators.

SHIRTS: Color-coded Nomex pullovers used by flight deck and aviation personnel for rapid identification of a sailor's job. Green: maintenance technicians. Brown: plane captains. White: safety and medical. Red: ordnance. Purple: Fuel. Yellow: flight deck supervisors and handlers.

SHOE: A black shoe, slang for a surface sailor or officer. In the modern era, hard to say since the day that brown shoes were authorized for wear by black shoes. No one knows why this happened. Wing envy is the best guess.

SIDEWINDER: Anti-air missile carried by U.S. fighters.

SIERRA: A subsurface contact.

SONOBUOYS: acoustic listening devices dropped in the water by ASW or USW aircraft.

SPARROW: Anti-air missile carried by U.S. fighters.

SPETZNAZ: The Russian version of SEALS, although the

term encompasses a number of different specialties.

SPOOKS: Slang for intelligence officers and enlisted sailors working in highly classified areas.

SUBLANT: Administrative command of all Atlantic submarine forces. On the West Coast, SUBPAC.

SWEET: When used in reference to a sonobuoy, indicates that the buoy is functioning properly, although not necessarily holding any contacts.

TACCO: Tactical control officer: the NFO in an S-3.

TACTICAL CIRCUIT: A term used in these books that encompasses a wide range of actual circuits used on board a carrier. There are a variety of C&R circuits (coordination and reporting), and occasionally for simplicity sake and to avoid classified material, I just use the world tactical.

TANKED, TANKER: Navy aircraft have the ability to refuel from a tanker, either Air Force or Navy, while airborne. One of the most terrifying routine evolutions a pilot performs.

TFCC: Tactical flag command center. A compartment in flag spaces from which the CVBG admiral controls the battle. Located immediately forward of the carrier's CDC.

TOMBSTONE: Nickname given to Vice Admiral Matthew Magruder.

TOP GUN: Advanced fighter training command.

UNDERSEA WARFARE COMMANDER: In a CVBG, normally the DESRON embarked on the carrier. Formerly called the ASW commander.

VDL: Video downlink. Transmission of targeting data from an aircraft to a submarine with OTH capabilities.

VF-95: Fighter squadron assigned to Airwing 14, normally embarked on USS *Jefferson*. The first two letters of a squadron designation reflect the type of aircraft flown: VF = fighters, VFA = Hornets, VS = S-3, etc.

VICTOR: Aging Russian fast attack submarines, still a potent threat.

VS-29: S-3 squadron assigned to Airwing 14, embarked on USS *Jefferson*.

VX-1: Test pilot squadron that develops envelopes after

Pax River evaluates aerodynamic characteristics of new aircraft. *see* envelopes

WHITE SHIRT: *see* shirts

WILCO: Short for "will comply." Used only by the aviator in command of the mission.

WINCHESTER: In aviation, it means out of weapons. A Winchester aircraft must normally RTB.

XO: Executive officer, the second in command.

YELLOW SHIRT: *see* shirts